D0388820

CONFESSIONS of an INNOCENT MAN

...

CONFESSIONS of an INNOCENT MAN

...

a novel

DAVID R. DOW

DUTTON

DUTTON
An imprint of Penguin Random House LLC
penguinrandomhouse.com

Copyright © 2019 by David R. Dow

DUTTON and the D colophon are registered trademarks of
Penguin Random House LLC.

Library of Congress Cataloging-in-Publication Data
Names: Dow, David R., author.
Title: Confessions of an innocent man: a novel / David R. Dow.
Description: New York, New York: Dutton, [2019]
Identifiers: LCCN 2018021426 (print) | LCCN 2018023786 (ebook) | ISBN 9781524743901 (ebook) | ISBN 9781524743888 (hc)
Subjects: | GSAFD: Suspense fiction.
Classification: LCC PS3604.O93826 (ebook) | LCC PS3604.O93826 M46 2019 (print) | DDC 813/.6—dc23
LC record available at https://lccn.loc.gov/2018021426

Printed in the United States of America
1   3   5   7   9   10   8   6   4   2

Book design by Elke Sigal

This book is a work of fiction. Names, characters, places, and incidents either are the product of the author's imagination or are used fictitiously, and any resemblance to actual persons, living or dead, business establishments, events, or locales is entirely coincidental.

For K and L, still my pillars,
and for D and S, the newest two

What she laments the most,
What makes her body tremble head to toe,
Is that tomorrow she will have to live,
And all tomorrows after—like ourselves.
  —Charles Baudelaire, "The Mask,"
    Les fleurs du mal

It is sometimes easier to make the world
a better place than to prove you have made
the world a better place.
  —Amos Tversky

CONFESSIONS of an INNOCENT MAN

. . .

PROLOGUE

∎ ∎ ∎

On the cinder-block wall, twelve feet away from the bars to the cages where my prisoners spend their days, a digital clock counts down toward zero. When they saw that clock for the first time, before I pressed the start button to get the numbers moving, it read 58656:00:00. That's how many hours they're going to be where they are: twenty-four hours a day, 365 days a year, for 2,444 days—six years, eight months, and eleven days. Today the clock says 49896:00:00. One year down, a bit more than five and a half to go. To celebrate, the three of us are having cake.

I say to prisoner number 1, whose name is Sarah, Happy anniversary.

She doesn't answer.

I say to prisoner number 2, whose name is Leonard, You too.

He doesn't say anything either.

I cut the cake in thirds and put their two pieces on two paper plates. I stick a plastic fork in each slice, like a birthday candle. I say, Y'all enjoy now.

I

And I slide each plate through the 4.25-inch space separating the bottom of the iron bars they're behind from the poured concrete floor of their cells. Once they have their pieces, I take a bite of mine.

I say, The cream cheese frosting doesn't have very much sugar; I don't like it too sweet. The black flecks are Madagascar vanilla, no expense spared.

I smile.

I say, Some recipes call for nutmeg, but I leave it out. I'm not a fan.

Neither Sarah nor Leonard replies.

I'm already planning ahead. I say, I'm thinking we'll have angel food next year, red velvet the year after that, followed by apple, then coconut for our fifth anniversary, and German chocolate, that's my favorite, for our sixth. But I'm open to suggestions.

More silence. I say, And we can have devil's food a few months later to commemorate your liberation. Funny, huh, devil's food?

Not even a smile. They're both in a bad mood today. I've gotten to where I can tell.

I made the cake myself. I'm not a particularly skilled pastry chef, savory was how I earned my stars, but I'm reasonably competent, and besides, somebody might notice if a single middle-aged man who appears to live like a hermit in perpetual mourning waltzed into a bakery and came out with a three-layer cake big enough to feed a family of eight.

They each put a piece on their forks at the same time. Sarah says thank you. Leonard still says nothing. We talk from time to time, arguments mostly, but my feelings haven't softened much. There's no reverse Stockholm syndrome happening here.

These people stole from me, and I am without qualm about stealing right back.

On the flat-screen TV molly-bolted to the steel-fronted cinder-block wall, CNN is advertising upcoming coverage of the tenth anniversary of Hurricane Katrina. I was still locked up when New Orleans got flooded, so I stood and watched video of a scene I'd never seen before. There were people on boats floating in the French Quarter, still photos of an abandoned amusement park, and what looked like a refugee camp inside the Superdome.

I said, Unbelievable.

Sarah and Leonard were watching the TV too, but neither one said anything back. I keep CNN running sixteen hours a day down here, off at eleven each night, on again at seven. The first week I had them, I asked whether they wanted Fox or MSNBC. I knew what their answer would be, but I asked anyway. I told them if their decision was not unanimous, I'd make the call on my own. They didn't express an opinion, so I said, *So be it,* and I put it on CNN.

They both have a pair of disposable earplugs, to block the sound if they feel like it, and an eye mask to keep out the light. I give them new earplugs every week. It's not like I plan on taking them to a doctor if they get an ear infection, but still, I'd rather they didn't. I guess if they were really bad, like oozing pus or running a burning fever, I'd fake a sore throat, go to a doc-in-the-box, get some penicillin, and treat them with that. So far, though, knock on wood, they've stayed pretty healthy.

I say, See you around, Your Honors.

Neither one of them laughs, but I do, just a little hint of a chuckle. *Your Honors.* I do still amuse myself.

I drop the rest of my cake into a plastic trash container I'll empty tomorrow or the next day, then I exit the open steel door, listen to it shut like a bank vault, turn the three bolts, and walk back upstairs. It takes me a while. I've gotten a bit out of shape, my knee is bad, and I've been feeling under the weather.

Also, their prison is six stories underground.

PART 1

...

If you ask a lucky person to tell you what happened on the worst day of his life, he can do so without hesitation. If you ask the same question to a homeless mother of three whose earthly possessions all fit in a stolen grocery cart, she won't have a clue. I know this is true, because I am one of the lucky ones, but my father was not.

Even by Mexican standards, we were poor. Our tiny three-room house constructed from bamboo and mud was hot in the summer, cold in the winter, and leaky when it rained. On a good day, we had two meals of frijoles and corn tortillas. My father never finished second grade. He couldn't read, and when I needed his signature on a form so I could get financial aid for college, he signed his name with an X. His job literally killed him, and his death killed my mom.

But when Papá rose at dawn he was singing, and at night after dinner he would take Mamá in his arms and dance with her on their rotted porch to the sound of Tejano music coming from the transistor radio by the stove. I saw him frown only once, and never heard him raise his voice. He was the most positive, upbeat person I have ever known. Twenty years after he died I figured out why.

The lucky or the rich can name their worst day because it is special. For people like my papá, daily challenge is mundane. The bad becomes invisible, and they can see only the good. Optimism is not a personality trait; it is a strategy for coping with your lot.

Mamá taught me English and Papá sent me to college. They made sure I was a lucky one. That is why I can tell you my worst day. It was the day someone murdered my wife.

I'm different from my father in a second way too. He was a good and decent man. I am not. It took me a while to admit that to myself. I doubt it will take you as long. What kind of man has sex a couple of times a month but never with his own wife?

I'll answer that question. I've had plenty of time to think. What kind of man am I? I am a shameful human being. You can call me the harshest name you like, and I will not disagree. I am all of those things and probably more, but there is one thing I am not.

I am not a murderer.

■ ■ ■

My wife's name was Tieresse. Eleven years ago an ex-con beat her to death with an antique silver-and-crystal candlestick we kept on a rolltop desk in the parlor adjacent to our bedroom where she did her work. I was not there, but my imagination was. An endless video loop of the scene plays in my head, and I wouldn't stop it even if I could. Some of it I know to be true. His back is to me. He's short and stocky, with greasy shoulder-length hair. He's wearing a denim jacket with no sleeves. A tattoo of a swastika dripping blood covers his upper arm. My wife lies on the floor, faceup, hands raised, her nose broken, a deep raw gash running down her left cheek from the corner of her eye to the cleft of her chin.

After we got married, I moved most of my things to Tieresse's house, but I kept the studio apartment on top of my restaurant. I stayed there when she was away for business, or when I was too tired or drunk after closing time to drive across town. That's where I was the night she died, in my apartment, having sex with one of my waitresses who was heading off to culinary school the following week.

Tieresse had seen the waitress several times. She knew her casually, knew her name, enough to say hello and exchange pleasantries, but she didn't know her well. She didn't care whether I slept with her. I promise she did not. At least I think she didn't care. Or I believed she didn't. I suppose the completely honest thing to say is I'd convinced myself she didn't. Selfish, insensitive people can delude themselves. It doesn't make them murderers.

At the trial my lawyer used the word *arrangement*. I felt an electric shock as the word hung in the air. The jurors had to have noticed, but I would not meet their eyes. My lawyer did not ask permission to offer that characterization. If he had, I would have said no. *Arrangement* is a grotesque and malevolent word. If Tieresse had been alive, hearing our relationship described that way would have wounded her. The fact she was dead didn't make it okay. I imagined her violently shaking her head, saying to the lawyer, to the jury, to everyone, *No, no, you do not understand at all.*

Tieresse was my love and my soul mate. I could not have

cared less about her money. Roll your eyes if you want to. I don't care. I adored her. We'd sit next to one another on our sofa for hours, our shoulders touching, and read or watch TV. She liked to watch YouTube videos of unknown lounge singers she'd seen in New Orleans or clips of old black-and-white television shows that were older than I was. We held hands in the movies like teenagers. She'd slip off her shoes and put her feet on top of mine under the table at the restaurants where she loved to eat and drink. She knew as much about contemporary art as a university scholar, and she could talk intelligently about anything—well, anything other than sports. Half the stories in the four news-papers she read every morning made her cry. She was my best friend and the kindest and most generous person I have ever known. She simply didn't like to have sex. It caused her enor-mous physical pain. There are people like that. I didn't use to know it either, but there are.

The waitress's name was Britanny. By the time my trial fi-nally started, more than a year after the murder, Britanny was married to an investment banker she had met her first week in New York, but she testified for me anyway. She had cut her hair very short and lost weight since I'd seen her. She cried softly as she spoke and had no reason to lie. I cried too. She alternated looking at the judge, the jurors, and me. It was obvious she was telling the truth. I don't know why the jury didn't believe her.

Tieresse was fifty-two when she died. I was thirty-eight. She inherited a small fortune from her dad, whose family had come over on the *Mayflower* and promptly begun acquiring timber land. Tieresse told me he fancied himself a baron and spoke with an exaggerated Brahmin accent. I'd never heard of such a thing. She tightened her mouth and said through a clenched jaw, *Dickens was far overrated as an author, dahling. He can't hold a candle to Jane Austen,* and she laughed and laughed. She said, *Mother sounded like the Upper West Side, but not on purpose. Father cultivated sounding different. He rehearsed in front of the bathroom mirror.* She did not exactly dislike him, but I wouldn't say she loved him either. He left her more than a hundred million dollars. She took that fortune and made it huge. She bought real estate and developed subdivisions all across the Midwest and western US. Her intuition about which cities were set to boom was so flawless a cottage industry of home builders, mortgage brokers, and real estate agents got rich just by following her moves.

Her dad had not been on the *Forbes* list of richest Americans, but she was. On the day she died, Tieresse was number ninety-nine. Along with Reinhardt, her twenty-five-year-old son from a first marriage that lasted less than a year, I was her only beneficiary, at least until they took it away.

Reinhardt used to hate me. When the police and prosecutors convince a young man his mom was beaten to death by her much younger husband who cheated on her serially and was with her only to take her money, it makes perfect sense for the son to hate the man. I would have hated me too. For seven years he spat my name if he used it at all. He detested every single thing about me. But not anymore. Now he hates the people who lied to him and railroaded me. That's another thing we have in common.

Until she and I got married at city hall in front of a justice of the peace and a witness we met on the way, Tieresse lived alone, dividing her time between New York, Houston, Paris, and Rome. The four best cities in the world for whiling away the hours in a sidewalk café, she used to say.

Houston? I had asked her. *It's like dining in a sauna.* She'd laughed and said, *Yes, you're right. In July and August, Tex-Mex, barbeque, and briny Gulf coast oysters do taste better in an air-conditioned room. But during the wintertime and spring, there's no place I'd rather be.*

That's how I met her: at one of those cafés she so very much loved. Actually, it wasn't truly a café. It was La Ventana, a small restaurant and bar I owned near the soccer stadium where real estate had once been cheap. When I bought the building with ten percent down and a small business loan, the ground floor had graffiti-covered sheets of plywood in place of windows, and the story above had moldy carpet covering wide oak-plank floors. I spent fourteen months restoring it myself. Every morning, seven days a week, I would drive my truck to a spot on Westpark where the day laborers waited for work, and at nightfall I would drive them back or offer to let them crash in sleeping bags on my floor. The day before Halloween, when the final lightbulb and framed black-and-white photographs were all in place, I bought a keg of beer and two hundred dollars' worth of pizza from Frank's and fed my crew and their friends. We had converted the second floor into a high-ceilinged loft where I'd live, and in the space below we'd installed a slate bar, ten tables, four booths, and a gleaming kitchen with a wall of glass. From late fall through early spring, when dining al fresco in Houston really can be grand, we added six more tables on a deck out front.

I'd been open less than six months when, on one of those days, a cool, crisp evening in early March, the tables were full. My general manager, Benita, ran into the kitchen and told me a guest wanted to see me right away. I peered out through the glass from my station behind the stove, and I saw a gorgeous woman with straight black hair, enormous lucent eyes, and cheekbones that cast shadows. My first thought was to wonder what such a person was doing dining alone.

Tieresse had ordered a red snapper sandwich on a house-made potato roll with fresh-fried garlic-laced potato chips on the side. She'd cut the sandwich in half, and I could see from where I stood that only a single bite was missing. Oil glistened on the tip of her index finger and a fleck of fleur de sel sat at the corner of her mouth where her upper and lower lips met.

I knew the fish was fresh. I'd bought it myself at the market that morning and had eaten a raw slice before I cut the filets for the early dinner crowd. I wondered whether I had missed a small bone.

Benita told me the guest's name, and I recognized it instantly. Everyone in Houston knew who she was. Her name was on museums, buildings at Rice University, food pantries, and shelters for battered women. I was prepared for this dazzling, imperious, obscenely rich philanthropist to tell me in great detail exactly what I had done wrong.

Her tongue flicked the salt crystal into her mouth, and she asked, Are you the owner?

I felt my knees start to buckle. I told her I was, and it took me some time to process her reply.

She said, I wanted to say this directly to you, not your wait-staff: I've never actually felt inclined to compliment a chef for a sandwich, but I must make an exception for this one. Everything about it is extraordinary. How do you manage to get a hint of lemon inside the filet?

I was paralyzed. I could not form the words to answer her. Benita came to my rescue. She said, He poaches it briefly in a Meyer lemon beurre blanc before moving it to the grill.

I stammered, Yes, that's what I do.

Tieresse said, Well, I might never be able to eat red snapper again.

She smiled. Her teeth sparkled. Her eyes were two shades of green. I wanted to say more but could only manage, Thank you.

She held out her hand, and I shook it. She told me her name. I said, *I know who you are,* and I told her mine. She said, *Well, Rafael Zhettah, it is a pleasure to make your acquaintance.*

I do not believe it is only in hindsight I am able to say I felt the magic right then, at that very first touch of her skin on mine, in the wake of words that surprised me yet that I immediately forgot.

I said, If you come back again it will be exactly the same.

And she said, Oh believe me. I intend to.

A month later, she was sipping a dirty martini on the La Ventana deck at half past five. I walked outside to check on her. She said she wanted to invest in me, and she asked whether I would like to open a bigger place.

I told her no. I liked my life. A bigger place would complicate it. The next day and the day after that, she asked again, and each time I said no. On that third day she said she understood, that she would not ask me anymore. The next day she came in again.

She said, I have a different question for you today.

I waited, surprised to realize I was nervous. She said, I apologize for prying. I asked Benita about your situation.

I felt my stomach lurch. My neck felt hot and damp. She asked whether I wanted to have a drink that evening after I closed. It was not the question I was expecting. I stood there mute.

She said, It's okay. Never mind. I shouldn't have asked.

I said, Yes I do. Very much. But we don't close tonight until midnight.

She said, Perfect. I'll see you then.

Tieresse had just turned fifty. She was nearly fifteen years older than I was. I had never been married. I had no children. I liked cooking, camping, reading, and canoeing. I lived like a graduate student. I had never known anyone like her. More money had slipped between the overstuffed sofa cushions in her den than I made in a year.

In other words, it was no surprise at all when, two years later, I was the first person police suspected when Tieresse was bludgeoned and killed. From the outside, I might have suspected me too. Being convicted, though, well, that was a different matter.

■ ■ ■

On our first date, Tieresse got to the restaurant a half hour before we closed and helped the busboys clear the final tables. I came out of the kitchen and saw what she was doing.

I said, Let me pour you a drink while we finish here.

She said, If I help out, you'll finish here sooner.

She smiled and dropped a handful of utensils and two water glasses into a square plastic container.

Later that night we sat outside and shared a bottle of prosecco with a slab of local cheese and a loaf of warm sourdough. She told me about her son, Reinhardt, twenty-two at the time, doing graduate work in computer science at MIT.

She said, We talk nearly every night. He tells me what he is working on, and I don't understand a word he says. I go to sleep smiling.

She asked whether I had children, and when I told her no, she asked whether I wanted them.

I said, Awfully intimate question for a first date, don't you think?

She said, Yes, I do.

She said, Well?

I told her for better or worse, I was not much of a planner.

I said, Possibly I'm Buddhist at heart, but I've never dreamed about the distant future. Even here, I think about what I am serving that night, and whether we have enough traffic for me to meet the payroll at the end of the month.

She said, Well, I think you should.

I should what?

Dream.

Before she climbed into the back seat of a town car an hour before dawn, she hugged me and said, Can we do this again?

I said, I sure hope so.

That night I couldn't fall asleep. Her words were ricocheting inside my brain. Yesterday there hadn't been anything missing in my life, then she asked me what else I wanted, and I realized not that there was, but that she had asked me a question I should have thought about before. A friend I had known since I was in college wondered what had happened to me, how I had been so smitten so fast.

I said, I realize it makes no sense, but when you fall in love, if you do, you fall in love. That's why it's called that. Until it happens to you, it's impossible to understand.

■ ■ ■

Valley Falls, Kansas, population fifteen hundred or so, straddles State Highways 4 and 16, thirty miles north of Topeka, in the northeast corner of the state. Four years before I opened La

Ventana I had been renting a two-room apartment in Olathe, just south of Kansas City, where I was in flight school getting certified to fly twin-engine planes. My dad taught me how to fly his boss's crop duster when I was a boy, and I had flown hundreds of hours, but I had never gotten around to getting my pilot's license. Being a chef was option b; my dream job was to sleep under the stars. So I planned to start a company supporting rafting and kayaking excursions in remote parts of the West. We'd land on a dirt strip near the river's put-in, and after spending the day on raging whitewater and exploring the canyons on foot, my clients would enjoy first-class catered meals. None of the other outfitters were doing it. But the investors I approached balked at the price of the insurance premiums and potential liability. My fledgling business never got off the ground. Yet I have no regrets. Flight training was its own reward.

One September day, on a cross-country training flight to Nebraska, my flight instructor pulled the power on both engines just south of the state line, simulating a double engine failure. I scanned the ground for a place to land. There are plenty of flat, treeless opportunities in Kansas, but not many are paved. I spotted what looked like an unused road and set the plane down there. The road was actually a mile-long driveway bisecting a hundred-acre wooded tract. It ended at what appeared to be a pasture of nothing.

My instructor congratulated me on both choice of spot and execution of the landing. We got out of the plane and walked around.

I said, Did you know this place was here when you pulled the power?

He said, I've never seen it before in my life.

■ ■ ■

During my sophomore year of college, I was on a second date with a girl I'd met in my accounting class. She was the youngest of eight siblings from a devout Mormon family. She sang in the choir and started the campus organization lobbying to end discrimination against same-sex couples. She asked about my family, and I told her. A few nights later I invited her to dinner again, and she demurred. I was surprised. I said, *I'm disappointed. I thought we'd had a nice time.* She said, *You know, Rafael, there are times you should dole out truth sparingly.*

If I'd learned my lesson, or been quicker to construct a lie, I might not have made the same mistake with Tieresse. It was our second date, too, when she asked me to tell her about my family. I told her I was an only child whose parents were dead. She asked how they died.

I said, My father was shot to death by Mexican drug agents during my freshman year of college.

Tieresse asked, He was a drug dealer?

I said, If you ask the DEA, they will say he was, but that's not exactly true. He was hired help. He flew a crop duster and sprayed the marijuana and cocaine crops with organic pesticides.

She said, There's such a thing as that?

I said, I have no idea.

She asked, For how long?

I said, For as long as I knew him. He couldn't read or write but he could fly in places only a crazy person would try. He wasn't macho. He was responsible. He did it for his family.

And your mom?

I said, She died two weeks later. The death certificate says it was a stroke. She was diabetic and pretty overweight. But it was a broken heart. After we buried my papá, Mamá got into bed and didn't get out.

Tieresse said, *That's awful. I'm so sorry.* And she placed her hand on mine. She said, Tell me more about them.

So I did. When Mamá was eight months pregnant, Papá put her in his plane, flew low across the border, landed in Laredo, refueled, and left her there, standing on the tarmac. I was born two days later, six weeks premature. But I was an American citizen. He'd done what he set out to. After two months in the ICU of a charity hospital, with my mamá sleeping in a lobby chair or a homeless-shelter cot, I was healthy enough to go home. I'm not sure how he got word to Mamá, but he did, and one evening, Mamá bundled me up and paid a farmworker to drive us to a small airport, and Papá came and picked us up. With money he borrowed from his boss at an interest rate people in America would go to prison for charging, he'd bought my mamá Indian jewelry and a trunk of new clothes. Later he told me, *Ella hace todo el trabajo duro.* It wasn't completely true. He did plenty of hard work. But he didn't see it that way.

Every week he deposited a few pesos into a savings account he'd opened in my name at a bank in Dallas. When I was fourteen, he told me, *Yo pienso que tú debes ir a la Universidad de Utah. Son amables con los mexicanos allí.* I asked him how he knew they were nice to Mexicans in Utah. He said, *Hijo, sé un montón de cosas.*

I told Tieresse, He did know some things. How he knew the Mormons would welcome a poor Mexican I have no idea. And I still even have fond feelings for that first girlfriend, despite the fact she ditched me because she thought I might be Michael Corleone.

Tieresse said, Lucky for me.

She asked whether the Mormons had sawed off my Spanish accent. I told her I never had one. My mother had been an English teacher and spoke to me in English at home whenever my father was not around. They met when a bus carrying her students back to school after a field trip to the forest broke down on a rutted dirt road and my father landed his plane in a field and helped them get on their way. My mother had said, *Hijo, I knew I wanted to marry him before I knew his name.* She quit at the end of the school year and moved to the village where I grew up. They dated for two weeks. In their married life, the only nights they ever spent apart were when my mother was in Texas for me to be born.

She asked how I ended up in culinary school. I said, *Because it was free,* and I told her why.

I'd been working evenings at a downtown restaurant. I couldn't believe how much food we threw away. I told Tieresse, *It wasn't rotten or spoiled or anything. We just didn't have any more dishes on the menu calling for it.* So I talked to my boss, and he hooked me up with some other chefs and grocery store managers. The group formed a co-op to give food that would otherwise be thrown out to the city's largest soup kitchen. A retired Hall of Fame basketball player donated moving vans to pick up the food every night and deliver it to the kitchen, and a local car dealer bought refrigerators and freezers so the kitchen could store it all. My contribution to the project was to write an app where administrators could enter the kinds of food they had and the quantities, and how many people they expected to serve; the app would then identify dishes they could prepare with what they had on hand. All the recipes were simple. Even someone with no kitchen training at all could follow them.

I said, Without telling me he was doing it, my boss entered the app in a scholarship competition, and my project won first prize. Tuition and room and board cost me nothing.

Later I would learn Tieresse called her lawyer the next morning and told him to let the mayors of twenty large cities know she would purchase all the necessary vehicles and refrigerators if they agreed to use the app to feed their city's hungry. But that evening, I was not yet aware that there was virtually no social program she declined to fund. So I said, Now you've heard my entire story. Your turn.

She said, My father sent me to school too. Boarding school in Switzerland, beginning in third grade. He and Mother would visit at Christmas. After she died my junior year, he would call instead. He deposited money in my bank account every week. He called it an allowance even though I did no chores and did not have to buy anything. When I mentioned the deposits to my roommate, a girl whose father was number two or three in the Saudi royal family, I never knew exactly which, she told me it was guilt money. I had no idea what she was talking about, but she sounded sure, so I didn't ask. He sent me new sweaters every winter, and my mother's jewelry for my birthday. I laughed. Even at Le Rosey, high school students had no occasion to wear a diamond brooch. I received packages every other day. I had to give things away, there was so much. The only thing my father didn't give me was love. In retrospect, I think I married Roland mainly because he was the exact opposite of my father in every respect except being rich. He dropped out of college, drank too much, used crude language, all of it. When my father met him for the first time he pulled me aside and said, *You cannot possibly be serious.* You know what I learned from all this?

I said, That men suck?

She laughed and said, Sort of.

Then she said, No, not really. What I learned is that every successful person is extreme in one way or another. Some drink too much. Some chase too many women. Some churn through employees. If a woman is content to be with a moderately successful man, then she can find many wonderful potential partners. But if she is drawn to an extremist, she must make sure his extremism is benign, or she will suffer every day.

I smiled and said, In other words, the bombshells should be with mediocre people like me.

She put her hand on top of mine and said, What is extreme about you, Rafael, is your modesty. That is about as benign as it gets.

I was not sure exactly what she meant, but she said it in a way that made me sure of one thing: that I wanted to see her again.

Two months later we had dinner one evening when my restaurant was dark. I told Tieresse to wear jeans and took her to a Mexican seafood dive on the east side where customers sat at long wooden tables next to strangers and ate whole fried red snapper, giant Gulf prawns, and grilled octopus, using mostly our fingers in lieu of forks. Hardly anyone spoke English, and everyone brought beer. The place had no liquor license. I'd brought a bottle of *añejo,* which we shared with the people sitting to our left and to our right. After, we went to a bar in Montrose and listened to a trio playing roots music on a banjo, viola, and mandolin. I had my arm around her shoulders as we walked to the car. She hooked her index finger into my mouth and pulled my face down toward hers, and I tasted cognac mixing with the mint she'd just swallowed.

Later at her house, we had sex for the first time. I fell asleep with her head on my shoulder and woke up seven hours later with it still there. She picked grapefruits from her tree and squeezed fresh juice. Her backyard sloped down to the bayou. We sat outside together in a glider, legs touching, and watched the muddy water flow south to the Gulf of Mexico. The look on her face was either worry or regret, and I didn't want to ask because I didn't want to know, until the silence grew more painful than knowledge, and at last I said, I take it not everything is okay.

She said, Since my divorce, I have had sex twice. I surprised myself last night. I'm supposed to live like a nun.

I said, A nun?

She told me she had endometriosis, a condition that made intercourse excruciatingly painful. She tried a variety of treatments, including drugs and holistic medicine. Nothing worked. Finally she agreed to have surgery. She said, The pain from the scar tissue is worse than what I had before.

I said, Why didn't you sue someone?

She said, Because it wouldn't fix the problem, and I don't need the money. I don't believe the doctor made any mistakes. Some people win the lottery, and when there is a one-in-a-thousand chance of postoperative complications, one in a thousand women will suffer. God drew my number.

I held her hand.

She said, I guess I am wondering whether that changes what you think about me, about us.

I said, I'm the one who doesn't make plans for the future.

She said, That's not an answer.

I said, Okay, I'll tell you my answer. I like you. I like going places with you. I like hanging out with you. So really the question is whether it's okay with you.

She said, What do you think?

A month or so later we slept together again. It would be the last time. Either she did a worse job of hiding the pain she was in than she had before, or I had become more attentive.

I said, *We don't have to do this,* and she leaned forward and kissed me.

Later that morning she said, You do know I am aware how much younger you are than I.

I smiled. I said, Yes, I am aware.

■ ■ ■

We spent every night together for the next month. She slept inside my arms. We did not have sex, but I still felt an intimacy I never had before. Late one Sunday morning, we were sitting outside, swinging our legs in unison up and down. Four wild parrots sat high in a pine watching three hummingbirds sip sugar water from a feeder hung from a branch.

Tieresse said, I don't mind if you sleep around every now and then with people your own age. I do not need to know. In fact, I do not want to know. But I will feel less guilty about your missing something important in life.

It took me a moment to get past the shock. In college I knew some polygamists, and their lifestyle baffled me. I said to Tieresse, I'm not missing anything. What is important in my life is to be with someone I love and care for, and I don't much want to have sex with anyone who doesn't fit that bill.

She said, Not now you don't. I've discovered things can change.

I sensed this conversation was not going to end until I conceded. To get it to conclude, I said, Whatever.

After that conversation, nothing changed. Unless I was too tired or had had too much to drink, I would go to her house after we'd cleaned and closed, arriving around twelve thirty or one. Half the time she'd be awake reading in bed, and we'd talk about the news or how things had gone at dinner service, or how she was liking her book. The other half the time she'd be sound asleep, and I would find a note on my pillow wishing me sweet dreams.

On a Friday evening in early May, a bachelorette party of sixteen twenty-somethings took up half my tables and stayed until we closed. They were still there after we'd cleaned all the other tables and swept the floor. Finally all but one departed in two stretch limos. The one came upstairs with me. When I put her in a cab at three thirty, she handed me her business card and said, *Thanks for the nightcap.* I felt shame.

I suspect Tieresse knew right away because my hair was still damp from the shower I did not customarily take before driving myself to her house. As I sunk into the bed beside her, my heart racing, guilt churning in my belly and bowels, she ran her fingers across the top of my head, and from deep down in her slumber she said to me, I love you.

Like all sins, it was easier the next time. People in the restaurant industry sleep around. Before Tieresse died, I had sex with four other women, including Britanny. I did not tell them, or anyone else, about my license. It wasn't their business. If they deemed me a lout, they had good reason. I did still feel guilty, I will admit that, but I did not think I was doing anything wrong.

I've had years to puzzle over that paradox. If there's a solution, I'm not smart enough to see it.

Tieresse liked to come to the restaurant in the late afternoons and sample the dishes for that evening with the waitstaff. As the early diners arrived, she would move to the bar and drink a snifter of cognac or a dirty martini. Two or three nights a week she would go to some social or philanthropic event. Once she said to me, I'm not going to ask you to accompany me to these horrid evenings because I do not want to pressure you to go somewhere you'd be bored and unhappy.

I said, How do you know I wouldn't enjoy it?

She raised her eyebrows and smiled.

She said, Do you want to test me?

Two nights later I went with her to a reception to raise money for somebody running for the US Senate in Missouri. The price of admission was more than I earned in a year. Not counting me and the people serving alcohol and hors d'oeuvres, everybody there was white, except for one Asian woman. All the men were dressed like they shopped at the same place: dark suits, white shirts, mostly solid red or blue ties, American flag lapel pins.

About fifteen minutes into it I brushed back Tieresse's hair, put my lips next to her right ear, and whispered, Uncle. I surrender. You were right.

She smiled and said, Then let's get out of here.

We went to a soul-food dive in the Third Ward and ate fried chicken, macaroni and cheese, and collard greens while still dressed in our fancy clothes. It was a favorite spot of mine, and I couldn't believe she knew anything about it.

I said, How on earth did you know I love this place?

She said, Do you mean to tell me you haven't googled me?

She smiled. I had, of course, but I was worried she would think I was creepy if I said so.

She said, You revealed all your secrets in the interview you gave to the paper last year.

I had forgotten I gave that interview.

I said, Of course I've googled you, beginning the day we met.

No matter the bedtime, Tieresse was an early riser. In the mornings she would go to the gym while I was still asleep. When she got home we'd play tennis in her backyard or float in her pool. We saw movies that started before noon. She was on the board at the museums, and so we had VIP tours of new exhibitions the day before they opened. La Ventana was dark on Sundays and Mondays. We usually ate out on one and stayed in and cooked on the other.

I'd always thought the woman I loved would be the only person I ever had sex with, not the one person with whom I never did. It was not a life I had either pictured or planned. Tieresse had a painting hanging above her fireplace. It was a young woman looking into a mirror. The side of her face was scarred, but the image in the mirror was not. Tieresse had said, *The difference between the life you have and the life you envision is equal to the distance between perfection and reality.* I had said, *Did you make that up?* She'd said, *It's what Reinhardt said when he saw the painting. I've never forgotten it.* I looked at the woman in the painting the morning after I betrayed Tieresse for the first time, and I saw myself.

The night we ducked out of the fund-raiser she said, I'm ahead by one in the contest of who knows whom.

I said, True.

She said, So your job is to take me somewhere I think I am going to hate but that you know I won't. Think you're up to it?

I smiled and said, No doubt.

■ ■ ■

We'd been seeing each other for six months when I told her I was playing my move. I invited her on a road trip. She asked where we were going and I told her to pack light and for the outdoors.

She said, That's all the information I'm getting?

I said, Yes, it is.

I picked her up and we drove to a hangar west of Houston adjacent to a three-thousand-foot grass strip where a friend of mine kept a plane he let me fly.

I said, You are going to love this place.

She had never been in a small plane and seemed nervous. I said, There's nothing to worry about.

She said, You're mistaking excitement for anxiety. I can't wait. You've already won. Can you teach me to fly?

We climbed past five thousand feet, high enough to be safe, low enough to see the countryside. Her face was glued to the window. Just north of Oklahoma she asked if she could fly, and she gently steered us through a series of S-turns as we followed the Cimarron River mostly north. She asked where we were going and I told her we were almost there. I turned toward that spot in northeast Kansas and landed on the same driveway where I'd made an emergency landing more than four years before. She had already unlatched her door before we came to a stop.

She said, This place is amazing.

We walked around the forest hand in hand and had a late, light lunch sitting by the creek. Later we put on swimsuits and went canoeing on the Delaware River. Early that evening, eating a picnic of ribs and Shiraz beneath the shade of a massive cottonwood just outside Ozawkie, she said to me, Kansas City barbeque isn't as good as Texas, but it sure ain't bad.

I said, Listen to you, saying *ain't*.

She said, Is the property where we landed for sale?

I said, I have no idea.

She said, If it is, let's buy it and get married.

I said, What?

She said, It's beautiful here, a combination of very remote and also manageable. What can I say? The geometry of the Midwest has always appealed to me. All these perfect right angles. I built my first subdivision near Lincoln, Nebraska.

I said, I was talking about the marriage part.

She said, Oh that. Quit being so damn Germanic already. Aren't you Latin men supposed to be impulsive?

Tieresse opened her tablet, spent five minutes doing some research, then reached for her phone. She asked three questions and after each said, *Yes, I see.* Before she hung up, she offered to buy the place with cash.

She said, I bought it, now close your eyes.

I said, Seriously?

She said, I mean it. Close them.

I went along. She said, *You can open your eyes now,* and when I did, she was holding out two rings she had fashioned from a half dozen pine needles she'd braided into a strand and tied in a loop. She said, *We can buy something more substantial when we get back to Houston. Now give me your hand.* I closed my eyes again, and she said, *Now what are you doing?* I said, *I'm making sure this is real.*

After that day, it became a private game of ours. If I was feeling stressed or down, she would say, *Close your eyes, amor,* and once I had she would place her hand on my face and say, *Now when I tell you to open, the world will be a better place.* It worked every time.

We spent the night in a cheap motel and began to sketch the house we planned to build on the back of an envelope. Tieresse hired an architect from Houston to move up to Kansas for half a year and supervise the construction.

At the end of the driveway we installed a prefabricated hangar and bought a single-engine turboprop plane for Tieresse's lessons. Leading west from the hangar, a covered path extended fifty meters to the spot where we built a three-thousand-square-foot rectangular house with a bedroom, living area, exercise room, library, and chef's kitchen. It had a porch that wrapped all the way around, well water, solar panels covering the roof, and a fireplace that doubled as a wood-burning oven. Across the garden was a small guesthouse just in case.

Tieresse was ready to move there, but I was scared. I worried about how La Ventana would survive. She said, *De Gaulle used to say the graveyards are full of indispensable men.* I wanted to change the subject. I said, *That's pretty sexist, don't you think?* She said, *Seriously, amor, your creation can run without your being there constantly.* I said, *If you want to know the truth, what I'm worried about is your running off if you have to be constantly with me.* And it was true. I was never someone who was falsely modest. I was simply aware she was too smart and too interesting not to get bored with me. She said,

For the first guy in his family to go to college, you appear to know nothing.

She liked to take long walks around the property at dawn and dusk, cutting trails through the forest. In the late winter, Tieresse spread wildflower seeds in the pasture, and in late June and early July we had an explosion of bird's-foot violets and purple poppy mallows.

It was the first and last flower season she spent there.

■ ■ ■

She sold all her houses except for the places in Houston and Kansas and put the profits straight into her charitable foundation. The only indulgence she couldn't bear to surrender was air travel. Tieresse said to me, *The very thought of these TSA agents passing around pictures of my bum gives me the willies.* I said, *I don't think they do that.* She said, *Ah, Rafa, your naïveté charms me,* and she kissed my nose, then my mouth. No matter where we went together, a private car took us to the airport, and a private jet flew us to our destination. Soon after our engagement, she wanted to watch Reinhardt defend his doctoral dissertation, so we headed off to Boston.

He looked nothing like the computer geek I expected. He looked instead like the middleweight college wrestler he had been. He said, *Nice to meet you,* and he shook my hand with a palm as calloused as my papá's had been. I said to Tieresse, *Why didn't you tell me he was an NCAA champion?* She said, *Because if you brag about too many qualities of those you love, other people will think you are either lying or delusional. It's the same reason I tell everyone you cook better than*

Escoffier, but I never say you're more handsome than George Clooney. The two hours we spent listening to Reinhardt discuss international financial security measures with four women and three men was like watching a movie in Urdu without subtitles. As we walked out I said, *I have no idea what I just observed.* He said, *What you just observed is a silly monastic ritual. I hope it was not insufferable. Let's go get pizza and beer.* At dinner we discovered we both love baseball and found ourselves debating which team was better, the 1939 Yankees or the 1908 Cubs. He said, *But best is not the same as favorite. For me, the 1978 Reds are it.* I said, *Ah yes, the Big Red Machine,* and Tieresse said, *I'm begging you both. Can we please talk about anything else?*

It helped that he was baby-faced and had the body of a high school athlete. It helped, too, that he knew so much about a feature of our world I associated with youngsters, and of course that we had baseball in common. But whatever the explanation, despite my worries, the fact that I was as close in age to him as I was to his mother caused no awkwardness. He walked us to our hotel that evening and brought bagels to our suite for breakfast in the morning. On the way back to Texas I said to Tieresse, *I didn't want to say anything before, but I was nervous about meeting Reinhardt. Now I feel silly. He put me completely at ease. I really like him.* Tieresse said, *Before Reinhardt was old enough to talk, he already knew when I was happy.* I said, *How do you know he wasn't sensing me?*

One Sunday evening we were at her house. She was sitting at the counter drinking a glass of wine while I cooked risotto. She said, *What's the matter?* I was singing an Otis Redding song when she asked. I said, *Some dogs have such a great sense of smell they know whether their masters will be in a good mood or a bad one while they are still sleeping.* She said, *Nice try. Now, spill it.* Resistance and denial would be futile. So I told her it had been bothering me that she knew all my friends, they all worked at La Ventana, but I did not know any of hers. I told her it made me feel like she was embarrassed.

She said, Rafa, I have acquaintances, scores, maybe hundreds of acquaintances, but they are not friends. My friends are Reinhardt and you.

I said, I think it's interesting that you had a shitty relationship with your parents and now have a wonderful relationship with your son, whereas I adored my mamá and papá and have no children at all.

She stared at me. I said, What? Did I say something wrong?

She said, I don't think you have any idea how smart you are.

The next night was the party for Britanny's going away.

■ ■ ■

Two detectives came to the restaurant at one. I was in the kitchen when Benita told me they were there. One of them, a fit-looking Navy SEAL type wearing a white T-shirt and jeans, introduced himself as Detective Pisarro and asked me whether I could answer a few questions. I said, About what?

They drove me across the bayou to the central station and left me in a windowless room. I lost track of time. I called Tieresse and got her voice mail. I called her again and again. I placed the phone on the table and kept my thumb on redial. To this day I do not know how many messages I left. The prosecutor would later say it was all a charade.

Pisarro's partner, Detective Cole, finally came into the

room, apparently to play the role of bad cop. In time I would find out it was no act. He was wearing a cotton knit squared-off tie, which he loosened as he plopped himself down in the interview room's other chair. He must have been spying on me from outside.

He said, It's a little late for an alibi.

I said, What?

Pisarro came back in. Good cop. He must have been spying too. He was looking right at me when he said to Cole, Maybe he's being sincere. Maybe he's repressed it. It happens.

I said, What in the world are you two talking about?

Cole said, We know you killed your wife.

That's when I fainted. I obviously do not remember being unconscious, but I have watched the videotape of the interrogation many times. I simply collapsed, like a tent whose poles snap in the wind. Pisarro walks out and only Cole is there when I come to. Pisarro walks back in and hands me a glass of water. I asked them where she was killed and how she died and who found her and when, my questions crowded together in too small a space. I said I wanted to see her. I said she had no enemies, everybody adored her.

Cole said, *Not everybody,* and I wanted to hurt him. They asked me questions about her life and her routine, her friends and her work. Then Cole asked where I had been.

My legs were shaking so hard the chair I was sitting in bounced and scratched. At some point Cole gave me a pen and a pad and asked me to put down my cell number, and I couldn't write.

I said, I am going to call a lawyer.

Cole said, You don't need a lawyer. Just tell us what happened.

I said, I have no idea what happened. I'm going home.

They did not try to stop me. Cole said, Her house is a crime scene. You can't enter. It's too late for you to clean up.

I said, She's my wife. It is our house.

Cole said, You'll feel better if you tell us what happened.

I said, Fuck you.

It was one A.M. I drove without intention or destination. I crept down Navigation, then Wayside. I turned west and went by La Ventana, surprised to see it clean and locked. I looked at my watch and remembered the time. I drove all night, circling the city on Loop 610. The eastern sky began to lighten. I went to Tieresse's house. Cole hadn't been lying. There was yellow tape blocking the yard and the door, and a squad car parked out front. I called Reinhardt.

I said, I am sorry to call so late. Or so early. I'm sorry. Your mother is dead. Tieresse is dead. Somebody killed her.

He asked how, and I told him what I knew, which was basically nothing. For a long moment the line was quiet. He said, I will fly down tomorrow.

I met him at the airport the next morning and told him what I had read in the paper earlier that day.

The housekeeper arrived at nine fifteen, her usual time. She saw that Tieresse had not squeezed juice, which was unusual, and the coffeepot was still full. She noted my car was not in the porte cochere, which was not unheard of. She called out to Tieresse and got no reply. A Modigliani hanging on the wall in the foyer to the parlor and bedroom was askew. The house-keeper went over to straighten it. Lying on the floor next to the desk was Tieresse, wearing her bathrobe, a damp towel on the floor beside her. The housekeeper screamed, dialed 911, and started to do CPR, until she realized Tieresse was already gone.

Reinhardt said, Nobody would want to kill her.

I said, I know. I told the police exactly that. They think I did it.

Reinhardt said, Did you?

I looked at him, not feigning pain.

He said, I'm sorry.

Later I would learn he had spent time with Detectives Pisarro and Cole while in town. All I knew then was he was going to ask the police when we could recover his mother so we could hold a ceremony.

I said, I can ask them that.

He said, She wasn't a fan of ritual, but I imagine there are quite a few people who would like a formal opportunity to tell her goodbye. It might speed things up if we are both on top of them.

Something about the way he said goodbye seemed unnatural to me, as if he was already reevaluating our own relationship. Granted, he did not know me well, but he knew me well enough. Yet anything I said would come off as desperate. I was already terrified and bereft. I didn't need to be desperate as well. So all I said was, Okay.

■ ■ ■

Then he asked the question I knew he would ask. Where was I? Why hadn't I been there, is what Reinhardt wanted to know.

How could I tell him?

The night of the murder was a Monday, when we are open only for private affairs. This particular Monday, we were hosting a party for one of our own. Britanny, a waitress for me since opening day, was heading off to the CIA. Tieresse stopped by in the late afternoon after signing papers in a lawyer's office to underwrite the construction of a new state-of-the-art laboratory at Houston's biggest cancer hospital. She walked into the kitchen as I was sliding a mustard-coated leg of lamb out of the oven. She said, *Julia Child's recipe?* And I said, *None better. Why don't you stay and join us?*

Tieresse said, As delicious as it smells in here, I have to be in San Antonio tomorrow morning at seven. I'll be having sweet dreams by the time you all call it a night.

She picked up a cashew crusted with pink salt and sesame seeds, studied it, and popped it in her mouth. I said, Delicious, right?

She looked through the glass into the dining room, where Britanny was sitting with Benita drinking wine. She said, That girl is far too pretty to be a spy.

I said, Hah, hah.

Tieresse said, And too hot to be a chef.

I didn't say anything in response to that.

She kissed me, and then she said, I'll stop by tomorrow night when I get back to town.

I walked her out then helped the gang put all the food on the banquette. People passed around platters of lamb and rice; a salad of cucumbers, tomato, and roasted lemon; eggplant tossed with tahini; and scratch-made pita prepared by a nineteen-year-old busboy from Beirut I'd hired the month before. We made toasts and told stories. My favorite was when Georgette recounted the night Britanny's hair caught fire when she bent too close over a flaming tableside dessert and, in her desperation to put it out, knocked over a decanter full of a three-thousand-dollar Bordeaux, spattering it across the seersucker suit of a retired federal judge.

At just past midnight, with the long rectangular table we had made by pushing six smaller tables together littered with a dozen empty wine bottles, two empty bottles of tequila, and an almost empty liter of cognac, I kicked everybody out. I said, You people need to go home and sleep it off. We can clean up this mess in the morning.

Everyone shuffled out and got in a cab or on the train. Everyone except Brittany. We woke up naked, hungover, and in my bed when we heard Esteban and Luis dropping bottles in the recycle bin the next morning at nine. She left through the back door, embarrassed to see the others, I suppose, and I did not see her again until over a year later, when she testified at my trial as a newlywed who worked as a sous chef in a three-star restaurant two blocks from Central Park.

So that, as I'm sure you can understand, is why I did not know quite how to answer Reinhardt's simple question.

■ ■ ■

In a testament to the talent of the cooks and floor managers I had hired, business went on at La Ventana exactly as it had before. It was yet another reminder of Tieresse, yet another thing she had been right about. I was dispensable. I would approve the menu in the morning and sign off on purchases, then climb the stairs to the second floor and stay in my apartment until the following day. I called the police every few hours to ask about progress. After a couple of days they stopped taking my calls. Reinhardt was staying at a downtown hotel. In retrospect, he might have seemed a bit cool toward me, but at the time, I believed he was suffering from the same shock I was. Three days after Tieresse's death he flew home, telling me he'd return once the body was released. I did not learn until later that the police had interviewed him for more than six hours over two days about my relationship with his mother.

Initially the local news media were kind to me, but the first suspect is always the spouse, and when the spouse is brown-skinned, over a decade younger, and billions of dollars poorer, he is also the second and the third. So I was not surprised when several parties canceled their reservations. It didn't matter, though. The tables remained filled with walk-ins. In fact, business actually picked up, from people wanting to show their support, I suppose. Once or twice I started downstairs to thank them, but I couldn't summon the will. So I sat on my bed, with the TV tuned to the local news and the volume on mute, ready to listen if the reporters started to talk about the case. The aroma of onions and garlic cooking in butter wafted up from below and made me queasy. I pressed pillows over my ears to muffle the sound of corks popping and dull the din of diners and drinkers enjoying themselves. When my stomach growled I brewed an espresso or ate tuna from a can or peanut butter from the jar.

Eight days after the crime, just as we were opening for lunch, Cole and Pisarro came to arrest me. Neither one was a good cop anymore. Pisarro said, *We are here to arrest you for murder.* They put handcuffs on my wrists and paraded me through my kitchen and dining room. People on my staff were crying. Diners put down their forks and stared.

They took me downtown and put me in the same room where they had interviewed me the last time. Cole had a theory. I was nervous Tieresse was going to divorce me. She had been angry I was flirting with Britanny and had gone home rather than stay at the party. I lured Britanny upstairs and got her drunk so she would pass out, and then I sneaked off, killed Tieresse, and crawled back into bed before Britanny awoke. I had ransacked Tieresse's closet and stolen gem-laden necklaces to make the motive appear to be robbery.

I said, That is ridiculous. Tieresse thought diamonds were an obscene indulgence and buying them provided blood money for despots and warlords. All her jewels were fake.

Cole said, But a thief would not know that. You're a deviously clever man.

Pisarro said, Your fingerprints and DNA were on the desk in the parlor and the murder weapon.

I said, I lived there. My DNA is all over the place.

Pisarro said, The housekeeper told us she has the same cleaning routine every week. You would know what it was.

I said, I am calling a lawyer.

The courts hadn't yet taken my money away. I called the only lawyer whose phone number I knew by heart, a friend who worked for a nonprofit, and asked him whom he would recommend. He mentioned two names, and I hired them both—a somewhat older white man from Houston named Jonathan who wears a bow tie with his three-piece suits and talks so softly you have to lean forward to hear him eviscerate the witnesses, and a German woman from New York named Heidi who specialized in representing accused Islamic terrorists and white nationalists and had reportedly never lost a case. They had worked together before, most recently winning an acquittal for a cattle rancher in Idaho accused of ambushing two federal agents attempting to serve a warrant. My lawyers persuaded the jury their client had believed these men wearing camouflage and carrying long guns aimed to rob him and had fired out his window in self-defense. I paid them each a quarter of a million dollars up front. I was in good hands.

Jonathan, whose office was a block away from the jail, arrived less than an hour after I called him just to introduce himself. The room grew quiet when he entered. He had a gleam in his eye, like he was having more fun than anyone alive. He explained I'd be booked into the county jail, but that he would be back first thing in the morning with his colleague to start planning our defense, and that I would be sleeping in my own bed the following day.

I said, I want you to know I did not kill my wife and have no idea who did.

He said, I believe you. It doesn't matter to me, but I know it matters to you. So yes, I believe you.

In the morning he was back with his colleague. Heidi did not ask whether I was guilty. She asked, *Where were you when it happened?*, and when I told her, she said, *That's going to be our biggest problem.* I asked what other problems there would be, and she said, *I'm not clairvoyant, I just know the math.* They explained to me a death penalty trial is actually two trials. At the first one the jury decides whether I committed the crime. If the jurors think I did, there is a second phase where the only question is whether the sentence is life or death. They said that in a typical death penalty case they would devote most of their energy to the punishment trial, but in my case they believed they could win an acquittal.

I said, That's why I hired you. I did not kill my wife.

Heidi had said, *God, you sounded just like Harrison Ford in* The Fugitive *when you said that.* I had seen the movie several times, but I did not know what line she was referring to, and didn't care enough to ask. So I just shook my head. Then she said something chilling.

She said, Here's the thing, Rafael. It doesn't matter. All that matters is what the jury thinks happened, and the prosecutors trying to put you away are very good, and they are going to tell the jury you are a broke Mexican who runs a small restaurant and fucks his waitresses and just waited for the chance to murder a cash cow you had hoodwinked and bamboozled.

I said, Oh my God, not a single word of that is true. I am a US citizen. I do not fuck my waitresses. They're not just hookers.

She said, I don't want to argue about verb choice here. That's not really my point.

And Jonathan said, I'm not sure you are understanding what we are telling you about how a trial works.

Then he said, But what we want to make sure you are comfortable with is our strategy. We both think our best chance is a not guilty verdict, because if the jury thinks you did it, they are going to hate you too much for us to be able to persuade them later they should do anything other than sentence you to death.

Heidi said, Apparently the police have already found four different women you have had sex with since the day you and Tieresse exchanged vows.

She stared at me, waiting for a reply. I felt my head drop. My neck and throat felt hot, and I suspected they were turning red. I do not know how to explain what I was feeling right then. It wasn't embarrassment or fear; it was more like shame. God, what could I possibly have been thinking? What kind of man treats the love of his life the way I treated mine? I said, *If they've already found four, they won't find any more.* I told them both about everything.

Heidi stopped writing. She put down her pen and folded her hands. She said, So, our biggest problem just got very much bigger.

Jonathan asked me, Are you comfortable with taking the enormous risk of concentrating our efforts on the guilt phase?

I said, I told you I am innocent.

He said, I heard you, but that is not an answer to the question I asked you.

I said, Yes I am comfortable with that. If the jury believes I could have done this to Tieresse, I do not care what else they do to me.

Heidi said, Okay, then. We have work to do.

They shook my hand and left, she bouncing on her toes, and he barely lifting his feet off the ground. Considering the stakes, I should have been nervous, but I wasn't. If a double murderer like OJ could get acquitted, then I, who had absolutely nothing to do with Tieresse's death, would surely be found innocent as well.

My lawyers were confident too. They had read out loud to me from notes that police and prosecutors had made from their interviews with witnesses. The statements were banal. My staff all talked about how in love Tieresse and I seemed to be. They told the story about how we had met, and how I did not care at all about money, so long as La Ventana brought in enough that I could pay my team a better salary than they could earn at any other restaurant in town. None of them had any doubt I adored my wife and could never harm her.

On the other side, Reinhardt said something similar about his mother. The interviews with him were recorded. You could hear in his voice disbelief that I could have been involved. Yes, he wavered when Detective Pisarro told him about my promiscuity, but he still resisted Pisarro's repeated if subtle efforts to get him to say Tieresse had expressed jealousy or worry about my motives in marrying her. He said, *I think she might have proposed to him. She started to act twenty years younger. She was in love, but also brilliant and clear-eyed. If Rafael had been a gold digger, my mother would have known instantly.* When he said my name, Rafael, there was no hint of enmity in his tone. It was only at the very end of their final conversation, when Detective Cole implied there was physical evidence implicating me in Tieresse's death, that Reinhardt equivocated. Initially he said, *What physical evidence? Rafael and my mother lived together.* Cole had said, *Exactly, we didn't find his DNA where we should have. It is because he did too good a job cleaning up the crime scene.* You could hear the blade of doubt even though the words were right. *Too good a job? What does that even mean?* But the barb was planted. The jury was already going to dislike me. That much was clear. But so long as Reinhardt assured them I loved Tieresse and could never do her harm, they'd put that dislike aside. If, however, the son was not going to stand shoulder to shoulder with his mother's husband, if even he had doubt, if he had any at all, the other bad evidence my lawyer had predicted had made its appearance.

■ ■ ■

The value of the estate Tieresse left me was more than two billion dollars. Reinhardt received an equal amount, and the remainder—almost five billion dollars more—was left to her charitable foundation. On paper I was one of the richest men in

America, but it was money I would never see if convicted of her murder.

I didn't need it, though. More than a year earlier Tieresse had moved two hundred and forty million dollars into a trust I controlled in several offshore accounts. I told her I had no need for such sums. She'd replied, *One never knows. If I get kidnapped on a trip to visit one of my orphanages, I'd like you to be able to quietly pay the ransom.* Laugh lines around her eyes crinkled when she smiled. Investments had swelled the trust's value to north of three hundred million dollars, and now, as it turned out, I was going to need the money for my own ransom, so I could post my bail and get back home.

At seven the next morning two burly deputies escorted me through a series of underground tunnels then up a freight elevator to the seventh floor of the criminal courts building where they put me in a holding cell with the names of lawyers and their phone numbers scratched into the gray paint cracking off the cinder-block wall. Usually these cages had twenty or twenty-five people crammed into them, but I was the only one there. I said, *Why so quiet?* But the deputies took their handcuffs and walked away without answering. Two hours later my lawyers arrived. My fingers were blue and my arms and neck were covered with goose bumps. Heidi said, *I can see my breath in here.* Jonathan said, *One of the deputies told me the boiler was broken.* My teeth chattered as they described to me how the hearing would proceed.

After another half hour, the deputies came back and walked me into the courtroom. I sat shivering between my lawyers. Six feet away the prosecutor stood behind a table covered with photographs of my dead wife. She held one up and told the judge I was a dangerous brutal killer who needed to be locked up. She said I was a flight risk who would find safe haven with my family in Mexico, and because the district attorney would be seeking the death penalty, Mexico might refuse to extradite me back to Texas if I were to flee. Jonathan rose to speak. His voice had a Texas twang that had not been there yesterday. He told the judge I was a US citizen and had not lived in Mexico since coming here for college more than twenty years before. He said I was a respected chef and small business owner, and my ties to the local community were deep. They were prepared to surrender my passport and have me wear an ankle bracelet and remain under house arrest. The judge asked the prosecutor whether those terms were acceptable to her if he set bail at five million dollars. She said no one knew how much money I had stolen from my wife and hidden away, so no, she said, those terms were not acceptable. The judge said, *I am persuaded*, and he ordered me held without bail. I gasped as they led me away.

We retraced our footsteps through the maze of underground tunnels and emerged into a new wing of the jail. They gave me an orange jumpsuit that smelled like bleach, plastic flip-flops, and a laminated ID. I was one of 9,416 inmates, half black, twenty percent Latino, ten percent Asian. Cell doors were electronically controlled. Most held two inmates, a few housed three. The one other inmate facing capital murder charges and I had cells to ourselves. Mine had a bunk, a sink, a toilet, and a metal shelf. Cells were arranged around a central area in an architecture that reminded me of the quadrangle where I'd gone to college. The common area had octagonal tables with attached stools bolted to the floor where we inmates would eat our meals after going through a cafeteria line with no choices and getting our trays. A TV tuned to a local station was on all the time. The diet was carbohydrate rich: rubbery pan-cakes and scrambled eggs, bologna sandwiches on pillowy white bread, Salisbury steaks with mashed potatoes from a box. Beverage choices included water, milk, instant coffee, and red punch from a plastic gallon jug. The other inmate facing death and I ate by ourselves in a separate room. After two days, his trial started, and when it ended two days after that, I never saw him again.

Five days a week at nine A.M. guards shackled me up and took me to a room where I met with my lawyers or members of their team until midafternoon. When I got my dinner tray at night, it also held the sandwich I had not eaten for lunch. By the time my trial finally began, I had lost sixteen pounds and grown flabby at the same time. During my thrice-weekly showers, I would look down at my concave chest and rounded belly and wonder how that was possible.

I was allowed to buy newspapers or books, but I did not have the concentration to read. I did purchase a spiral notebook and made notes of things I needed to tell my lawyer. I slept a lot. Escaping into unconsciousness is how I avoided fixating on how suddenly and without warning my entire life had gone from privileged to bereft.

My legal team wanted to delay the trial so they could talk to people who had known my family in Mexico, but I said no. Nothing my aunts or uncles or cousins might have to say had anything to do with my case. I didn't even know if any of them were still alive.

Given the circumstances, my complete confidence might surprise you. But I knew the truth, and I still had faith in the system. I was positive the jury would find me innocent, because I didn't do it. So when my lawyers suggested a three-month delay, I said, Not a chance, or you're both fired. Let's get this show on the road.

■ ■ ■

Early one Monday morning, after I'd spent more than thirteen months in jail, a female guard brought me a suit and a tie and told me to be dressed in fifteen minutes. It was not yet dawn. Two heavyset deputies carrying Mace and armed with holstered .45s came for me and walked me through the same set of underground tunnels I'd been through before. In the holding cell I practiced looking worried yet confident. I'd heard jurors form an impression about guilt or innocence right away, merely by looking at the defendant, before they have heard even a single shred of testimony. I wanted them to see an innocent man when they looked at me—scared and uncomprehending, but innocent. I opened my eyes wide, then narrowed them a bit. I rubbed them until they were swollen and red. My palms were wet and I wiped them on my wool trousers. The suit was navy blue and off-the-rack. Whichever member of my legal team picked it out had done a good job.

By the third day of jury selection I worried I was looking bored. Here's the way it worked: Sixty people with *Harris County Juror* stickers affixed to their shirts or blouses packed the courtroom's benches. The judge talked to them first, then the prosecutor, then my lawyer. They asked questions like, *Are any of you related to the defendant or the victim in this case? Have any of you or a member of your immediate family been convicted of a crime? Have you served on a capital murder jury before?* Questioning went on like this for half a day. Before court ended that afternoon, the lawyers stood whispering in front of the judge, and a few minutes later, the judge called out the numbers of eight of the potential jurors and told them they were released, and all the others should return the next morning at eight.

On day two, jurors came into the courtroom one at a time. They were individually questioned at great length by the lawyers and the judge on topics ranging from their attitude toward the death penalty to what television shows they watch. The lawyers asked them what books and magazines they read, which websites they visit, where they go out to dinner, how often they attend church, whether they follow sports, and how they felt about defense lawyers and police. They could have been filling out online applications for a dating site. You might be surprised to learn that many Americans think someone is guilty if he gets arrested and the prosecutors take him to trial. My side didn't want those people on our jury. Their side did. They were looking for people who trust that the police get it right. My side preferred jurors who are skeptical of government. Their ideal jurors were people who demand an eye for an eye. We wanted women and men who know couples consisting of very different social and economic backgrounds. They wanted people who support building a border wall. The prosecutor would try to identify jurors who were against the death penalty, and then corner that juror into saying she could never sentence someone to death, the result being she was disqualified from serving on the jury. My lawyers would try to get the same person to admit she could listen to all the evidence and evaluate it impartially, and sentence someone to die if the circumstances warranted that punishment. It was a verbal chess match between the lawyers, who were manipulating potential jurors like pawns on the board. For part of the first day I marveled, but soon it became tiresome, and then I grew alarmed my future depended entirely on guessing right.

The scripts did not change. By the time the prosecutor was asking the fifth potential juror whether he could sentence a defendant to death if that defendant had never before committed a crime but had bludgeoned his wife to death to collect an inheritance, I was already losing the battle to keep an engaged expression on my face. And yet we were just getting started. These individual colloquies lasted three and a half weeks. I actually looked forward to going back to my jail cell at the end of the day. I wondered what the jurors would think if I fell asleep at my own trial.

Then, midday on a Thursday afternoon, the judge banged his gavel and we had a jury: six white men, four white women, one black woman, and one Latina, ranging in age from twenty-eight to sixty-four. When they took their seats, the black woman stared straight at me. The other eleven looked away. The judge gave them some instructions, told them he had some technical matters to go over with the lawyers the following day, wished them a pleasant weekend, instructed them not to watch the news or read the paper about the case, and directed they be in their seats first thing Monday morning. They murmured among themselves as they filed out. Heidi watched them leave. Jonathan looked at her and said, *So?* She said, *It's rare I find myself counting on the men. But all we need is one.* They were not talking to me, but I offered an opinion anyway. I said, *I think three of the women looked sympathetic.* Heidi said, *Maybe so.* She was just being polite.

Whatever my lawyers were doing that weekend to prepare for Monday's start apparently didn't require me, so the jailers left me in my cell. I lay on the bunk, stared at the wall, and had the first of what would become many fantasies of escape. I wondered what the guards earned in a year. Twenty-five, maybe thirty thousand dollars? What could I offer one to bring me jeans and a shirt and turn me loose? How could I transfer the money? How could I be sure they'd do what they promised once I had paid? If I did escape where would I go? Are there some countries that would refuse to send me home? On Sunday afternoon, with a local pastor preaching on TV, I said out loud, *This is ridiculous. There is no way the jury won't know I'm innocent.* I finally fell asleep and didn't wake until the guards came for me on Monday morning at half past five.

Jonathan reminded me to keep my face open and warm, especially if anyone said anything untrue. Heidi said, *The jury will watch how you react. They'll know if you're faking.* Their advice made me self-conscious and nervous, but once the witnesses finally started to testify, it was easy to be sincere. Tieresse's housekeeper, Stella, was first to take the stand. She explained she had been working for Tieresse for almost fifteen years, that she usually arrived at work shortly after nine and stayed until five thirty or six, that she did housekeeping and laundry, ran errands, and sometimes cooked. She said Tieresse was an early riser who had already gone to an exercise class at the gym by the time she got to the house but that I would usually still be sleeping when she arrived. She spoke with a heavy Latvian accent and the judge kept reminding her to speak up and slow down. She said she was confused the day of the murder because Tieresse was not there and the door to the parlor was ajar. Sometimes, she told the jury, Tieresse and I would be swimming. She kept the water heated all year round. But the pool was empty. The coffeepot was on a timer, and the carafe was full, with not a single cup gone. Usually there was freshly squeezed grapefruit juice in a carafe with ice, but the pitcher wasn't on the counter, and there were no fruit rinds in the sink. At first she thought the exercise class had run late, or that Tieresse had stopped to buy bagels on the way home, but she went into the garage and saw Tieresse's car parked and empty. That was when she began to worry.

The prosecutor showed Stella a photo of Tieresse, with her head resting in a pool of black blood, and asked whether that was how my wife had looked when Stella found her. Stella choked up and looked straight at me. She said I was there most mornings but not that day. A buzzing started inside my head. I concentrated on maintaining a neutral face. I glanced quickly at the jurors. They were all focused on the witness. One man and two women were leaning forward in their chairs. I saw Stella's lips moving and two jurors nod, but I could not hear what she was saying. Then the prosecutor sat and my lawyer stood, and it was quiet again. Heidi asked Stella whether she ever witnessed us fight. Stella said, *You mean like did he hit her?* My lawyer said, *Yes, did you ever see my client hit his wife or even raise his voice to her?* Stella said, *Mr. Rafael? No, ma'am. Never. He love her.* Heidi asked her whether Tieresse was happy, but the prosecutor objected, and the judge would not let her answer, even though she had already started to vigorously nod. When it was the prosecutor's turn again she asked whether I ever had strange women over to the house, and Stella looked at the judge, confused. The prosecutor said, *I want to know whether you ever saw the defendant at the victim's house with another woman.* Stella said no, never. The prosecutor said, *You understand that I am asking you because the defendant has admitted to having sexual affairs with at least four women during the time he was dating or married to your employer. I*

am trying to learn whether you witnessed any of these liaisons.
Jonathan objected, and the prosecutor withdrew the question,
but it was too late for me to hide the shame that had spread
across my face. When Stella stepped down, she left without
looking my way. I felt jurors staring at me, but could not force
myself to return their gaze.

Three police officers testified next. Two were the lead homicide detectives, Cole and Pisarro. The other was the patrol
officer who had been the first to arrive at the house in response
to the 911 call. He recounted how he checked to make sure the
victim was dead and upon finding no pulse secured the crime
scene and called for support. He described finding the candlestick next to the body and said it was covered with blood,
strands of hair, and pieces of Tieresse's scalp. My lawyer objected and the judge said, *Sustained.* The prosecutor showed
him photographs he had taken of open jewelry boxes scattered
on the closet floor and asked if that was how he had found
them. She asked him, *Officer, have you investigated robberies
before?* He said he had. She said, *Did this look like a robbery
to you?* My lawyer objected but the judge said, *Overruled,* and
told the officer he could answer. The policeman said, *No
ma'am. Usually a thief makes a mess. In this case, except for
the jewelry boxes, the rest of the house was pristine.* She said,
*No more questions for this witness, Your Honor. Thank you,
Officer.*

It was my lawyer's turn. Jonathan established the officer
was a six-year veteran who had investigated a dozen home robberies or burglaries and had testified previously in eight trials.
He said, *Do you consider yourself skilled as a robbery investigator?* and the officer said he did. My lawyer asked, *Officer, if a
thief was planning to steal a butcher knife, would you expect*

him to make a mess in the bedroom? The policeman said probably not. My lawyer said, *And if the thief was looking to steal a shoe, would you expect a mess in the kitchen?* The police officer looked at the prosecutor. She remained seated. He said, *Probably not.* Jonathan took a swallow of water then said, *Are you married, sir?* The prosecutor objected. My lawyer said, *I will get to the point quickly, Your Honor.* The judge told the policeman to answer. The policeman said yes he was, that he had been married for eleven years. My lawyer asked, *And does your wife have any jewelry?* He said, *Yes, her wedding ring, a couple of others, some earrings, a few necklaces.* My lawyer said, *Where does she keep it?* The police officer looked at the prosecutor again, but she did not stand up. My lawyer said, *You may answer, sir,* and the policeman said, *In our closet.*

Detective Cole was next, followed by Pisarro. They confirmed that crime scene photos shown to the jury reflected the way Tieresse's body looked when they found her. Cole described how he and two crime scene technicians had dusted for fingerprints in various locations, including the doorknobs, desktop, bathroom, and closet. Pisarro said they had made a mold of a shoe impression in the flower bed adjacent to the front door, but the impression turned out to belong to a yard worker. The most damning testimony came from Cole. Earlier, Stella had said she assumed Tieresse had already gone to and returned from her exercise class because the house alarm was turned off. Cole testified that after he and Pisarro had interviewed Stella, and she had told them the alarm was off when she got to the house that morning, they examined it and found it to be in working order. The prosecutor asked, *What conclusion do you draw from that, Detective?* Cole said, *Well, ma'am, it means someone who knew the code turned it off.* She said, *Do you know who had the* code? Cole said, *The homeowner, the housekeeper, the alarm company, and the defendant.*

Before the prosecutor had a chance to sit down, my lawyer was already on her feet. Heidi said, *It is possible, isn't it Detective Cole, the alarm was never turned on.* Cole said, *The housekeeper told us the victim always turned on the alarm before retiring.* My lawyer asked, *But it is possible she didn't that night, isn't that true?* Cole said, *I suppose. Almost anything is possible.* My lawyer said, *And what time did the victim retire the night before she was killed?* Cole said he didn't know. She said, *Well, Detective, if the victim turned on the alarm before retiring, and the thief broke in before she went to retire, you would expect the alarm not to be set, isn't that so?* Cole said, *I do not think the homeowner pulled all-nighters.* My lawyer objected and the judge said, *Sustained.* My lawyer said, *Please answer my question, Detective: If the thief was already in the house before the victim got ready for bed, the alarm would be off in the morning, isn't that so?* He said, *Yes ma'am.* My lawyer nodded, as if to say, *Exactly,* and she sat back down.

The prosecutor asked, *Did the defendant have the alarm code, Detective Cole?* Cole said, *He told my partner and me he did, and the housekeeper confirmed as much, so I assume so.* She said, *Thank you, Detective.*

Opening day's final witness was the coroner. He testified that Tieresse had died from blunt trauma. Her skull had been fractured and showed evidence of at least thirteen blows. I held my head in my hands. He said that Tieresse's left wrist and right hand were shattered, indicating she had tried to fight the intruder off. I inhaled sharply, and for the first time since her death, I felt unable to control my rage. I gripped the arms of my chair. My lawyer said, *Look at me,* and when I did, she whispered, *I need you not to look angry. I need you to relax.* I dropped my head into the crook of my right arm and squeezed shut my eyes. I felt Jonathan touching my arm and Heidi's fingers on my back. It was the first sign of affection anyone had shown me since the day of my arrest. I felt the black juror staring at me, but I didn't look back. The prosecutor asked the medical examiner approximately what time Tieresse had died. The coroner said, *Based on the temperature of the liver as well as indicia of rigor and livor mortis— essentially, the color and rigidity of the body—death appears to have occurred between ten at night and three* A.M.

I do not know how the jury reacted to this testimony because I was not watching them. I was not concentrating on my expression. I think Jonathan was asking him questions, but I was not listening any longer. Instead, I was thinking to myself. I was thinking how Tieresse was fighting for her life at the very moment I was in bed with a waitress, and I didn't care anymore what the jury decided. Nothing they could do to me would be punishment enough. Maybe I hadn't killed her, but I hadn't saved her either.

The judge reminded the jurors not to watch the news or read the paper, and he sent them home for the evening. The lawyers sparred over some technical issues about jury instructions. The two deputies came over with their handcuffs. Before they took me back to jail, I told my lawyers I wanted to change my plea to guilty.

■　■　■

Instead of taking me to my cell, the deputies put me in a room where I would meet with members of my legal team. A moment later, Heidi walked in. She said, You are in charge. If you want to change your plea you can. Did you beat your wife to death?

Everything I had been doing to hold myself together failed at once. I sobbed so violently I could neither catch my breath nor speak an answer to her question. I shook my head, and Heidi said, *Don't worry about it. I know the answer to that question.* She placed her hand on top of mine, banged on the door to let the deputies know we were through, and said, *See you in the morning, Rafael.*

The prosecutor had told the jury before even a single witness was called that the case against me was entirely circumstantial. There were no eyewitnesses, no damning calls to 911, no videotape, no physical evidence. She said, *It was a case of the dog not barking.* Whoever killed Tieresse knew the code to turn off the alarm. Whoever killed her knew exactly where she kept her jewelry. Whoever killed her knew when she would be alone. Whoever killed her knew that what looked like a delicate antique candlestick was actually a rock-hard potential murder weapon. She said, *There is only one person in the world who has all those characteristics, and he is sitting there in front of you.* She pointed at me and let her arm float in the air as she walked backward to her chair.

She said, *Of course, there is always a motive,* and I knew what she was going to say, and I wanted to look down, but even more than shame, I felt anger. This person accusing me of a violence beyond my capacity had no idea how I adored my wife, how the best part of my day was seeing her and the worst part was telling her goodbye. Her entire case depended on portraying me as a caricature. She said, *People of all stations loved this generous woman. Who on earth would have butchered her, other than a much younger husband, a serial philanderer, a struggling line cook who had lived hand to mouth for his entire life and now stood to inherit billions—billions she had worked hard for?* She paused, pretending she needed to catch her breath, then she whispered again, *Who else on earth?* Pointing again at me she said, *No one.*

If the theme of the first day's testimony had been, *This is how you know the husband did it,* the theme of the second day was, *And this is why.* The prosecutor put up a video screen and showed a picture of Tieresse and me walking out of city hall after our wedding. Underneath was the date. The state then called a succession of three women, who all testified they had sex with me in between the day of my wedding and the day Tieresse was killed. The prosecutors did not call Britanny, however, and that omission gave me hope. It shouldn't have. They were lying in wait.

My lawyers asked each of the women the same set of questions: *Did you know he was married? Did Rafael say anything about leaving his wife? Did it feel like anything more than a one-night stand to you?* They all answered the same way: *Yes, I knew he was married because he was wearing a ring. No, he did not say anything negative about his wife or that he was going to leave her. No, it was just sex.* Three of the jurors stared at me, and I could sense disgust. But I didn't care. I didn't care if they deemed my behavior the worst sort of infidelity. It was, after all. In truth, I didn't care what they thought of me. I confess I hoped these strangers could see I did not kill my wife, but all I really cared about was that they know how much I loved her.

On the third day of the trial, it was finally our turn. The prosecutor might have had passion on her side, but we had the truth on ours. My lawyers called as witnesses neighbors who had known Tieresse for twenty years and me for two. They had seen us together and been to our home. Maybe they could not swear that I did not do it, but they could swear it was unimaginable. They called people who had worked at La Ventana since the day we opened. They also could not swear to a negative, but they could say they had never seen me happier since the day Tieresse and I went on our first date, and they did.

Benita was also my business manager, and her testimony was a direct rebuttal to the prosecution's case. She testified we had never struggled financially. Since being on the *New York Times* list of ten places to watch, we had a four-month waiting list for reservations. She told the jury how Tieresse had asked me not just once, but at least three times, to open more restaurants using her money, and how I had declined each and every offer. She was sincere and angry, and I loved her for it.

Many of the witnesses cried. They looked me in the eye when they first took the stand, and they stared straight at the jurors when saying there was no way I could have done this. I wanted to hug every one of them.

We saved the star witness for the next day. Britanny was my alibi. That was the good news. The bad news is that her testimony certainly wasn't going to cause the jurors to like me. Jonathan had tried to lay the groundwork during his opening statement. He told the jury they would hear from some women I had sex with since getting married. He said the prosecution would make it sound as if I were a gold digger who had been cheating on my wife since the first day of our marriage. But I hadn't, Jonathan said. According to my lawyer, who held a thick *Physicians' Desk Reference* in his hand, Tieresse was a *non-libidoist*—someone who got no pleasure from sex. Even worse, because of a series of unfortunate medical decisions, having sex caused her agonizing pain. She knew that about herself, and she had given me permission to sleep with others. *They had an arrangement,* he said, and when he used that word, I shuddered. I leaned over to Heidi and whispered, *That is not what it was at all,* and Heidi patted my knee and whispered back, *Let us be the lawyers here, okay?*

Britanny's husband was in the courtroom, sitting in the first row, watching his newlywed tell the jury about her final fling before meeting him. She told them about the going-away party, how the entire La Ventana staff, from the cooks and waitstaff to the Hispanic kids who bus the tables and keep the water glasses full, sat around a giant makeshift table and ate and drank and told stories about obnoxious guests. She told the story about her hair catching on fire. She told them I brought the finest bottles of wine up from the cellar and passed around the most expensive liquor we poured. She told the jury everyone at the restaurant knew I sometimes had lady friends upstairs to my loft and they suspected Tieresse knew as well. The prosecutor objected, and the judge instructed the jury to disregard Britanny's speculation. She seemed rattled. She sipped from her water glass and wiped her palms on her skirt. She told the jurors she had not planned on staying. She said, *Things just happened, I wasn't expecting it, and the next morning, Rafael told me to please stay in touch, and I told him I would. He was my friend. He still is my friend.* When she said that, she looked first at the jury, and then to me.

Every word she said was the truth. There is no way anybody could think she was lying. Why would she? She had absolutely nothing to gain. My lawyer thanked her for her testimony, and it was the prosecutor's turn.

What time did you fall asleep? the prosecutor asked her. I didn't remember. Britanny didn't either. The prosecutor said, *Do you have a lot of one-night stands?* Heidi objected and the prosecutor withdrew the question. She asked, *What time did you leave in the morning?* Britanny told her it was around nine. I looked over at the jury. I was wondering what any of these questions had to do with anything, but I was worried because the jurors appeared interested. She asked, *Had you been to the defendant's house prior to that evening?* Brittany said, *You mean his house house, or his apartment above the restaurant?* The prosecutor smiled. The fish had taken the bait. She said, *Oh, so you know he had two houses. Is the answer to one different from the other?* Britanny stammered. She was nervous. Finally she said, *I'd never been to either.* The prosecutor said, *Do you have any idea how long it takes to drive from La Ventana to the defendant's house?* She drew out the word *house* as if it had three syllables. Brittany said she didn't. The prosecutor asked whether she would be surprised to learn the drive was less than ten minutes, and Britanny shook her head. The judge asked her to speak up, and Britanny said, *No, I would not be surprised. I did not know where their house was.*

In her closing argument the next morning, the prosecutor would say I had at least two hours, and possibly closer to four, to drive to the house, murder my wife, clean myself up, and drive back. She used our star witness to make her timeline plausible. She said, *Could that have happened?* Britanny said, *No, that didn't happen.* The prosecutor said, *Do you know what is happening around you while you are asleep?* Britanny said nothing. The prosecutor said, *I am asking you whether it could have happened,* and when Britanny still said nothing, the judge told her to answer. The judge said, *Ma'am, you have to speak up.* My lawyer objected and the judge overruled it and told her to answer. Britanny said, *No, I do not know what happens*

when I am asleep. I do know Rafael is not capable of this.
The prosecutor said, *The jury will decide that issue, miss. My
question for you is whether you slept more than four hours that
evening after your rollicking party.* Britanny said, *Yes. I did.*
Britanny looked softly at me as she left the witness stand, apol-
ogizing, I think, for not being helpful, and I shook my head,
meaning to say, *No, you did fine.* When the judge sent the jury
home, not a single juror met my eyes.

That night I didn't sleep at all. The next morning, Friday,
the lawyers gave their closing arguments. The jury started delib-
erating at eleven o'clock. Not counting the days spent picking the
jury, the entire trial had taken less than four entire days. Shortly
before six they came back. The judge asked the foreman whether
they had reached a verdict, and he said they had. The judge
asked him to read it aloud, and he didn't even say my name. He
said, *Will the defendant please rise?* I stood flanked by my
lawyers and looked at the foreman. He was staring straight
down. None of the jurors was looking at me. The foreman read,
*We, the jury, find the defendant, Rafael Zhettah, guilty of
capital murder.* His pronunciation of my name was perfect. I
collapsed into my chair.

For the next few moments, I heard many voices, but I did
not comprehend any of what they said. I heard the sounds of
the judge talking to the jury, my lawyers talking to the judge,
the jurors talking to my lawyers, my lawyers talking to each
other. Then the judge banged his gavel, and I was present again,
in time to hear him tell the twelve who believed me a murderer
he would see them Monday morning at nine, and as they filed
out Heidi slumped into the chair next to me and began to explain what would happen next. Jonathan stared blankly at the
empty jury box.

Until I became a defendant, my knowledge of criminal trials came from reading *To Kill a Mockingbird* and watching *A Few Good Men* every time it was on TV. Atticus Finch had a human relationship with his client Tom Robinson, and Tom Cruise struggled to connect with the marines he was defending. The central relationship in both stories was the one between lawyers and their clients. What I never noticed was the importance of the relationship between the lawyers and the women and men who would judge their clients. That night in my cell, though, it hit me. The trust between the lawyers and the jury matters way more than the trust between the lawyers and the client, and my lawyers had none left. They promised the jury I had nothing to do with Tieresse's murder, and the jury hadn't believed them. Their credibility was spent, and credibility was all they'd ever had.

In a room at the jail reserved for inmates to meet with their attorneys I sat in silence while my legal team desperately debated what kind of lifesaving narrative to construct. It would have been hopeless even if they'd had a month. They had sixty hours. Their only option was to use my neighbors, colleagues, and employees to beg the jury to spare my life, but those same witnesses had already testified I was innocent, and the jurors hadn't believed them the first time. I asked the deputy to take me back to my cell and left them there without saying goodbye.

If I slept at all the next three nights, it was only for an hour or two a day. My plan was to be so tired on Monday that I would literally fall asleep during the trial. I could think of no more powerful way to communicate to the jury how little I cared about what they thought.

The prosecution called Reinhardt as their first witness. He testified about how he had been raised by a single mother who

managed to build a business behemoth and cook him breakfast
every morning. Twice he stopped to compose himself. He did
not look at me even once. After he stepped down, a parade of
philanthropists told the jury Tieresse was an innovator who
inspired them to give more to the community. More than one
said she was irreplaceable. I did not resent any of the state's
witnesses. If asked, I would have said the exact same things.

Before lunch on Tuesday the state rested its case, and it was
our turn. An expert on the prison system explained to the jury
I would never get out of prison if sentenced to life instead of
death, and there was no reason to believe I would be dangerous
either to guards or to other inmates inside. The point of his
testimony was to make the jury feel like they could lock me up
and throw away the key and not worry they were taking the
risk I would injure someone else. For our second witness, my
lawyer called me to the stand.

The night before, in the county jail, I skipped dinner and
met until midnight with Heidi and Jonathan. They had a script,
and we practiced my answers to their questions half a dozen
times. They coached me on inflection, pace, and when to look
at the jury and when to look at them. I worried I would sound
practiced or robotic, but I shouldn't have. The next day, when I
raised my right hand and swore to tell the truth, I felt drops of
sweat sliding down my spine and my hands were shaking so
hard I sloshed water out of the cup when I picked it up to drink.
My voice was a rasp when Jonathan asked me my name.

I didn't sound rehearsed because I couldn't remember a
single thing they had told me. The first thing he asked me was
how to pronounce my name, and then he said, *Did you kill
your wife?* I think the prosecutor objected, but I'm not sure,
because I was so shocked by the question. I am positive we

hadn't gone over it before. How could he have the audacity? I felt flushed with anger. There must have been some sort of argument among the lawyers because what happened next was the judge said, *Mr. Zhettah,* and I turned toward him, and he said, *I've ruled, you may answer the question.* I said, *I'm sorry, what was the question?* Jonathan repeated it. I wanted to say, *Fuck you,* and stand up and leave. Let the deputies tackle me. I was done with this circus. But I did not. I said, *No sir. I loved my wife.*

He asked how we had met, what sort of things we did together, what we talked about, where we liked to go. At some point I was delivering a eulogy in a question-and-answer format, and for a moment a wave of overwhelming sadness rose up inside me, but then I realized I was given this opportunity to tell twelve strangers and a room full of reporters who knew nothing about her except that she was rich what a special creature she was.

I said, You hear about people like Mother Teresa who devote their lives to the poor. I don't mean any disrespect, but I can guarantee you Tieresse was every bit as angelic as Mother Teresa. She could have walled herself off from the rest of the world if she'd wanted to, lived in a castle, vacationed on private islands, given up on the world. Instead she went on a mission to improve it.

I said, I am the saddest person in this room, I don't care whether you believe that or not. I am also the luckiest.

We had not rehearsed that, either. And I saw Jonathan freeze and Heidi's mouth open, and I had no idea whether that was a good sign or a bad. But when at last I finished talking, and the prosecutor had no more questions either, Jonathan came up to the chair where I was sitting between a court reporter and the judge, and he placed his hand on top of mine, and I felt the jurors watching me, and I believed they knew their earlier verdict was wrong.

My lawyers and the prosecutor made closing arguments. The prosecutor said I was a conniving, deceitful predator. My lawyers said nobody was duplicitous enough to fool as many people as had testified on my behalf. I thought the black juror was staring at me, but when I followed her line of sight, I realized she was looking at Reinhardt, who was sitting in the second row. The judge read the jury their instructions and told them deliberations would begin in the morning.

Back at the jail on Tuesday night, I paced in my cell. I could hear an infomercial for a treadmill playing at three A.M. on the TV that was never turned off. On Wednesday morning I drank a cup of instant coffee but vomited it back up before the guards came for me at seven. I sat there, while Heidi and Jonathan tended to other matters, other clients, on their mobile phones. Before the lunch hour, the judge's law clerk let both sides know the jury had reached a verdict. I stood up, flanked by my lawyers, and the courtroom was completely still. Then the judge said something and the foreman rose and spoke, but I didn't hear a thing, except for a gasp from Heidi when the foreman sat back down and the judge told me I had been sentenced to death.

PART 2

...

Once in Kansas I saw a tornado. I watched it through binoculars from a mile away. Even at that distance I could hear A-frame trusses exploding and the hiss of gas as propane tanks were ripped from their concrete pads. On my side of the street it didn't even rain. You can be cheek by jowl with mayhem and simultaneously a thousand miles away.

I lost track of place and time. Jonathan was talking to me, I think. The black woman on the jury might have been crying. The court reporter's hands were frozen above her stenotype, or perhaps someone was still talking. I didn't hear the deputy instruct me to stand, so he and another yanked me from my chair, slapped cuffs on my wrists, and double-timed me back to the county jail. Two more deputies joined them, and the four took me out back into an alleyway and loaded me into the second row of a windowless van.

Two men were already sitting in the front, separated from me by a plexiglass shield. I was no longer any old prisoner. I was about to become death row inmate number 0002647, and all the rules had changed.

One deputy sat to my right, another to my left. My wrists, still cuffed together, were chained to a leather belt cinching my waist. My ankle restraints attached to a thick metal grommet welded to the floor. The guard to my right held up a bottle of water and asked if I wanted a swallow. I was parched with fear.

I said, No thank you.

I heard my voice quaver, and I felt my thighs tremble, and I said, *On second thought, yes, please.* He held it to my mouth and tipped it back. Halfway to Livingston, home to death row, we pulled off the highway and parked by a fast-food restaurant. The driver left the engine running and went inside.

When I was a boy, and my papá was at work, Mamá took me to the market where she bought masa and dried beans. The man who handed her back her change leered at her in a way I already knew was a crude assault. She said something to him, and he licked his lips and did it again. He had a raised scar on his forehead and was missing a top front tooth.

That night, when Papá got home, I heard him and Mamá whispering on the porch. He kissed me after dinner, got on his motorbike, and rode away. I heard him quietly return in the middle of the night. The next morning Mamá and I bought our supplies at the same *almacén* we had been at the day before, but we handed our money to a new proprietor. I never again saw the man who had disrespected my mamá, but I remembered the way he had looked at her when the guard sitting in the front seat turned around and took off his shades and ran his eyes from my toes to my mouth.

The driver returned. The guards ate their hamburgers and fries and licked grease and salt from their fingers. The driver said, *Buckle up, ladies,* and we took a two-lane highway across a muddy creek. Through the windshield I saw a motorboat speeding across an enormous lake. The road turned sharply to the right, and a squat red-topped water tower came into view. Through the driver's closed window I could hear barking dogs in a metal prefab building behind a row of rusted barbed wire. The van pulled up to a gate guarded by a man on horseback cradling a rifle and another sitting in a weathered plastic chair wearing a holstered .45. The seated guard stood and approached the driver's side window. He looked at the IDs the deputies carried, made some notes on a form attached to his clipboard, and asked how long they intended to be. The driver said, *However long it takes you people to get this guy unloaded. We're off the clock in an hour.*

The guard said, Your lucky day. Row's on lockdown. Won't take long to get this one processed.

Then he turned his gaze to me. He said, Welcome to death row, son.

We pulled up to a loading dock, where two guards from death row were waiting. One was a chicken-necked white kid with a splotch of acne on his forehead and braces on his lower teeth. The other was a thick black woman who was twirling a mahogany baton. The deputy sitting to my right got out of the van, and the guard in the passenger seat looked at me and said, *Your turn.* He stepped out at the same time as I did and pulled a pouch of tobacco from his pocket. He said to the white kid, *Shift's over. Y'all got an issue me dippin' here?* The CO said, *Nope, so long as the warden don't come out,* and he spat a glob of thick yellow mucus onto the pavement beside my right foot. The black woman slid the baton into a leather loop, then manacled me in the prison's own hardware. She unlocked the other set of cuffs and chains and they fell to the ground. The guard who had sat next to me and offered me water picked them up and tossed them onto the floorboard in the back of the van. Then he said, *May God grant you mercy, young man,* and I realized for the first time he had white hair at his temples and his two-day beard was flecked with gray. The guard whose eyes had roamed over me snorted and said, *Shit, old-timer, let's go get a beer.* They were laughing as they left.

A third corrections officer appeared. Although I did not yet recognize the insignia signaling rank, it was obvious he was in charge even before the kid with acne called him *Captain.* He checked the cuffs on my hands and dropped a second chain from the leather belt to the loops on my ankles. It happened very fast. The captain said, *Welcome to your new world, inmate.* His tone was not facetious, and his eyes were sincere. The black woman smelled like lilac. She said, *Ready, Captain,* and he said, *We are, Sergeant.*

Lilac led the way, with Captain and Kid on my left and right. The buildings were concrete and steel, forming a U-shape surrounding a neatly manicured lawn being tended to by a gaunt middle-aged black guy wearing a white cotton shirt that said *Trustee.* Even from up close, the square single-paned windows were as small as portholes on the lower deck of a cargo ship. Their scarred plexiglass, I would learn by morning, turned the sunlight into a broken spectrum comprising different shades of dirty bathwater. I looked down and saw my reflection in the manacle, startled to see deep lines cutting into the face of a man who had aged thirty years in thirteen months. I shuffled along, because shuffling was the only way to move, and because I didn't want to get wherever I was going. The captain said, Inmate, you're going to have to learn to move faster than that.

We arrived at a cage, eight feet by eight, with a drain in the center of the floor and steel bars for all four walls. Lilac nudged me in, gently I thought, then all three guards stepped back as the door swung shut. The Kid reached through the bars to unlock the chains and told me to remove my clothes. Lilac picked up what looked like a fire hose and blasted me with warm water mixed with bleach and soap. She told me to face forward and lift my scrotum, and then to turn around, squat, and spread my cheeks, and she blasted me again. Perspiration mixed with the water dripping from my pits. Lilac told the captain I was clean, and he said, Good job, Sergeant.

To my left was a booth with a single guard watching four twenty-year-old computer monitors and manipulating a row of joysticks. A digital clock read 4:47 P.M. They left me there for two hours. It grew dark. A row of incandescent bulbs in sockets protected by chicken-wire orbs clicked on. I heard doors slam and men laughing. I smelled mustard greens cooking in grease.

New guards came to get me: Their name tags said *Sanchez, Forester,* and *Meggyesfalvi.* I stared at the laminated ID with the surname I couldn't pronounce. He said, *Inmate, have you got a problem?* And he handed me a white cotton jumpsuit with the letters *DR* stenciled on the back, a pair of polyester boxer shorts, a crew-neck T-shirt, shower slippers, and a plastic ID with my name, photo, personal information, and inmate number. His accent was Eastern European, Hungarian, maybe. In my mind I named him Bela.

Earlier, after Lilac had hosed me down, the Kid had asked, *Protestant, Catholic, Muslim, or Jew?* I told him none of the above. He elbowed Lilac and laughed. He said, *How come the terrorists brag about being Muslim and the Jews pretend they ain't nothing?* The captain grinned.

I said, My mother was Jewish, my father was not. I practice no faith.

The captain said, Suit yourself, inmate. We'll put you down as Jew. You make hebe number three.

The kid wearing braces laughed and said, That's a good one, Cap'n, hebe number three.

The captain glared at him, and the Kid got quiet.

According to my ID, I was *Rafael Zhettah, 6'1", 175, Caucasian-J, DOB 7–18–66, no. 0002647.* The photo was a head shot, taken when I was preparing to be hosed down. I looked at my eyes and saw the terror I had been too numb to feel.

Bela said, Inmate Zhettah, hands.

He pronounced it *za-heater.* I said, It's pronounced *je-tah.*

Bela said, *I promise you, inmate, how I say your name in here is the least of your fucking problems. Now give me your goddamn hands.* I dropped my hands in front of me and pressed my belly against the bars. Bela said, *Are you seriously a goddamn retard, za-heater? Turn your ass around.* I said, *Sorry, this is a different routine from county.* I faced away and felt Bela's warm damp breath on my neck. He said, *Damn straight it is, numb nuts. Welcome to the major leagues,* and he snapped the cuffs on my wrists.

They walked me down a long corridor, through two electronic solid steel doors operated by guards in a booth like the one I had seen before. I was carrying a small mesh sack with toiletries and a moleskin notebook Lilac had examined carefully when I arrived. I said to my escorts, *Is it possible for me to get a pencil or pen?* Nobody answered. Inmates were banging on their cell doors and there was a hissing sound coming from an area I later learned was the shower. I smelled ammonia mixed with urine. Bela said, *Here's your house, Inmate za-heater. Welcome to the neighborhood.* Forester made a call on a two-way radio then used a key to open the sliding door to my cell: unit 11J on B-pod, one of six wings here on death row.

We inmates call the cells our *houses,* as if naming a cage something desirable can make it so. It was four strides from front to back, and not quite three from left to right, approximately sixty square feet. My closet in Tieresse's house had been substantially larger. With my back to the door, a metal cot hung by chains from the wall on the right. Behind it was a shelf for my books. To the left, a stainless-steel sink and toilet. Next to it, a single outlet where I could plug in a hot plate to make coffee or heat beans purchased from the prison commissary, if I had any funds in my inmate account.

Forester told me to squat, *With your back to me,* he said, and when I did, he reached through the beanhole—that's what you call the slot in the door—and removed the cuffs. I felt him slip a felt-tipped pen into my hand.

It was nearly seven P.M. I'd missed dinner but I wasn't hungry. I spread a stained polyester sheet over a quarter-inch pad atop the metal bunk, lay down with my head on a thin foam pillow, covered myself with a scratchy gray fleece blanket, and listened to the sounds of my new home. I took out my notebook and made the first entry in my diary.

Day 1: My celebrity preceded me. There's a guy in the cell next door screaming that he doesn't want a Mexican lady killer as his neighbor. He's saying, *Put the spic with his own. I ain't gonna live next to no Mexican.* I'm not sure who he was talking to, but I heard someone else scream, *Shut your mouth, Adolf,* and then the guy next to me said, *Fuck you, nigger lover.* I wonder how they know anything about me. I wonder if I should worry about my neighbor. Less than ten hours ago I was in

Houston wearing a suit. Five days ago I was ready to go home. Now I am here, in a dark and cramped space, unsure of my neighbors and wary of the guards, smelling of sulfur, and shivering from either cold or fear. After the deaths of Tieresse and my *padres*, it's the fourth-worst night of my life. I wonder why, as much as I want to, I am unable to cry.

■ ■ ■

I still remember the first night. On the first night, I noticed the sounds.

In the county jail where I had spent more than a year, the inmates had hope. They dreamed of being acquitted. They planned to go home. In the county jail, once the lights clicked off at ten, commotion stopped. Crazy guys got taken somewhere else. A few night owls sat up and whispered or read by lamp, but most of us slept. Deputies kept their radio volume low and left us inmates to ourselves. They knew the gig was temporary, that they'd be back riding patrol in a week or two, so they didn't need to prove how different they were from the inmates by constantly beating us down. We couldn't leave when we wanted, but we all knew we'd be leaving. It was guaranteed. What made us peaceful, almost serene, was the existence of hope.

Men do not go crazy from being locked in a cage. They do not go crazy from the outside pushing in. They crack from the inside pushing out. When you take away hope, madness fills its place, and madness is loud. Death row is the loudest thing I ever experienced, louder than anything in the free world, louder than a concert, louder than a jet, louder than a firecracker exploding inside your ear; and it is loud all the time, morning, day, and night. We do not count down the days until we will be free in here. We count them down to our deaths. Making noise is the proof you aren't yet dead. In place of hope there is anger, and anger, too, is very loud.

If you listen carefully, you can hear layers of sound: crazy inmates screaming and banging on solid steel cell doors, white guys blasting country music on transistor radios they're allowed to buy so long as they are well behaved, Jesus freaks praying for salvation while listening to Christian talk, static-laced intercom messages announcing shift changes, and hourly reminders to conduct a count. The guards are different too. They're not like the deputies in the county jail who were marking time before leaving the asylum and heading back out to the streets. These guards are lifers. Their future is nearly as dismal as ours. Out of malice or ennui, COs check on prisoners by lifting up then slamming shut the cover to the beanhole, ensuring (perversely, I know) we are still alive. They ram meal carts into steel doors. They add to the cacophony as part of their jobs.

That first night, even more than freedom, I prayed for earplugs.

Some people say the first night is the worst, but I disagree. What it is is different. It is unlike anything you have ever known. But once you get accustomed to the constant din, to the menacing white supremacists and sadistic COs, to incoherent babbling and inexplicable shrieks, once you get used to all that, every night is the worst.

■ ■ ■

Day 2: Morning came, my first morning on death row, soiled sunlight slicing into my cell, and I had not even closed my eyes.

77

I pulled my knees to my chest and rolled off my bunk. I examined the bolts holding the toilet to the floor and then looked to see if it was possible to use a paper clip to jimmy open the door. If it was possible, it was beyond my skill set, but it didn't matter, because I didn't have a paper clip anyway. I craned my neck to see where I would be if I managed to lose enough weight to shimmy through the tiny window. (I would have been on a walkway lined with a twelve-foot razor-topped fence.) These were fantasies. No one had ever escaped from this prison or even managed to slip out of his cell. But I'd have these fantasies, and others like them, a dozen times a day for every day I was here, every last one.

Breakfast was powdered eggs and a slice of untoasted white bread that contained more chemicals than wheat. I had a single swallow of juice from a box. When the guards came for the trays later that morning, the guy in the cell next door to mine started demanding again that they move him. I did not yet know all their names, but the kid with braces I'd met the day before lifted up the beanhole and told the guy to shut up. Then he said, *By the way, Taylor, he ain't only Mexican, your neighbor's also a Jew. Guess you're a two-time loser.* He banged shut the beanhole, and I heard him laugh. Taylor screamed, *Tell the captain I want an I-90, you hear me, bitch?* A few days later I learned an I-90 is a form inmates fill out when they have a complaint about something. It was pretty obvious what Taylor's complaint was, but just in case, he made it clear to me. He said, *It ain't nothin' personal, Chavez. All you got to do is read the Bible. God says we ain't s'posed to be mixin' with the niggers and the spics. Live and let live.* I wanted to tell him God also says you're not supposed to murder. Instead I said, *My name isn't Chavez.*

Later that day, the transport team came for me. I was still not familiar with the routine. I said, *What am I supposed to do?* A CO named McKenzie said, *Put your ID in your pocket and your dick in your pants.* I said, *What?* He said, *Turn around, dumb ass, and show me your hands.* He, the acne-scarred kid, and Lilac took me through a series of six doors and three corridors until we arrived at an area that could have been a decaying city high school. McKenzie knocked on a door and in an obsequious tone told a woman who turned out to be the warden's secretary we were there. She steered us into a room. The warden was wearing boots, a plaid western shirt, and polyester slacks straining at the waist. He looked at McKenzie and said, *Prison rodeo's today.* Then he introduced himself to me, told me we won't have any problems getting along if I follow the rules, and asked whether I had any questions. I did. I wanted someone to explain to me how this nightmare was happening. I said, *No sir.* On the walk back, the kid with braces asked McKenzie, *Does the warden compete in the rodeo?* McKenzie said, *How the fuck should I know?*

When I arrived at the prison, Texas was executing people faster than it was sending new guys to death row. There was spare capacity. The cell directly across from mine and the one to the left were both empty. As the kid was opening my door, McKenzie made a joke about the vacant houses being a sign of a bad economy. He blamed it on the president. The kid forced a laugh. Lilac pressed her lips together. They left, and once again, Taylor and I had the wing to ourselves.

Somebody had left a yellowed newspaper article about Taylor's case on top of my bunk. According to the story, Taylor, who was thirty-eight years old, had spent twenty-one of those years in prison. His first stint came after he was convicted of firebombing a black church near Dallas. While inside, he founded the prison's Aryan Brotherhood gang and negotiated a treaty with the KKK. After being paroled, he was suspected of having killed two black neighborhood political organizers in the East Texas town of Vidor but was never charged with that crime. He was later convicted of murdering three Jewish doctors in their homes in an affluent San Antonio neighborhood, claiming they were aborting white Christian babies without the mothers' consent.

Lilac checked on me that afternoon. She lifted the beanhole. I said, *I'm here.* She said, *One thing we got in common, Inmate za-heater, is your new neighbor hates you as much as he hates me.* Forester was with her. He added, *Tell you the truth, inmate, most of the guards here, myself included, don't much care for the guy, but we ain't gonna interrupt our lunch if you get shanked. Do me a favor though and don't let it happen on my shift, 'cause the paperwork's a bitch.* Lilac said, *I know that's right.* I said, *Did one of you leave a newspaper on my bunk?* They closed the beanhole and I heard Taylor scream, *You're all a bunch of lyin' motherfuckers, all of ya.*

Later that night I heard rhythmic tapping that might have been Morse code. I did not yet have a handle on the acoustics inside this place. The sounds could have been coming from next door, or from above me, or from a mile away. I said out loud, If that's code, I don't understand what whoever you are is saying.

The tapping stopped, then a voice whispered, *It's me.* I said, *Who?* He said, *Me, asshole. Your neighbor.* It was Taylor. I didn't know what to say. He said, *Sadist motherfuckin' COs just like to stir the pot. Did the warden give you his live-and-let-live diatribe? It's all a bunch of bullshit. I ain't a racist. I just told them I don't want to live in a nigger neighborhood, same as they don't wanna live in mine. Ain't nothin' personal.*

It sounded like he was lying on the floor of his cell, with his head at the bottom of the solid steel door. I lay down on my belly and said, I'm not sure I like any of these neighborhoods. Are there black guys around here?

He said, What is it with you people and the niggers?

I said, Not sure what you mean by *you people.* I'm not really anything.

Taylor said, Not yet you're not. Talk to me in a year, assumin' we're still around.

Minutes passed. I thought he had gone to sleep, and I started to make a note about our conversation in my journal, but fifteen minutes later he asked, You play hearts?

I said, Uh-uh.

He said, You want to learn you let me know. Got to do something to keep you sharp. Push-ups and hearts, key to longevity.

I said, Are you being ironic?

He said, What?

I said, Nothing. Thanks for the advice.

■ ■ ■

Once I realized the routine, I stopped being worried about Taylor. They keep us in solitary confinement. Even if you don't like your neighbor, you're not going to have a chance to kill him. Sometimes the guards will put two inmates who don't get along in adjacent dayrooms, or march them past one another on the way to or from the shower, just to amuse themselves and laugh at our impotence, but our hands are cuffed or we're sep-arated by bars. The worst that happens is someone spits on you.

The only real crime on death row is committed by the guards. Every few days or weeks, teams of three COs, wearing helmets and face masks and carrying Mace and shields, burst unannounced into our cells. They say they are looking for contraband—maybe a toothbrush handle whittled down to a point, or a piece of jagged plastic broken off the corner of a food tray. But the contraband they find is usually a transistor radio jury-rigged to pull in a jazz station from Houston, or a gallon of home-brewed moonshine distilled from a carton of lemonade and a box of raisins. If they find drugs, they're finding some-thing we bought from a peddling CO.

During week two, my house got tossed for the first time. The sergeant said my copy of *Sports Illustrated* could be used to start a fire. He took it and stood outside my cell reading an article about motorcycle racing while his minions poked their fat fingers down into a jar of instant coffee and emptied into the commode a box of stale saltines. On their way out, one of the COs said, *Get this mess cleaned by dinner, za-heater, or I'll write your ass up.* Next they went into Taylor's house. He greeted them by flinging at his cell door feces he'd mixed with urine in an empty bottle of juice. The COs left him to sit there in squalor for four hours, and they put the rest of the pod on lockdown for a week. I heard a guy from the Muslim Brotherhood called the COs a bunch of pinhead fascists. There's nothing like communal punishment to make pris-oners who hate each other into loyal allies.

Day 23: Lockdown officially ended this morning. When the trustee came for my lunch tray, he said guards would be taking me to rec this afternoon and to the shower to-morrow. The written regs say we're supposed to get an hour a day outside our sixty-square-foot cell and four showers a week. We get maybe half that, but most guys don't complain. They'd rather sleep.

A little past three, the transport team came for me. It was Lilac, Forester, and McKenzie. I turned and squatted and offered my wrists before they could ask, and Forester laughed. *Eager beaver,* he said. We walked down the hall, turned left at a sign reading C-pod—*All inmates must be in restraints,* and turned left again. Directly in front of me was another cage. It was a disco-size dance floor of concrete enclosed by a double-layered floor-to-ceiling fence. It was completely empty.

I said, This is rec?

McKenzie said, Is it just me, Forester, or are the inmates getting dumber?

I looked at Lilac. She looked away.

I spent my exercise time walking around the perimeter of the cage, changing directions every five laps. After every ten laps I did push-ups. I hadn't done a push-up since high school gym class. I managed two sets of ten, then seven on the third set, and five on the last. My arms were shaking after three. When they came back for me I said, *Has it already been an hour?* McKenzie said, *It's been twenty-five minutes, macho man. Time to go.* That night I slept in my sweaty shirt. I was too sore to take it off.

I was scheduled for a shower the next day. Lots of guys skip them because the water is either scalding hot or freezing cold, and the guards can leave you in the cubicle for a couple of hours before they take you back to your cell. But I wasn't thinking about that. I was thinking about how good it would feel to have hot water melting the knots out of my back. Plus, since the day they blasted me with soapy disinfectant on my arrival, my hygiene had consisted of bathing in my sink. I desperately needed a shower. So when the team came to get me, I squatted next to the door before they asked to offer my wrists. The guard looking through the beanhole said, Inmate za-heater, you might want to grab ahold of your towel and soap first, 'cause we ain't your fucking butlers.

The water dripped from the head, and the temperature veered from hot to cold and back again. I leaned forward and lifted my arms and placed my palms flat against the tile. I had been all by myself in the world since the day Tieresse died, but at that moment, in the moldy cubicle with lukewarm water trickling from the pipe and temporarily muffling the inmates' din, I felt entirely alone for the very first time. I turned off the water and sat down on the concrete bench. I think the guards sensed my despair. They left me there for only forty-five minutes before shackling me back up and walking me home.

We passed in front of Taylor's cell. His radio was playing country music and the air was thick with the smell of raw sewage. Bela said, *What the fuck?* McKenzie lifted the beanhole and slammed it shut almost right away. Taylor had tried to fling excrement again. McKenzie said to Bela, *If my reflexes had been slower I would have killed him.* Bela said, *You'd of had plenty of help, sir.* Taylor screamed, *You people better listen. There ain't gonna be no peace until the neighborhood gets clean.* Then I heard him muttering to himself, but I could not make out the words. McKenzie said, *You are one slow learner, inmate, an embarrassment to your people. I'll be back.* Taylor said, *Fuck you, McKenzie, and get fucking Che Guevara off this pod. I ain't gonna put up with no more goddamn harassment.* Despite the solid steel door separating us, I felt fear. He said, *You laughing, Che Guevara? Then fuck you too. Move him the hell out of here, McKenzie, or get me up to level.*

We have three levels here. Level 1 is where I was. Level 2 is where guys who commit a minor infraction get sent. Level 3 is the hole. Inmates on level 3 lose their radios, if they have them, and they don't get to exercise or shower or buy anything from the commissary. Eventually I would experience those consequences firsthand, but at the time, I simply wondered whether I should tell Taylor I hadn't been laughing. As we waited for Lilac to open my cell door, McKenzie told Bela to call an extraction team. It was the first time I'd heard that expression, but it didn't seem the right time to ask them what they meant. Bela closed and locked my door and took his hardware without saying another word.

Laughter was coming from behind the cell door directly across from mine. Apparently I had a new neighbor. He must have moved in while I was in the shower. He was too comfortable to be a new guy. He probably came from another pod. A high-pitched voice with what sounded like a fake lisp said, *I missed you up on level, amor,* and he made a kissing sound. He said, *Did you miss me too, Adolf?*

Taylor said, Fuck you, asshole.

The other inmate laughed and said, 'Spite the fact you're the dumbest guy in all of TDC, Adolf, I'm still gonna be muy triste when they fry your Nazi ass. That means really sad, moron. I mean it. In the meantime, though, I'm gonna sit here and munch on my popcorn and watch 'em gas you 'til you cry like a bitch.

Taylor said, Bastards know I'm ready to rumble. They ain't gonna mess with me today.

The new inmate said, *Goddamn you're a dumb-ass, Taylor.* Then he said, What about you, new guy? You ready to watch?

Moments later, four COs appeared outside Taylor's cell.

I watched through the slit above the beanhole. Three were wearing black ninja outfits and helmets and carrying Mylar shields. A fourth held a video camera in one hand and an aerosol can in the other. One of the ninjas shouted *Now,* then lifted the beanhole and tossed something inside. I heard a muffled explosion and smelled cordite. Taylor screamed, *Hey, hey, chill motherfuckers.* The guy in the cell across the corridor said, *Olé, Adolf, stun grenades. Otra vez, comandante.* The guard with the can counted to ten, then a ninja opened the beanhole and the guard shot in a stream of spray. Taylor said, *It's enough. I can't see. This is excessive force. I wanna see the captain.* I heard him coughing. The guard with the can said, *Sure, I'll get right on it, inmate,* then he nodded at a ninja, who opened the beanhole again, and the guard sprayed Taylor one more time. He stood to the side and held the video camera up to his eye, and the three ninjas rushed in. One was saying, *Get down, get down, get down,* and I heard a brief commotion, and then I saw Taylor, naked, lying on his belly on the run, with his hands cuffed behind him, and the foot of a ninja planted in the small of his back. It all happened in seconds. Two trustees appeared from the other direction and removed the mattress, towel, and clothes from Taylor's cell. Taylor said, *Nigger collaborators is all y'all are.* One of the ninjas kicked him in the head. The guard with the video camera told the trustees to take all the possessions to the burn area and set it all on fire. The ninjas pushed Taylor back into his cell. The guard with the video camera said, *You can sleep on the floor 'til your house is clean. Here's a mop.* He pointed the camera at a watch and announced the time, and then the four of them were gone.

The guy across the way said, Now that's entertainment.

■ ■ ■

Two hours later a piece of lined notebook paper folded into a tight isosceles triangle skidded under the solid steel door and into my cell, coming to rest when it rebounded off the metal commode. I opened it carefully. Written in pencil, in a third-grade scrawl, was a message: *Welcome to hell, new guy. I'm el águila. Your neighbor is a skinhead, probably 'cause he's ugly, got a tat of that Nazi symbol on his face. Name's Taylor. Don't worry 'bout him though. He just talks. Rumor is you're the rich dude killed his old lady. Do you play chess? If so, my opening move is e4. Where you from?* It was signed with a happy face.

My first instinct was to ignore it. I did not want to make any friends here, and I definitely did not want to make the wrong friends. But unlike Taylor, this guy did not appear to be insane, and I liked the challenge of trying to play chess without a board. I turned the paper over and wrote on the back. *It's been a long time. Go easy on me. I'm Zhettah. I'm from Houston. Also, I thought guys didn't ask why other guys are here. e5.* I refolded it, lay down on the ground, trying to see under the door, and flicked it across the floor with my middle finger. I heard Águila say, *Nice shot, new guy.* For a moment, I felt proud.

It came back in less than two minutes. Águila had written: *I didn't ask you nothin' new guy. And what kind a name is that? I'll call you Cazador, cool? I like King's Gambit. f4.*

I wrote back, *You're right, you didn't. But in case you are interested, I'm innocent. Where are you from? exf4.*

He said, *OK, whatever, jefe. I ain't really from no place. Moved around a lot. Born in Laredo though. Nf3.*

My stomach sank. In the county jail, they had a cop in the cell next to mine pretending to be an inmate, hoping I'd spill my guts to him. I recognized all the tricks, the fast camaraderie, the evasions and non sequiturs. But I couldn't figure out why they'd still be trying to get me to confess now. I was already convicted. I was already sentenced. I was already here. It didn't make any sense. I wrote, *You all have been trying for a year to get me to say I did something I didn't. It isn't going to happen. I loved my wife.* I underlined the last sentence. I added, *d6. p.s. I ain't a rich guy.*

He wrote back immediately, *Long time my ass. That's the Fischer Defense. You might actually know the game. I got to think on it 'til tomorrow. Been a while since I seen that opening. And you got to chill, cazador. What you didn't do don't mean shit to me. Buenas noches, Inocente.*

Immediately I realized I had misread him. I'd apologize in the morning. I glanced at my watch. Hours had somehow passed. It was almost midnight. Through my plexiglass window I saw a pure white glow, and for the briefest moment I marveled at the brightness of the moon, until I remembered I was seeing the security lights atop the prison wall. I brushed my teeth, washed my face, and lay back down. I closed my eyes. When the beanhole banged open at four fifteen and a trustee slid me my breakfast of powdered eggs, lukewarm instant coffee, and an untoasted slice of packaged white bread, I'd been sound asleep for four solid hours, and I felt more rested than I had in nearly two years.

■ ■ ■

In the county jail, the TVs in the common area were always tuned in the afternoons to shows of judges presiding over disputes about somebody's dog who pissed too often on the neighbor's lawn or a teenager whose garage band played hip-hop in a suburb where bluegrass was king. The inmates would laugh at the feigned toughness of these bogus jurists, recognizing them as the bullies they are, mocking weaker people who are not allowed to answer them and dismissing these plebeian grievances as unworthy of their wisdom. I hated those shows. Now I missed them. Death row doesn't have TVs.

The morning after Taylor got gassed, Lilac came by at eight and told me I had a visitor, to gather up my things and put on my shoes. I did not have any things, and I did not expect any visitors.

I said, Are you sure? For me?

She said, Grab your materials or we'll take you out there without them.

I said, I do not have any materials.

She said, Hands.

I turned around and squatted, and she reached into the cell and clicked on the cuffs. She said, Stand back.

When the cell door swung open, there were three other guards, the transport team. As soon as they pulled me out, Águila shouted, *Be nice to the new guy. He's innocent.* I heard him laugh. One guard led the way, the other two followed behind with their hands on my shoulders. We walked down the corridor and through two electronic doors, and then we were outside. I could see the sky. We were in a narrow space, perhaps four feet wide, with twelve-foot cyclone fences topped with rolls of razor wire on either side. The guard ahead of me held his ID up to a small video camera, and another electronic door slid open. A blast of cold air rushed out. We entered another hall, with single-person visiting cells to my left. They opened a door marked 3B and waited for me to enter. The door was not electronic. One of the guards closed it and padlocked it shut from the outside. I squatted, and one of the guards reached through the slot and took off my cuffs.

On the other side of thick, wire-laced glass, three people were waiting for me: a woman with thick auburn hair who appeared to be in her thirties, a black guy with a shaved head, and a woman in her early twenties with an earring piercing her purple-glossed lower lip. Behind them I could see two female guards wearing jackets and observing the visitors. Auburn hair pointed to a phone on my side of the glass, and I held it to my ear.

She said, My name is Olvido. I wrote you a letter two weeks ago introducing myself. I am your habeas lawyer.

I said, I got your letter. I didn't hire you.

She said, I know. Inmates sentenced to death have an automatic appeal. The judge appointed me and my team to handle it. If you would prefer to hire someone of your own choosing, you may do so.

I said, I'm in here because I used my own judgment to hire lawyers once before.

She said, Okay, then.

She introduced her two colleagues, Luther and Laura. They simultaneously said, *Nice to meet you*. I said, *Likewise*. Olvido told me they would file an appeal within nine months, that the district attorney would respond within six months, and that the court would decide in another year.

I said, You're telling me I will be here for two and a half or three years even if I win.

She said, Yes.

I said, And what if I lose?

Olvido explained I would have another appeal in federal court, and that if we got to that point, I could decide whether I wanted her to continue as my lawyer or replace her with somebody else.

Luther said, Of course, we might not get to that point.

Laura said, Luther is the optimist on the team.

She and Olvido smiled. I just nodded. They had caught me by surprise. Nobody told me my lawyer would just show up one day.

I said, Sorry, I was not expecting any visitors.

Behind them, one of the guards took a picture of an attractive woman standing in front of the glass separating her from the young black man she was visiting. He was leaning forward, close enough to touch her, except for the shield between them. The guard handed the photo to the woman, and I could read the woman's lips. She said, *Thank you.* The guard smiled.

I said to Olvido, How long have you been doing this?

Olvido said, I look younger than I am. I've been doing death penalty work a long time. Luther and Laura not so long. But they are both terrific, which is why I hired them.

I said, Okay.

A trick I used when hiring a new chef was to say, *Cook me an omelet,* and once she had the eggs in the pan, I'd walk away from the fish I was grilling and the sauce I was making and say, *And take care of my things too.* Some cooks panic in the face of unexpected chaos. It's better to learn that during an interview than at service on a busy Saturday night. I was meeting in an area of the prison I'd never been before with lawyers I was not expecting and whom I didn't even know I had, and I was failing the test. What were we talking about? I looked again over Luther's shoulder. Some of the inmates were visiting with older people, who might have been their parents, and others with much younger people, who might have been their kids. One black inmate was talking to a Hispanic man wearing a cross and reading from a leather-bound Bible, and an obese white guy with green tattoos covering his arms was sitting across from a tiny nun being swallowed by her habit.

Luther turned around, seeing what I was. He said, America's melting pot, just like the NFL.

I think he was kidding, but I couldn't be sure, so I just said, *Yeah, I guess.* Behind him I saw vending machines holding soda, candy, sandwiches, and chips. Laura asked me if I wanted anything to eat or drink. I told her thank you, but I wasn't hungry. Olvido said, *If you'd rather we come back another day, that's fine, but at some point I want to hear about your life before the trial.*

I said, Before my trial I was married to the love of my life. I did not kill her.

It had not occurred to me she did not already know everything about me, but why should she? I started to tell them about the day I learned Tieresse had been murdered, but Olvido interrupted. She said, Tell me first about how you met her.

Five hours later, I had told them about how I met Tieresse and our life together. I told them about my parents and my childhood. I told them about my restaurant and my career. I told them about the places Tieresse loved and the charities and causes she supported. I told them almost everything.

Gradually the room grew more quiet and dark. The booths emptied, and the visitors returned to the free world. At five o'clock, a guard knocked on the door behind Olvido, and Luther swung it open. Olvido greeted the guard by name. The guard smiled, said something I could not make out, and pointed at her watch. My lawyers stood up.

Laura said, We did not tell them our legal visit would last past regular hours, but we'll be back soon.

Olvido said, Before we leave, do you have any questions for me?

I said, How are you going to prove my innocence?

She said, I don't know yet. What else?

I said, Can I sign a document allowing you to move money from my bank account to my commissary? They took my inheritance, but I have several assets left. I'd like to buy a radio and some books, and some edible food.

My plan was to live on tuna fish, peanut butter, pinto beans, corn tortillas, bottled salsa, and prewashed salads in plastic bags, all of which I could buy by filling out a form and giving it to the guard who checked in on me every morning. Texas planned to execute me in six or seven years, but I wasn't going to let their diet kill me first.

I said, I have a neighbor who showed me how to fill out the forms to get stuff and he let me borrow some cash from him, but I don't have any money in my account.

Luther said, Sure, that's not a problem.

He opened a slot at the bottom of the glass separating us, reached into his bag, and slid me a document. I signed it and gave it back. I asked, Is that all I have to do?

Luther said, You'll have money in less than a week.

Olvido said, Last call.

I said, Is it possible the guy in the cell next to mine is an informant?

Laura might have laughed. Olvido said, No, not a chance. You are on death row, in case you haven't noticed. They don't need an informant anymore.

I said, I definitely have noticed.

They stood up and touched their hands to the glass. I supposed I was expected to touch it back, so I did. A metal door slid open, and they were gone.

For more than two hours I sat there and waited. The next time I had a visit, I'd remember to go to the bathroom first. The guards had not forgotten about me. They just weren't in a hurry. When I got back to my cell, a plastic tray lay there with a cold mound of what might have been beef stew. I examined a gray-green object I think was a pea and flushed it all down the commode. I replayed in my mind the conversation with the lawyers, and I realized I had done all the talking. Should I have asked them about themselves? Nobody teaches you the etiquette of being a prisoner.

Águila accepted my apology with grace. He said, *You ain't been here long enough yet to be going loco, muchacho. No me molesta.* He also sent me a kite with his suggestions about what kind of soap, razors, and shower shoes to buy, and warning me about which guards screw the cuffs too tight, which leave you in the shower for an hour or more after you're done, and which you can bribe to look the other way if they spot your home-distilled hooch or to score you some drugs.

Most death row inmates have no idea what the others have done, but Águila said they all knew about me. They'd followed my case on the nightly radio news. I was famous before I got here because of the fame of my victim. Águila said, This ain't a place you want to be famous, Inocente.

I got down on the floor and quietly asked him if he knew

how much some Valium would cost, and how I could pay for it until somebody outside had time to make the transfer for me. He said, loud enough for anyone to hear, *In that case, Cazador, you're screwed.* A moment later he kited a triangle of tightly folded notebook paper under my door. Inside he'd drawn a smiley face, and he'd enclosed six small white pills. I wrote *Gracias,* and I kited it back.

The next morning, on the ninth move, Águila played Bxf4. After I looked at it I said, Queen to e8.

He said, Fuck. Nice move, Inocente. I'll get back to you.

■ ■ ■

In the first four months, I left my cell thirty-three times: eighteen for an hour of rec, twelve for a shower, once to visit the warden, and twice for legal visits that totaled 17 hours, including the time I sat waiting to be brought back home. All told, I spent 50 hours, give or take, somewhere else. Other than that, for 2,878, I was alone in my sixty-square-foot cell. My next month, I wouldn't leave at all.

Day 123: Until today, about ten percent of the guys on the row had cell phones. I did not have one, but I knew about them. Everybody did. The inmates bought them from guards for a grand apiece, paid for in cash by the inmates' families, and they hid them in hollowed-out books, inside typewriters, or in other places COs didn't look. The operation was discovered when an inmate known as Chief Notebook placed a telephone call at seven thirty P.M. on a Tuesday night to the chairman of the Texas Senate's Committee on Criminal Justice. He apparently called the senator at home just as the senator was sitting down with his first vodka martini. No one knows how Notebook got the senator's unpublished number. He introduced himself, said he was calling from his cell, and complained about the lack of computers and exercise equipment, sadistic guards, absurd mealtimes, and the lack of all-natural chunky peanut butter. According to most versions of the story I heard, the senator said, *Who is this again?* and Chief Notebook repeated his name and his inmate number and asked how soon the problems might be redressed.

About fifteen minutes after the senator's cocktail hour was interrupted, guards began the process of tossing every cell on the row. It took a few days. There were 378 death-sentenced inmates at the time. By dawn, they had found fourteen cell phones. By dinner the next day they had twenty-three. When they finally finished, they had thirty-one, including one hidden in a wheelchair-bound inmate's rectum and another under the folds of belly fat of an obese guy named Big Al. I know for a fact they didn't find them all.

Four guards got fired. The guys with phones got sent up to level 3 for ninety days, where they got no showers, no exercise, and no outside food. All the rest of us were on lockdown for thirty, meaning we were confined to our cells twenty-four/seven. I'm not sure what the penological theory of communal punishment is, but I do know not letting us out of our houses made us forget how mad we were at Notebook.

The day before Notebook made his call, Águila flicked me a kite that said, *Hah, I got you now. Qf3.* I wrote, *Kd8,* and sent it back immediately. He groaned. He wrote, *Damn. Rematch?*

During our month of lockdown, we played fourteen more games. Two were draws. Two I won. He won the rest. On the thirty-first day, the same day lockdown ended, the captain came by Águila's cell and spoke to him too softly for me to hear. I asked him what was up.

He said, Captain came by to tell me I got a date. Looks like you're gonna have to find some other maestro to school your ass.

I was quiet, trying to imagine how that conversation went. I said, So when do they move you?

He said, Captain told me they got to leave me in my house on account a the death-watch cells have some kind a infestation. He wanted to know if I minded. For a supposably smart hombre, he asks some dumb-ass questions.

He turned on his radio. I heard water dripping from somewhere. I said, Tell me about your family?

He said, Escuche, Inocente, don't be gettin' all sentimental on me now. Everybody you know here's gonna get the juice.

I said, I know, but tell me anyway.

He said, Maybe some other time.

The next morning I asked again. He said, You writin' a book or something?

I said, Why are you asking me that?

He said. No reason. Are you?

I said, I write in my journal. I'm thinking about writing the judges. That's the only writing I do. You think it would do any good?

He said, What? A book? Or writing the judges?

I said, The judges.

He laughed. He said, Shit, Inocente, what I heard is they don't even read what the lawyers write.

But I persisted, and eventually he told me. He was born in Chicago, the youngest of thirteen siblings born to illegal immigrants. He said, *'Til I was ten, I thought my oldest brother was my father. He was fifteen years older than me, but the reason I thought he was my dad is on account of I never saw my dad.* Águila's father worked in a grocery store bakery at night, making bread and doughnuts, and during the day bused tables at a downtown diner. He said, *You know how many hours a week a man getting paid seven bucks a hour needs to work to pay the rent and feed thirteen kids?* He didn't wait for me to guess. He said, *More than there is, that's how many.* His mother attended mass every morning, then spent the rest of the day cleaning the house and cooking pinto beans, nopalito, and tortillas. On Sunday mornings the entire family went to church at eight. Águila said the pews were packed with brown-skinned people, and the priest's sermons, always delivered in Spanish, warned that homo-sexuals could be cured, that abortion was murder, and that birth control was a mortal sin. Águila said, *Mi padre dejó de ir a la iglesia, but he didn't stop fuckin', that's for sure. Matter of fact, I might even have some half siblings runnin' around. No estoy seguro.* To my ear, his laugh was wistful. I asked how he ended up in Texas. This time his laugh was bitter.

When Águila was in third grade, a rival gang killed two of his brothers and wounded a third. The family packed their belongings into a van and drove all day and straight through the night until they reached a small rancho in central Mexico where they moved in with his mother's parents. On his fifteenth birthday, he came to Texas to look for work. He lived in a housing project in San Antonio, worked in a garage, and sent most of his paycheck home to his family. One evening at a bar a friend offered him a thousand dollars to open the garage at night so some thieves could chop up stolen cars and sell the parts. Águila said, *Mil dolares. For real. Is this a great country or what? Mis padres siempre estaban cansados, tired of never having no money and not enough food, and here I was, getting paid to just open a door and turn on the lights.* A few weeks later, Águila was smoking a cigarette in the garage's small office while his friends were removing wheel rims made from aircraft aluminum they intended to sell for five thousand dollars apiece. Two Honduran guys wearing balaclavas and carrying Uzis burst in and ordered everybody to lie down. Águila opened the desk drawer and removed a Heckler & Koch 9 mm handgun. He pulled back the slide, stepped from the office, and emptied the weapon. The brown-skinned guys who had burst into the garage were undercover drug agents. Águila had killed two cops.

He said, So that's my life story. I got time for one more game. You can play white.

After six moves he said, *If I'd a been wearin' glasses I'd a probably seen their IDs. So in a ways, I blame my bein' here on not havin' no health insurance.* Before I could say anything he laughed. A pawn up, I offered him a draw on the twenty-second move. He said, *Play on, Inocente.* Seven moves later, I resigned.

On a Thursday morning in May they took him to the Walls Unit to die. He asked the guard to lift the beanhole to my cell, then he said, Hey Inocente, here's a copy of my last will and testament, I think you call it. Gomez knows to give you my chess set, all right? Vaya con Dios, amigo. I'll miss you.

I said, I'll miss you too.

He said, Shit, inmate, you got more important matters to worry about.

He raised his shackled hands to his sternum, bent over at the waist, and, as best as he could, saluted me goodbye.

Two years earlier I wouldn't have hired a guy like Águila to mop my floors. That night, number 213, I cried for the first time since I'd arrived on the row.

■ ■ ■

Day 277: They put a new guy in the cell across from mine. Until today it had remained empty since they killed Águila. I heard somebody trading insults with Sergeant McKenzie. It had to be an inmate. Being that McKenzie is dumb, sadistic, and vindictive, I pretty much liked this new neighbor before I knew who he was.

He was quoting the Bible and using words I hadn't heard since Tieresse and I used to watch old YouTube clips of William F. Buckley debating Gore Vidal in the sixties. The new guy called McKenzie a crypto-Nazi, and McKenzie laughed the way people who don't understand something laugh to pretend they do. Peering through the slit above the beanhole, I could see that the new guy's wrists were cuffed so tight his hands were pale from lack of blood. He was black, with a shaved head and muscles that pulsed beneath thin, almost translucent skin.

When the cell door opened, McKenzie karate kicked the new guy behind his left knee. The new guy buckled only slightly and said, Fat man, you kick like a girl in elementary school, but I'm impressed you could even lift your leg that far off the ground.

I heard McKenzie say, Tell me again how many times you had to repeat first grade, dumb-ass?

The door closed behind him, and the new guy said, There you go again, fat man. A fool giving vent to his rage. Proverbs 29. Look it up.

One of the COs with McKenzie snapped the cuffs off the new guy, and the guards marched on down the block.

Later that night a kite came skittering under my door. It said, *I'm Sargent. It's a name, not a rank. You know you got a Nazi skinhead motherfucker next door, right? I think you and*

I got the same lawyer, Cuban chick with big ole tits, smartest and toughest one around. Your luck might be turning. Peace. It wasn't signed. I wrote back and said, *I'm Zhettah. I know about Taylor. I like my lawyer, but this shit takes too long.* I flicked it back.

He answered, *I know who you are. Long day for me. Buenas noches, compadre.*

Five minutes later I heard him snoring, but when I woke up at three to use the toilet, I heard him chanting in his cell. Taylor was hissing, *Shut the fuck up nigger, it's the middle of the night,* but Sargent either didn't hear him or didn't care, or maybe both. I put in earplugs and went back to sleep.

Day 290: I finally got to have what passes here for a normal conversation with Sargent, because he and I were in adjacent dayrooms. He asked whether I wanted to work out with him. I said sure, even though I had no idea how it would work. He said, Get on the ground and do some push-ups.

He then started to run. He ran four laps, stopped, and said, *Your turn.* So I ran four laps. We alternated this way for forty-five minutes. He'd run while I did push-ups, then we'd switch. It took him half as long to run his laps as it took me, and he did six times as many push-ups per set as I did, but every few minutes he'd say, *Nice job, Zhettah, nice job.* He pronounced my name correctly.

We talked about Águila. He and Sargent had known each other for years. Sargent called him Molina, which was apparently his actual name.

Sargent said, Hombre killed two cops and got life, but then came over here 'cause he killed an AB motherfucker in general. You got baby killers live here twenty years, and they go ahead and execute a dude who got rid of a piece of scum. How fucked up is that, Inocente?

I said, That's what Águila called me. Or Molina, I mean.

Sargent said, Duh. I know that, Zhettah. Molina told me you're the only guy he knows here who don't belong. I promised him I'd look after you, as best I can anyways.

I said, Taylor's Aryan Brotherhood. I guess that's why he didn't like Molina.

Sargent said, Inocente, your skinhead neighbor don't like nobody who ain't as ignorant as he is, which don't leave him too many brothers to like.

A couple of days later, Sargent's cell got tossed. The lieutenant found his speed, and they busted him up to level 3. Sargent was laughing during the search, because he knew why they were there. He had bought the stuff from McKenzie. We all did. I'd been buying from him since my third month here. He hated Sargent, and Sargent acted like he hated McKenzie, but the inside narcotics trade was an emotionless business. Being a prisoner, you learn to be accepting, or maybe just nuanced. If you want something, and the only person who can get it for you is someone you detest, and buying it from him means helping him profit, what do you do? The only people who think there is not an obvious answer to that question haven't been here.

On his way out, Sargent said, Catch you in thirty, Inocente.

But Sargent was mistaken. He was gone for two months rather than one. Twenty-nine days into his sentence, he refused an officer's order to shave on the grounds Muslims do not shave during Ramadan. The CO told Sargent he wasn't Muslim. Sargent said, *I am what I am,* which even I recognized as a Bible reference. On day 354, when they brought Sargent back, I sent him a kite. I wrote, *Welcome home. Rumor is you finally went around the bend up there <smile>. Tell me the truth: Are you crazy or is it just an act?*

He sent me back a picture of a smiley face winking.

Sargent said, Molina and I was neighbors during your trial. We listened to the updates on Pacifica every night. I won a hundred eight balls off him on account a the wager we made. He said you'd get off. I said no fucking way. We'd be seeing you in our hood.

I said, How come you bet against me?

He said, Spic kills a rich white lady? I don't need to know nothin' else.

I said, Yeah, but I didn't actually kill her.

He laughed. He said, Shit motherfucker, like that's gonna matter.

■ ■ ■

Nights and days passed without signification. If the leaves changed color, I didn't know. You can tell the season from the angle the sun shines, but only if you can see the sunlight. For long stretches of time the cell block was so hot my thin mattress stayed damp and moldy. Then for a week it would be so cold you could see your breath. For a month it would be comfortable. And then it would again be hot. East Texas has its own seasons.

We measured our lives not by the month, but by what sport was being played. Guys bet commissary items on basketball games, then turned to baseball, and football after that. People wouldn't say, *I got a date in August;* they'd say, *I'm gonna miss the NFL.* After his visit from the warden, Águila said to me, *Shit, Inocente, I'm gonna miss the World Cup. Como siempre, mi corazón dice México, but the boys just don't have it this year. So go on ahead and bet the bank on Italy, you feel me?* Italy squeaked by France in the finals of that year's cup, winning five to three on penalty kicks after extra time ended in a one-to-one tie.

My lawyers wrote me regularly and came to visit once a month even though they had no news. Over time these visits grew less awkward. I learned one of the lawyers on my team, Luther, had been a US Marine, and the other, Laura, a professional musician. Sargent told me my lead lawyer, Olvido, was filthy rich from being a big-shot corporate lawyer before she started representing us inmates. I asked Sargent if he knew why she had made the trade. He said, Is it sexist to say she might have herself a bit of a Jesus complex?

During our third meeting Olvido said, It's a myth that most guys on death row claim to be innocent. I've been doing this work many years and you're just the second one.

I had said, I am innocent.

She said, I know you are. And that's the reason I have to ask you a really hard question.

Here's what she explained: Lawyers representing death row inmates raise two broad kinds of challenges. One attacks the jury's guilty verdict. The other attacks the death sentence. For nearly all her clients, the goal was to win the second claim, and the attempt to undermine the verdict was designed mostly to gain leverage in avoiding an execution. And that strategy appealed to her clients, because all they wanted was a life sentence instead of being put to death. She said, *My clients tell me all they want is to see their families and die of a heart attack playing handball with the guys.* But my case presented an unusual problem, because I did not want to spend my life in prison for a crime I did not do. The dilemma my lawyers faced was that if they decided to raise both kinds of challenges, a court might be just worried enough about my guilt that it would grant me relief from my sentence. She said, *That way, in case you are guilty, the judge is not responsible for putting a murderer back on the street, but if it turns out you didn't do it, the judge has not allowed the execution of an innocent man.* I said, *That makes no sense.* She said, *Legally that's true, but it might make emotional sense. How would you like to order the execution of somebody who didn't commit a crime?*

She said, So what I need to know is whether you want to run the risk that the judge decides to split the baby by leaving your guilty verdict intact but throwing out the death sentence.

I said, No way. Either you hit a grand slam or you strike out. I'm not playing for a single.

She said, I'm not just covering my ass here, but I have to make sure you realize this is a decision you can't take back.

I tried to imagine living in prison for forty years. Across the visiting area an Asian inmate was talking on the phone to a petite woman bouncing two toddlers on her knees. Olvido turned around, saw what I was looking at, then turned back. Maybe being alive would be better than being dead, even if it meant living like an animal in a poorly run zoo. I wondered whether those two Asian kids would be able to remember whether they ever touched their dad.

She said, If you decide now not to raise certain issues, I don't get to raise them later. You'd be betting your life on the one issue, and I have to tell you it's much harder for a man to prove he's not guilty than it is for the government to send someone who's innocent to death row.

I said, This is an easy call for me.

She said, It's not for me.

I had said, But I get to make the decision, right?

She said, Yes, you do.

I said, Then prove I'm innocent. If you can't, let them kill me.

I stood up and touched my fist to the glass. I said, *I'm sorry to lay this on you,* and I meant it. Still, on the walk back to my cell, I felt the inner calm that accompanies the certainty you've made the absolutely right call.

■ ■ ■

Every other month, a new inmate would arrive. Every three weeks, one would depart. We'd always be on lockdown on execution day. I'd lie on my bunk and listen to a radio show from Houston that counted down the minutes to the execution, and once the time of death was announced, the host would play a tape of a recording he had made with the inmate earlier that week. They sounded on tape just the way they had in real life. The host of the show would talk to the guys about whether they were scared, what their lives had been like, and what they had done to get here. It was the first time I knew the details of the murders these friends of mine had committed.

The morning after one of these shows, I had said to Sargent, I know this violates the inmate code, but can I ask you why you're here? I pestered Águila until he told me his story.

Sargent said, Molina.

I said, Yeah, Molina. Either way, it bothers me when I listen to Ray on the radio on execution days and hear about it. It makes me want to replay every conversation I had with the guy and try to reinterpret it, or understand it in a different way. Does that make sense?

Sargent said, Inocente, you cain't be all mawkish and shit in here.

But he told me anyway. He was a drug dealer. He said he

had killed more people than the police gave him credit for. He wasn't bragging. He said, Most of them deserved it.

I said, Most?

He said, Yeah, most.

It's unusual for a drug dealer to end up on death row for killing another drug dealer, but that's not why Sargent was here. He had also killed his girlfriend's mother and sister. He whispered when he told me. I asked him why.

He said, I ain't got no fuckin' clue. How messed up is that?

He said, I hate rememberin' that day. Matter a fact, I started tryin' to forget as soon as I booked on outta that house. They was good people. I don't hate myself like a lot a the brothers in here, but I do hate some a the things I done.

He said, I got a daughter who don't talk to me. No matter how they kill me, it ain't gonna hurt more than that.

If I'd met Sargent anywhere else we'd have passed without exchanging a word. I probably would have been scared of him. Same goes for Águila. We definitely would not have been friends. But here, inside, Sargent and I had two things in common. We had the same lawyer, and we liked each other.

I was getting six or eight letters a week from people in Europe, mostly women. Most of the guys on the row had one or two pen pals, but I was as famous as Ted Bundy, according to Sargent, so my mail never stopped. Some of the women sent revealing photos of themselves, but I never saw them. By the time the letters reached me, some guard was using them as pinups. I threw all the letters away.

Sargent said, Cruel not to write 'em back.

I said, More cruel to answer.

He said, True that, Inocente.

One woman from Hungary wrote me three months after her

first unanswered letter arrived and said, *fuck you you airogant prix. I new you murdered of your wife.* Someone from Holland sent Bible verses with hand-drawn illustrations. I showed Sargent a pencil sketch of Jesus walking across the Sea of Galilee, and he asked if he could have it. A woman from England wrote me a letter every week for almost three years. She wrote in long looping script on paper too thick to fold. The letters were filled with mundane details of her life—what she had cooked for dinner, what she had watched on TV, what was happening in the world of politics, what her new puppy had chewed up. I marveled at her tenacity, but still I wrote no reply. A month had passed without my hearing from her when I received another letter on the same thick stationery, this one written by the woman's grown-up daughter. She was writing to let me know her mother had passed away. She asked how she could transfer to my prison ledger a few hundred pounds her mother had left to me. It was the only letter I answered. I wrote, *Your mother made my days here immeasurably brighter. I will miss our correspondence dearly. I wish you and your family the very best,* and I gave her instructions for adding money to a numbered account she didn't know belonged to Sargent, not to me.

Sleep was how I passed time. Outside prison, I slept like a normal person. Here, I sometimes slept fourteen hours a day. I took up yoga. I ordered volumes of poetry and spent time working on my memory. It could take me an entire day to learn a single sonnet. I memorized pi to seventy-three places. I did these things for myself, to keep my brain and body from atrophy, because I intended to get out of here. I did not know how or when, but I knew. I was not going to die in prison.

Other things I did as a service. I wrote a cookbook of dishes inmates could build from items in the commissary, using their hot plates to prepare: potato-chip-crusted hot dogs atop a frijoles-and-salsa reduction; kung pao tuna salad with Asian vinaigrette (basically, bottled Italian dressing spiked with soy sauce); cheddar-stuffed turkey cutlets (made by placing shredded cheddar between double slices of packaged turkey and browning on the hot plate). The recipes were passed along the row by kite and word of mouth. The friendly guards started calling me Inmate Chef. Sargent asked me if I could come up with a soul-food recipe, so I dreamed up smothered pork chop, which consisted of a ham steak cooked with spinach leaves (from the spinach salad), braised with juice from squeezing cherry to-matoes.

It occurred to me a life sentence might not be that bad. And I hated myself for having the thought.

Day 1,067: My lawyers' prediction about how long the legal proceedings would take was proving astonishingly accurate. They came by to tell me the state court had ruled against me, finding the evidence sufficient to support my guilt.

I said, What evidence?

Olvido said, Physical evidence placing you at the murder scene.

I said, But I lived there.

Olvido said, I know.

They told me I was entitled to a new lawyer for federal court, and the new lawyer could try to raise issues they had not raised by arguing they had been incompetent, and it had been a mistake not to challenge the death sentence.

I said, You did what I asked you to do. I want you all to keep being my lawyers. Is that allowed?

Olvido told me it was, and my team got up to leave. Luther still walked erect, but Olvido and Laura appeared deflated, like their clothes were two sizes too large. I banged on the glass and Olvido turned back around and picked up the phone.

I said, When you're relying on me to lift your spirits, you might as well be flying on a plane with a pilot who's blind. But I still want to make sure you know how much I appreciate you. It's not your fault I'm here. Everybody here knows, including me, if you can't win, it means nobody can. Capiche?

I touched my hand to the glass.

She said, Mr. Zhettah, you're a prince.

I said, I asked you to please call me Rafael.

She said, Yes, you did. Rafael, you are a prince.

She smiled, and I smiled in return.

On the walk back to my cell, I decided to surrender.

■ ■ ■

Before they left, my lawyers gave me a copy of the court's ruling. The decision against me had not been unanimous. One judge said in his view, the evidence used to convict was inadequate. There had been no eyewitnesses. There was no physical evidence. I even had an alibi. All indications were Tieresse and I had a warm and loving marriage. *Yes there was philandery,* the judge wrote, *but if sexual promiscuity were proof of murder, Lord Byron himself would have stood trial.* Two other judges disagreed. One said the absence of evidence proved only that I was a cold and calculating planner. The other said I would have known when Tieresse was going to be alone, how to turn off the alarm, and how much time I would have to clean up the scene. *Sometimes,* she wrote, *the obvious suspect is obvious precisely because he is guilty.*

When the Mexican agents shot and killed my father, I was only a college freshman, so I never got to see him age. If my natural life span was going to be roughly the same as his, I had no way of knowing what that number was. But that night, two weeks after my forty-second birthday, I sat on my bunk, convinced I had passed my life's halfway point, and I sobbed. I heard Sargent saying, *Talk to me, Inocente.* But I was too deep in my hole. I said, *Maybe later. I'm not ready yet.*

Early the next morning, though, when I should have been getting breakfast, a transport team showed up and told me to pack my things. They moved me off B-pod at dawn. The COs do that, move people around a lot, and at random. Team shows up at your door, says pack your house, links you up, and puts you someplace else. Supposedly it's for security, but that's BS. It's just a way for the guards to harass the inmates. Being moved with no warning bothers some guys. They get to know their neighbors, and then they're not neighbors anymore; they fix up their cell, get it all clean and arranged, then they have to start over. It didn't bother me, though. I didn't want to feel comfortable here. Everything they could do to make my life miserable I welcomed. The team showed up, and I said, Buenos días, jefe. What took y'all so long?

Sargent heard me packing up. I told him about what my lawyers had said. He said, Did you know Gandhi was against hunger strikes?

I said, What are you talking about?

He said, Gandhi thought people who went on hunger strikes in prison were attempting to coerce the jailers to improve conditions or release them early. He was against any kind of coercion.

I said, So I should walk to the gurney instead of making them carry me?

Sargent said, Shit, Inocente, you're like some motherfuckin' logician. Hell no, you shouldn't walk. What I'm sayin' is the only thing you can control is whether you're true to yourself, you feel me?

I said, Yeah I do. Thanks, Sargent.

He said, Peace, brother. Catch up with you later when the Brownshirts here move us again.

■ ■ ■

They took me to D-pod. Looking back, I believe it was D-pod that turned me into who I am today. It obliterated the categories I had used to make sense of the world. Until then, I was just a visitor here. I didn't belong. But on D-pod, the last vestige of the chef and husband and friend I had been were erased, and I became someone whose entire identity is his tribe.

I wanted to ask Sargent whether that was Gandhi's point, but Sargent, of course, wasn't here. I missed him already. I missed Águila too.

When Lilac left me in my new cell, she handed me earplugs, and soon I learned why. At nine that night, the guy next door started talking in tongues. I hollered, *Kindly keep it down, brother,* and he responded with a series of clicks I didn't understand. I inserted the earplugs and went to sleep. I woke the next morning when the trustee passing out breakfast sounded an alarm. Moments later, three helmeted COs rushed into my neighbor's cell. He'd used a cereal spoon to gouge out his one good eye, then he ate it. They took him by helicopter to a psychiatric unit an hour south of Houston, and they told the rest of us we'd be on lockdown for a week.

Later that day, the oldest guy on the row died in his sleep. He was a seventy-four-year-old white guy from Dallas who'd been confined to a wheelchair since having a stroke two years before. When they rolled him to the dayroom he cradled a canister of oxygen in his lap. The captain announced lockdown would last an additional seven days.

A guy who called himself Preacher Bob grew agitated. He told the captain even God had spared the righteous before He destroyed Sodom and Gomorrah. The captain said, *Whatever, inmate,* and walked away. Preacher Bob head butted his door and launched into an incoherent sermon that lasted more than seven hours. Despite my earplugs, his ranting kept me awake all night. I sent him a kite that said, *Fidel Castro's rambling speeches are shorter than your mumbo jumbo. How about at least turning down the volume so we can get some sleep?* He wrote back and said, *Who's that, the Mexican guy on A-pod?*

I decided to fast for a week just to see if the guards would notice. I don't know how much weight I lost, it's not like we can just step on a scale, but my boxer shorts were suddenly too large, and I could see my hip bones and count my ribs. Nobody said a word. I opened a book Sargent had given me by someone named Beccaria, but my mind wandered, and I couldn't remember what I'd read. On the eighth day of lockdown I decided not to shave. When I had the beginnings of a beard, the CO ordered me to get rid of it. I told him I didn't have a razor. He brought me one that afternoon and ordered me again to lose the beard. I ignored him. He said, *Last warning, inmate. Do it now.* I felt him watching me. I heard Preacher Bob quoting Jeremiah. *Do not be afraid of them. They will fight against you but not overcome you, for I shall rescue you.* I rubbed my eyes so hard I could see floaters. It got very quiet. I looked out my cell and saw three guards wearing helmets and a fourth holding a video camera, a clipboard, and a can that looked like it held bug spray. I said, *Is there an issue here?* and then I thought to myself, *So this is how it happens.* One of them opened the beanhole and hit me with a burst of tear gas mixed with Mace. Water poured from my eyes and I felt bile rise in my throat. I dry heaved. Someone shouted to move away from the door, and then the beanhole opened again and a second stream hit me on my cheek. I heard a guard say, *Three, two, one,* then the door banged open and the three helmeted COs crashed in and threw me to the floor. I was on my stomach, struggling to get a breath. I felt a knee in my back and a sharp edge where my front tooth had broken. They tore off my jumpsuit and cuffed my hands, then hustled me to another cage with a drain in the floor. A female guard blasted me with a fire hose while the CO with the video camera continued to record. The CO who had ordered me to shave said, *Last warning means last warning, inmate.* Still cuffed, and now naked and dripping wet, I sat on my ass in the detox cage until two new COs arrived and marched me to a cell on the upper floor. The door slid shut behind me and I said, *Hey, where's my stuff?* The mattress had no sheets and I had no clothes. I sat on the floor and hugged my knees to my chest, trying to get warm.

That night the beanhole opened and McKenzie threw me a jumpsuit and a bologna sandwich. I ate a bite. It tasted like pennies, and I threw the rest away. He said, Welcome to level 3, asshole. You want to act like a goddamn camel jockey, we'll treat you like one.

They gave me a toothbrush, a bar of soap, and a razor. I flushed it down the commode. A week later I had my second gassing. The drill was the same. While I was still coughing, they ran in, tackled me, and stripped off my clothes. This time I was careful not to break another tooth. After hosing me down, they took me to a brightly lit room with a single metal chair bolted to the floor. I said, *Is this left over from when y'all used the gas chamber?* The young guard wearing braces whom I hadn't seen in a while said, *Did we used to gas people here, Lieutenant?* The lieutenant said, *We're corrections officers, Sergeant, not Nazis.* I said, *My my, young fella, congratulations on the promotion.* He started to answer, but then caught the lieutenant's eye, and didn't. My hands were cuffed in front, and I used my thumb to squeeze a drop of water from my belly button. A thick leather strap across my thighs hid my genitals and kept me from standing. A trustee from general population used shears and an electric razor to shave me clean. I could not stop coughing. If the trustee had been using a blade, I'd have been sliced wide-open.

McKenzie walked in and nodded to the lieutenant. He said, You're a slow learner, ain't you, za-heater?

When they moved me back to B-pod Sargent was still across the hall. I told him about my time up on level. He said, You know what your problem is, Inocente? You think it matters to these people who you are.

Another spasm of coughs shook me. Sargent said, If that gas is still in your lungs, you might want to see the nurse.

I said, It's not the gas. I just have a cold, and I don't think she's a real nurse.

Sargent said, True that, Inocente, but she got herself a scrip pad and she dresses like one. Ain't that enough?

I said, *No, not today it isn't,* and I started hacking again.

■ ■ ■

Being on death row alters your perception of time. When you're still naïve and hopeful and believe justice will prevail, the clock slows down. Once you realize the game is rigged, the weeks fly by.

During my state court appeal, I woke up every morning thinking some CO would lift the beanhole and say, *Hey za-heater, did you hear the news? You won.* I was in a hurry for the judges to declare me innocent, positive today would be the day. Yet that day never came, and the weeks dragged on, taunting me with their monotony, until at last Olvido showed up to tell me we had lost.

Immediately my world started to spin too fast. Texas executed a woman, and the guys here protested like she was one of our own. The skinniest guy on the row got stuck in a pipe trying to escape from the shower. He had a heart attack and died as the COs frantically struggled to pull him out. A Thai inmate who learned Spanish from a cholo in a Salvadoran gang fell in love with a German serial killer whose parents had been missionaries in Mexico, and they romanced one another in perfect Spanish with accents that made me laugh. One day a Unitarian pastor stood outside the dayroom and presided as the two got married. A week later, they were executed on consecutive days, with the same pastor standing at both their feet.

So it went. An execution a week, a dead guy's voice on the radio filling the row, another empty cell.

I prayed for time to slow down, desperate for someone to take however long was needed to realize I did not kill my wife. But when the federal court ruled against me, taking roughly the same amount of time as the state court had, it felt like it happened overnight. My legal team came to tell me the only appeal left was with the Supreme Court. They said the justices wouldn't be interested in my case because it didn't present any interesting or challenging legal issues.

I said, It's not an interesting legal challenge that I'm innocent?

Luther, the former marine, had said, Nope. It's tragic, sure, but not very interesting.

Olvido encouraged me to write the court and ask for new lawyers on the grounds that she and her team had made a terrible mistake by raising only a single claim. She said it was a long shot, but if the court agreed and gave me new counsel, I would get to start all over.

I said, I understand that for most of your clients, time is your friend. I wish you would understand that for me, time is the enemy.

I stood up and shouted for a guard. I was ready to go. I said to Olvido, I don't blame you for anything. You've done exactly what I've asked. I'm sorry for lashing out. I just don't have anyone else.

■ ■ ■

Summer came. The commissary now sold fans with plastic blades. I bought one for everybody on B-pod. I had never had dreams before, but I started to have them now. At the restaurant, the biggest fear we had was an infestation of roaches or rats.

Even though it was a health code violation, we fed two stray cats anyway to entice them to patrol the kitchen and pantry. In my prison dreams, cockroaches came pouring out of a slit in my mattress and covered me like fur.

Day 1,699: Guard Johnson came by and told me I had a visitor. Guard Johnson was the only CO in the facility who said my name correctly. When she first saw my ID, she asked what kind of name it was and how to pronounce it. She practiced saying it in my presence until she had it down. I've never heard her curse, and I think she knows by name every last one of the more than three hundred inmates who call death row home. If I had even the barest desire to normalize my life here, I'd start by talking to her.

Guard Johnson stood there waiting for me to squat so she could cuff me and take me out to visitation. But nobody except my lawyer and people on her team ever came to see me, and (except for their initial visit) they always wrote first. That meant whoever wanted to visit was somebody from the media or some death penalty opponent who likes to meet with inmates to try to keep us from going insane, or maybe one of the pen pals whose letters I had ignored. Either way, I wasn't interested. So I said to Officer Johnson, Please put me down as RV. I'm going to stay here and do my rec.

Officer Johnson said, Please don't refuse the visit, Inmate Zhettah. It's your lawyer.

As I was being pulled out of my cell, Sargent said, *Tell her I send my love.* From anybody else it would have been lewd, but Sargent was sincere.

Olvido was sitting in the booth twirling a pen between her thumb and index finger, occasionally pausing to mark a passage in a document she was reading. She did not waste any time.

She said, Supreme Court turned down your appeal this morning. We'll keep trying to find another argument, or another angle on one we've raised, but I wanted to let you know your case is now at the point that the DA's office in Houston will set an execution date.

I said, This is totally fucking unbelievable. I did not kill anybody. Why can't I wake up from this?

She did not say anything. I didn't expect her to.

I said, I'm sorry. How long?

She said, They have to give you at least ninety days' notice, but I hear through the grapevine your ex-wife's son calls the DA all the time.

I said, Reinhardt?

She said, Yeah, him. So I would not be surprised if they move fairly soon. We'll file something else, even though I don't know yet what it will be, but we're digging through the oldest muck at the bottom of the oldest barrel, so it will be nothing more than a prayer dressed inside a bunch of legalese.

I said, I know.

She nodded at the vending machines and said, Anything I can get you?

I said, A suit, maybe a tie, and keys.

She smiled. I stood up and touched my hand to the glass. She touched it back. She tried to hide it, but before she turned to leave, I saw a tear spill from her eye.

The transport team came to get me right away. Sargent was back in his house, fresh from the shower. He asked what the visit was about and I told him. He said, You hear that Tigres del Norte coming from Martinez's house?

Yeah.

He said, Well, that ain't the fat lady.

■ ■ ■

For four days after my lawyer gave me the news I didn't leave my cell. I said no to rec. I skipped the shower. I didn't shave. On the fifth day McKenzie tossed my cell with two new COs, but they didn't make a mess. He told me to lose the facial hair. I didn't even respond, and he didn't write me up. When I grew so hungry I ached, I would eat a bite or two of whatever was on the meal tray. I had a six-pack of tuna and three cans of pinto beans, but I couldn't find my can opener. Maybe McKenzie had taken it and I hadn't noticed. I thought about ordering another.

I knew a guy who got exonerated after a dozen years and three execution dates. Now he runs a charitable foundation. In an interview on NPR, he talked about the resiliency of the human spirit. He recounted all the occasions he could have folded but didn't, all the indignities that didn't break him. But he was just a fool who got lucky. I got arrested and thought I would never stand trial. I went to trial and thought I'd be found innocent. I came to death row and believed a court would right the wrong. Resilient is just another word for insane. The more powerful force is delusion, more powerful by a million miles. Sargent had said it isn't over 'til it's over, but I wasn't going to be one of those guys sitting in the holding cell waiting for the call to come minutes before six saying I'd been saved. Fuck it. There was nothing left to do. Unless God decided to flood the state and anoint me Noah, I was going to be executed for something

I swear on my papá's grave I did not do. I'm not strong enough not to fold. I'm not.

I said, *I'm sorry, Tieresse.* It was the first time I'd spoken to her since getting here. I hadn't wanted her name or memory to be inside this place. I said again, *I'm sorry.*

When I lived in the free world I watched a video of a terrorist beheading an American hostage. Maybe on the inside he was terrified, but to me, the hostage seemed fearless. In my imagination, before the camera started to roll, he spat on the hooded thug holding the blade. The thug pulled a pistol from his belt and whipped the butt across the bound man's head. The hostage listed, but he did not fall.

It had been a mistake to watch. There are some images your brain cannot erase.

On day 1,707 I had a dream. The hostage video was playing again. The terrorist, wearing a mask, drew his knife across a whetstone. The hostage, wearing an orange jumpsuit, was kneeling before him. His hands were bound. He was insolent and lithe. Off camera somebody said something in a foreign language, Arabic perhaps, and the hostage looked up at him. The face on the hostage was mine. I bolted awake. It was nine A.M. The captain was standing at my door.

The captain said, Good morning, Inmate Zhettah. Warden's got something to tell you.

■ ■ ■

He moved aside and the warden stepped forward. I was sitting on the edge of my bunk. The warden said he'd get right to it. He told me the judge had set my execution date. It was four months away. He said I'd stay where I was until thirty days out then they'd move me. He didn't say, *To a cell we call suicide watch,* but that's what he meant. He handed me a piece of paper, the court order, said he'd be back in a few days to go over procedures, and he and the captain turned and left.

Sargent said, What was that about?

I said, I have close to five hundred million dollars in offshore banks the authorities never found. You want it?

■ ■ ■

Sargent said, Here's what we're gonna do. You get a day to memorize a sonnet, then I get a day. We alternate 'til they move you. Whoever makes the fewest number of mistakes 'tween now and then gets to write your final statement. Deal?

I said, You are a sick and morbid motherfucker.

He said, True that, Inocente. Now is it a deal or ain't it?

I said, Bring it.

Sargent went first. He chose sonnet 117. He licked every note. I said, I love that line, *Shoot not at me in your wakened hate.*

He said, First poem I ever memorized. Read it right before I quit eighth grade.

I said, Well then that's cheating.

He said, Might be. Your turn.

I went with the eighteenth. I nailed it too.

Sargent said, Nice, but a little obvious, don't you think?

I said, Maybe, but I'd never paid much attention to the lines at the end, I forget what you call it.

Sargent said, The couplet.

I said, Yeah, couplet. *So long as men can breathe.*

Sargent said, Tell you what, you start getting all lachrymose on me, we're gonna have to change the rules so I pick yours and vice versa, you feel me?

If Sargent had an objective other than to be my friend, I do not know what it was. If his goal was to distract me, I suppose he succeeded. But if his plan was to get me to dig in my heels and fight, it was a bust. Any fight I'd ever had I'd left up on level 3. On the day they came to move me, Sargent told me the score. We'd each made four mistakes.

I've heard two different explanations for the new routine. Some guys say you get special treatment because you no longer have anything to lose. Others say it's because they want to make sure you don't kill yourself before the state gets to do it. Either way, Lilac and McKenzie were unusually quiet when they came to transfer me to a different cell.

Sargent said, Listen up, Inocente, tie goes to the dead guy, but I might have a suggestion or two, all right?

I said, You earned it hermano.

■ ■ ■

The cells on death watch are the same size as the others, but they're on their own pod. The pod is adjacent to a room where two guards sit monitoring a panel of seven screens. Six of them have displays that rotate every fifteen seconds: the shower, the dayrooms, the corridors, the visiting booths, the perimeter, the roof. They show every area of death row except the inside of the inmates' cells. The seventh screen shows a constant feed from a small camera recessed into the ceiling of the cell that would be the last place on earth where I lived. They watch you eat, sleep, and use the toilet. They watch you brush your teeth and shave, and a guard comes in to confiscate the toothbrush and razor when you're done. They watch you all the time.

Sargent might not have made it past middle school, but he read a book every other day. The year before he had been enamored of the French intelligentsia. Those are the intellectuals, he told me. In France, the public holds them in high esteem. One day he was droning on about a book by some French philosopher named René Girard. France does not have the death penalty anymore, but it did until recently. Girard supposedly compared executions to ritualistic human sacrifice. I told Sargent I'm no genius, but I know hogwash when I hear it. Then all of a sudden the prison officials started to care about whether I might kill myself, and I understood exactly what he was saying. I wanted to tell him I'd learned something important, to thank him, but he was too far away, and I didn't trust the COs to deliver a kite.

They let me keep my new can opener, but they took away my hot plate. I ate beans from a can with a plastic spoon. I bought a box of graham crackers but my mouth stopped making saliva so I had to throw them away. I would break off a piece of a chocolate bar and let it melt in my mouth.

I was no longer permitted out of my cell to exercise. On shower days, the transport team stood three feet away for the four minutes I was allowed under the spray. A chaplain I had seen in the visiting area several times came by my cell to ask me whether I wanted to visit. I said no thank you. I slept even more than before, sometimes up to eighteen hours a day. I still had my radio, but I could not concentrate on any of the shows. The only reason I was not bored is that I was so terribly scared.

If I had been the hostage in the video, you would have heard me wail.

I passed the time trying to memorize more sonnets, but without the competition with Sargent, it took me three times as long. My brain was failing me, but I spoke out loud to Tieresse. I said, *If you read this line, remember not / The hand that writ it, for I love you so, / That I in your sweet thoughts would be forgot, / If thinking on me then should make you woe.* I wrote a letter to Sargent, telling him our lawyer had news for him, and I wrote letters to two COs who had been kind and decent to me. I wrote four letters to Reinhardt, and tore up every one. I couldn't get it right. It probably didn't matter, because I doubted he'd read it. On the fifth effort, it was close enough. I told him he was the only person I wanted to prove myself to. I told him I hoped one day the truth would come out, and until it did, I understood exactly how he felt about me, because I would have felt the same way.

I addressed the letter to my attorney and asked her to please try to deliver it. I also gave her additional details about my financial resources and authorized her to distribute to herself and her legal team ten million dollars. I requested she set aside another five million dollars for Sargent, and upon his death to Sargent's daughter, and to give all the rest to legal aid organizations and public defender offices.

I wrote, *Nothing makes it clearer where money is needed most than for the people who need it to be the same ones in whose hands your own life depends.*

I told her how grateful I was to her and her legal team. After I signed it, I cried for the third time since I arrived.

Thumbtacks are considered contraband, so I used tape to hang three stacks of ten pages each on the wall above my bunk. I pulled down one each day, in reverse order, starting with 30.

On day 13 the transport team came by and told me I had a phone call. It had to be one of my lawyers, because they were the only people I was allowed to talk to on the phone. They took me to a tiny office down the hall from the warden's suite. It was empty except for a small bridge table with folding legs and an olive-green rotary-dial phone. It rang as soon as we entered. One of the COs answered, identified himself, and handed the receiver to me.

She skipped any pleasantries. She told me her office had received a form letter from the district attorney's office. The letter was sent to all attorneys who represented people whose cases had been investigated by a particular homicide detective. It was Detective Cole, the bad cop from my case. This detective, according to the letter, had stored physical evidence from several of the cases he investigated in cardboard bankers' boxes inside his garage. It was unknown whether any of this evidence had been wrongfully withheld from defense lawyers or was even relevant to any of the cases. The letter from the DA said defense lawyers were being notified *out of an abundance of caution.*

Detective Cole's unorthodox practice was discovered after he died of a heart attack three days before his fifty-sixth birthday and his second wife decided to move to North Carolina to be closer to her children. While packing her possessions, she opened an unfamiliar box. Inside she found a bloodstained ball-peen hammer, a rape kit in a plastic baggie with an unbroken seal, and a thrift store's worth of clothes. She panicked and called the detective's former partner, Detective Pisarro. He said he had no idea what was going on, and he called the police chief and the district attorney right away. That afternoon, police officers, lab technicians, and prosecutors put up crime scene tape and sifted through everything in the garage and inside the former detective's den. They emerged with a total of eleven boxes full of evidence. By the time the last vehicle drove off that evening, satellite units from five local news stations were broadcasting from the driveway live.

There was no reason to think any of the evidence had anything to do with my case, Olvido told me. My lawyer was calling just to let me know I might get contacted by reporters, because Cole had been the lead investigator on my case, and I of course was set to die in less than two weeks.

She said, I apologize for calling with non-news. I thought about waiting until we know more, but I didn't want you to get your hopes up if some TV crew comes to visit.

I said, I don't talk to the media.

She said, I know. It's just that once guys have dates, the reporters can be relentless.

We said our goodbyes, and the same CO who had handed me the phone materialized at my side and took it back. I was probably just imagining, but he seemed to look at me with sympathy, and I wondered whether he had been able to hear the call. Then I wondered whether the guards who would drive me to the execution chamber, and the others who would strap me to the gurney, would also look at me with sympathy, or whether steeliness was a prerequisite for the job.

Back in my cell I washed my face and neck in the sink. I put on a clean shirt and lay down on my bunk. I ate six potato chips. I tried to drink the iced tea that had come with my dinner, but it was as sweet as dessert, so I poured it through my fingers to save the ice and filled the plastic cup with water from the tap. Before dawn a CO banged open the beanhole to make sure I was alive. I raised my head and said, *Just sleeping,* then rolled over, pulled my knees to my chest, and slept until the middle of the afternoon.

If I'd had the ability to concentrate, I would have written a catalogue of everything that had surprised me over the preceding seven years, beginning with the day I shook Tieresse's hand and felt a love I had been unable even to imagine, and ending with the final moment I held the pen in my hand. Seven days before my date, my legal team showed up with yet another.

Olvido spoke. She said, Did you know the police found a bandana in the backyard of Tieresse's house when they were investigating her murder?

I said, No.

She said, Neither did we. It's not logged as evidence. There's a reference to it on a page of a police report that's misfiled.

I said, So what?

Olvido said, Did you wear a bandana at home or the restaurant?

I was not sure if her question was rhetorical.

I said, A bandana? Like a cowboy? Are you serious?

Luther said, The bandana was in one of the boxes in the detective's garage. Pisarro was the one who found it. We talked to him yesterday. He assumed it had been given to the lab techs. Turns out, it's still in an evidence bag. The seal isn't broken. It's never been tested for DNA.

Maybe I was unusually slow from not eating. The three of them were grinning like they had won the lotto, but I did not see why any of this mattered. Laura said, If there is DNA on the bandana, and the DNA matches the unknown DNA from the murder weapon, you're getting out of here.

My heart started to race. They explained to me the procedure. They would ask the trial judge to order testing on the bandana. If for some reason he refused, they would appeal to the state court. If for some reason they lost again, they would go to federal court. I thought to myself, So this is what they sound like when they think they might win.

I said, I am not getting my hopes up.

Since I arrived here, the state of Texas had carried out 115 executions. Most of those guys I didn't know very well, but 13 I did, and 12 of the 13 were less scary than inmates I met in the county jail. This entire place made no sense to me. To be optimistic, I'd have to see logic or rationality where I never had before.

Olvido said, Neither would I. But this is the sharpest arrow we've had in our quiver since the day we got appointed. We'll be in touch.

Before they stood up to go I put my left palm against the glass and said, No matter what, thank you.

Olvido said, Don't thank us quite yet.

But she was smiling when she said it.

■　■　■

Earlier I was going to tell you that Tieresse had cancer. For several months she kept it from me. A few weeks before our wedding, she confessed she'd been hiding a secret. I braced for something awful. Her secret was melanoma. It had spread to her liver and lungs, but a year before, her doctors in Houston used their clout and hers to get into an immunotherapy trial being run out of a cancer hospital in Atlanta. Twice a week she flew in for an injection. After eight months of shots, she was cancer-free. Her prognosis was terrific, but the doctors were reluctant to say she had been cured. Perhaps the cancer would return. Those oncologists have good reason to be the world's biggest pessimists. Tieresse wanted me to know.

I said, Why in the world would you keep that from me?

She said, Because if you knew, you would have felt like you were abandoning me if we hadn't worked out. I didn't want you to stay with me just out of guilt.

I said, The Jewish guilt gene from my mother wasn't passed down to me. I'd stay with you no matter what because you're my partner.

She said, Okay, vaquero. Anyway, now you know.

By the next morning, I had a list of questions. I asked about the length of the treatment, how the vaccines were formulated, which lab did the work, how many milligrams she received, what were the sixth-month, one-year, and five-year survival rates, on and on. She smiled patiently, and in response to every question I asked, she told me she didn't know. I was speechless. This amazing woman could tell me how many and what kind of roofing nails were used to pound shingles into a spec house she'd built five years ago in a subdivision in Des Moines, but she didn't know the answers to any of my questions about her treatment and prognosis. I was frustrated and stunned.

I used to call her Reesa when I was angry. I said, Reesa, this is your life.

She had said, Amor, I just told them I was not ready to die, to please do whatever they could to save me, and I followed their advice. What do I know about T cells and proteins? They are the experts. I put my life in their hands. I'm not indifferent. I'm just aware of my limitations.

She leaned forward and kissed me, and my anger turned to awe.

Walking back to my cell, I recalled the feeling I had that day. Some of the guys on death row spend hours every week writing letters to their lawyers offering suggestions and advice for which issues to pursue and how to raise them. If the lawyers don't listen, the guys get mad. Not me. I had learned my lesson. You have to trust the specialists. I told all my lawyers I was innocent, probably more often than they wanted to hear, but Tieresse was the smartest person I ever knew, and I was at least smart enough to know that. Not once was I even slightly tempted to give my legal team practical advice.

Sargent told me that when Águila was executed, his case was still pending before the Supreme Court. I had said, *That can't be right. They can't kill you until your case is over.* Sargent had laughed. He'd replied, *Shit, Inocente, ain't you been here long enough to get over bein' so ingenuous?* When it comes to the legal technicalities, I hadn't. And actually, I'm still not. But what follows is my layman's understanding of what happened over the next seven months.

Two days after they came to see me, with five days to go before my scheduled execution, my legal team filed an appeal asking the court to grant a stay and order DNA testing on the bandana. Reinhardt attended the hearing. The district attorney said this was a delay tactic. He told the judge there was not any proof there was DNA on the bandana, and even if there were, it would not establish anything because there was proof I was there. But the trial judge did not see it that way. He asked the district attorney, If there is DNA on the bandana that matches DNA found on the murder weapon, is there a better explanation than that whoever killed the victim was wearing the bandana?

The judge did not wait for an answer. He said he was granting a stay of execution and ordering forensic analysis of the bandana. As soon as he banged the gavel, the prosecutor hustled out of the courtroom, with Reinhardt at his side. An hour later the district attorney's office filed an appeal.

It was Thursday afternoon when Olvido called me to explain. My execution date, scheduled for Wednesday of the following week, was still almost a week away, so I asked, Why can't you all just go ahead and test the bandana for DNA anyway and then figure out what it all means later?

Olvido said, We offered, but the district attorney controls the evidence and he refuses to release it until ordered to do so. Your wife's son does not seem to care for you.

Sargent must have bribed McKenzie to deliver a kite, because when I got back to my cell, a tightly folded triangle was peeking out from under my pillow. Sargent had written, *Rumor is something's cooking.* I briefly summarized what was happening, and left the folded kite on my dinner tray. Sargent wrote back, *If it would help, you know I'd pray for you, Inocente.* He signed it with a drawing of a raised fist.

On Monday, with two days to go, the warden came by to explain the routine. He stood in front of me while I sat on my bunk. He was wearing khaki trousers, a blue shirt with an open neck, a tan corduroy coat with patches on the elbows, and suede ankle boots. I expected him to take a puff on a pipe. He looked like a college professor.

He addressed me by my name. He said I could have my usual visits on execution day until noon. I told him I do not have any visits. He looked at the captain, who was standing in the doorway. It was the first time I noticed him there. The warden said in that case they might transport me to the *other unit* as early as ten. He said it like that, *other unit,* and for a moment I was transported in space and time. It was a month before I opened La Ventana. I was in a tiny village in northern China, shopping at the local market. I do not speak a word of Chinese. The vendors I met didn't speak a word of English. I had no idea what I was buying, whether it was bitter or sweet, whether to cook it or eat it raw, whether it might cause me to fall ill or die. But it was exciting, because I knew I would be going home tomorrow with a story to tell.

Somebody was shaking me by my shoulders, and I was back in my cell. The warden was asking, *Rafael, Mr. Zhettah, is everything all right?* I came to, and I thought to myself, *Seriously, you are going to ask me that?* but I just nodded and said, *Yes, sir.* I noticed the captain hadn't moved, still standing there, with his hands clasped behind his back. I wondered whether he was holding Mace. What would they do if I grabbed a shank and held the warden hostage? He told me there was a form I could use to leave my personal property to other inmates, and he asked whether I had made arrangements. I blinked and he said, *For after.* Who would even attend my funeral, if I had one? A wall of cold air poured in through the open door. I could hear the air compressor click on, and I shivered.

He was looking at me, waiting. I hadn't thought about my

body, I don't really believe in all that, but for some reason, I didn't want to be buried at the prison. I asked whether I could leave my body to a medical school. He glanced at the captain, who shook his head. I said I would ask my lawyer to take care of it. He told me there would be a chaplain, if I wanted one, and the staff at the *other facility* would be able to provide a sedative. He asked if I had any questions, and I shook my head. He took half a step toward the door, giving me room to stand. I wondered whether I should shake his hand. He said, *Please be sure to let me know if you need anything,* and then he was gone.

I looked around my cell. I had the chess set Águila left me, but I didn't know anyone who played. I'd give my book of Shakespeare sonnets and Rilke poems to Sargent, except he probably had them already, perhaps even had all of them memorized. It occurred to me he had sandbagged me in our competition. I laughed. For a year I'd lived next door to a Cambodian guy I'd hear crying every night. McKenzie called him Chairman Mao. One day I said, *Mao was Chinese,* and McKenzie said, *What the fuck is it to you, za-heater?* I decided I'd give Mao my hot plate and radio even though I never heard him speak a single word of English. I was racking my brain trying to think who might want my legal materials or my lamp when another blast of cold air swept in under the door. I was suddenly nauseated and kneeled before the toilet in case I threw up. I said, *Why's it so cold in here?* Nobody answered, but a few minutes later Guard Johnson raised the beanhole and handed me a styrofoam cup of tea. I said, *Thank you, ma'am,* and she said, *You're welcome, son.* It was foggy outside—I could tell by the halos surrounding the perimeter lights—and unusually quiet on the row. From right outside my door, an overhead fluorescent bulb crackled and buzzed. I fell instantly into a dreamless slumber. I awoke briefly when a trustee passed a dinner tray into my cell, but I was too deep inside my sleep to eat it.

When the transport team came by early the next morning to tell me I had a call, I was filling out the form the warden had left behind. Olvido reported there had been no word from the Supreme Criminal Court. She explained the court usually handed down opinions only on Wednesdays, but given how Wednesday was my execution date, she had expected to hear something sooner. She told me that her team already had the papers ready to appeal to federal court but there was no point to doing so as long as what they had already filed was still pending.

I said, But what if it's still pending?

She said, It won't be.

I said, I found out there was a guy I knew who got injected while his appeal was being considered.

She said, That was a different situation.

I said, My trial lawyer told me I probably wouldn't be convicted, and definitely wouldn't be sentenced to death.

She said, Juries are unpredictable. But judges have a job.

I said, That's true, but their interpretation of the description might be different from yours and mine.

I was trying for levity, but she did not respond. She might not have heard me.

She said, I will call as soon as there is news.

The COs checked on me every hour. Sometimes they would pretend not to, raising the beanhole and asking, *Anything you need?* Other times I would hear them whispering outside my door.

Tieresse's charitable foundation financed some researchers

interested in the psychology of political dissidents in authoritarian countries. They wanted to understand how some men and women refuse to wilt. One of those they studied was a Russian physicist named Sharansky. He had spent years in a Soviet-style gulag, sentenced to hard labor. Even from Siberia, he never stopped his agitation. Eventually, bowing to pressure from President Reagan, the Russians released him. The KGB drove him to a bridge connecting East and West Berlin and instructed him to walk directly across and not look back. Sharansky walked backward into West Berlin, zigzagging the entire way. Tieresse met him a few months later in Israel.

She said to me, When I met him, I was expecting someone imposing. Instead, I shook the hand of a bald ectomorph. I don't think he weighed a hundred and twenty pounds. I asked him what had sustained him. He told me resistance is simple when the evil is everywhere.

I knew that when they came for me the following day I wouldn't resist. I would walk to my death as if unaware of my fate. I had twenty pounds on Sharansky, and a twentieth of his will. Less, probably. You can't will yourself to be a genius. It's the same with courage.

Some people will want to know whether I went to sleep. No, I did not. On Wednesday morning at eight when my cell door opened I was trying to meditate. The captain handed me the handset to a cordless phone. Olvido said they were filing something in the federal court so it would already be there if the Texas court did not intervene by noon.

My papá would have said what was happening to me was impossible in America. Until seven years ago, I would have been sure he was right. But at ten on the button, the transport team told me to pack my things. We'd be leaving in an hour.

As I shuffled out of my cell, I heard voices coming from behind the other doors. I heard things banging, inmates protesting the only way we can, my neighbors telling me goodbye. They walked me through B-pod, past my old cell, on the way to my death. Through the cacophony I made out Sargent's voice. He was saying, *Illegitimi non carborundum.*

I shouted, What the hell does that mean?

He said, Stare the motherfuckers straight in the eye, Inocente, straight in the eye.

They walked me out the same door through which I had come nearly six years before. I could see the overcast sky. Rain mixed with sleet, and a CO kindly draped a yellow slicker over my shoulders. McKenzie was there too, but he wouldn't be making the drive to the Walls Unit, where the execution would occur. He mispronounced my name for what I figured was the final time, and told me he would pray to God to be merciful on my soul.

Already waiting in the van was a CO in the driver's seat and another riding shotgun. The guard on my left pushed my head down and guided me into the back, where there was an upholstered bench perpendicular to the vehicle's other seats. The guard used a pair of handcuffs to clip a leather belt encircling my waist to a D bolt welded to the floor. Then he backed out and another guard climbed in and said to the driver, Let's roll.

No one spoke, except to give reports on our speed and location over a two-way radio to guards at both the prison we were heading to and the one we had left. I did not know how much time had passed, but when we got to the new prison, a clock on the facade read twenty minutes before one. I'd been in the van an hour and a half.

Four guards and the warden met us in the loading dock. They shackled me with their own set of irons, then removed the others and handed them to the guards who had brought me. The new warden introduced himself and told me the drill. I could shower and change. I said no thanks. He said I would be served dinner at three. I told him no thanks. He said they would bring it anyway, and I could eat it or not. He asked whether I had a spiritual adviser. I said no, and he asked whether I wanted one. He told me if I changed my mind to let the team know.

When the jury sentenced me to death all those years ago, it didn't matter. I had already heard the word *guilty,* and once I did, everything else was white noise. With the warden there, it happened when he said *team.* He meant the tie-down team, the men who would cinch leather straps tight to pin me to the gurney and slide intravenous needles into my veins. By the time I realized nobody was talking, the warden was no longer there.

One guard led, one followed, and the two others were on my sides. We crossed a tiny manicured courtyard as wide as I was tall with blue and yellow winter pansies growing along the edge. I said, *You guys actually plant flowers here?* Nobody bothered to answer. The guard in front used a key to open three bolts on a heavy non-electronic door with a single wire-laced pane. There was the holding cell, the same size as my cell on the row, except it had bars wrapped with chicken wire in place of solid steel. The door leading in was open. To the right was a cot bolted to the wall, and next to it a stainless-steel toilet and sink. They unshackled me, backed out, and closed the door. A guard used a key to turn a lock and slid a rod into a notch from right to left.

They stood to the side and talked softly among themselves, every so often glancing my way. I paced three steps one way and three steps back. I took deep breaths. Sargent's shout echoed in my head. *Look them in the eye, Inocente.* I wasn't sure I could.

I was not expecting anyone to visit, but at four the warden walked in, followed by Luther and another CO. Luther handed me a copy of the state court's opinion. I had lost. By a vote of two to one, the court concluded I was not entitled to last-minute DNA testing for two reasons. First, the judges said, I could not prove the bandana had not been planted or adulterated during the preceding six years. Second, they continued, it would not matter anyway, because the evidence of my guilt was overwhelming. They wrote, *This eleventh-hour fishing expedition is nothing more than a thinly veiled attempt to delay and avoid the justice long overdue to this cold-blooded murderer.*

The sole dissenting judge was incredulous. He pointed out that scores of people had been released from death row after their innocence was established. He wrote, *To assume our criminal justice system to be infallible is the height of arrogance, and to indulge such arrogance when a human life is at stake—a potentially innocent life—is abhorrent. If Mr. Zhettah is guilty, there will be plenty of time to carry out his death sentence later; but if he is not, we will have committed simple murder, which cannot be excused or taken back.*

Luther said, We already filed a petition in federal court.

I said, Please promise me that no matter what happens, you will have the bandana tested.

He said, We are going to get you a stay.

I said, Promise me.

He said, I promise.

A trustee brought in a tray of food. A guard looked at his watch and said, *You're late.* The trustee shrugged and said, *I came over when they tole me to.* I said I was not hungry, and the same guard told the trustee to take it away. The trustee looked at me for a long moment, pleading, I thought, then took the tray and rolled the cart away. Luther had been standing there silent. He put his hand to the chicken wire and left. A pastor came in and introduced himself. I said, *No offense, sir, but no thank you,* and he too looked at me with pity before turning back in the direction from which he had come. At five the warden entered and asked if I wanted a sedative. I told him no. He left a plastic pill case with one of the guards.

On the gray wall across from my cell, the second hand on the clock clicked each time it jerked a notch forward, while the minute hand slid around in stealth. The warden had said they would move me into the execution chamber at ten 'til six, but at 6:05 I was still in my cell. A red phone without a dial sat atop a dirty plastic lawn chair adjacent to the door. At 6:07 I jumped when it rang. A guard answered, said his name, then quietly said, *One moment please.* My heart was beating ten times faster than it should. I heard *whoosh whoosh whoosh* in my ears. The guard handed me the receiver through a hole in the chicken wire that appeared to have been cut for exactly this reason. It nearly fell from my slippery hand.

Olvido said, Tonight is not the night you will die. The federal district judge just granted you a stay and the court of appeals upheld it. The attorney general told me they will not be appealing to the Supreme Court. They'll be taking you back to death row shortly. I'll be up to see you tomorrow.

■ ■ ■

When you're expecting to die and you don't, you can forget to do the small things. So I had made a list of the things that matter. *Say goodbyes, express thanks, remind them I'm innocent, say let's get this show on the road.* It had been Sargent's idea to tell them they were killing an innocent man. To me, the most important part was the thanks. I wanted to thank Olvido for everything she and the others had done for me, or tried to do, and I knew I'd be nervous. I worried the nearness of death would make me forgetful or mute, or maybe both. That's why, starting the day before, I rehearsed the speech, memorizing a brief statement of gratitude, despite the ultimate failure. I planned to recite it when she called to tell me the Supreme Court had turned me down. I hoped she wouldn't cry.

On the drive back to death row at eight o'clock that night, I could not recall whether I had thanked her for saving my life. I could barely remember our conversation at all.

The three COs whose plans had been to lead me to the gurney instead waited for someone to unlock the door to the courtyard, and then led me as we retraced our route, only this time in reverse. I said, *How often y'all walk this way?* Nobody answered. It was too dark to make out the flowers. When we got to the loading dock the warden was there. He said, *Thank you, inmate, for your composure and deportment,* and then I was sitting in a van again, this time one with windows, accompanied by three guards who did not speak. We pulled onto a wide esplanade with towering oaks. Despite the hour, a couple went jogging by, the man pushing a baby stroller in front of them. I smelled a mixture of hickory and oak. My stomach grumbled, and I wondered how far we were from the pit where briskets and ribs were being smoked. A half dozen college students were throwing a Frisbee on a soccer field illuminated by deco lamps. The death penalty protestors, pro and con, had all gone home, but poster boards with hand-scrawled slogans blew down the sidewalk in the breeze. I looked up, and through a thin scrim of wispy cirrus clouds I saw a triangle connecting Venus, Mars, and the crescent moon. It was the first time I had seen the moon in five years. In an hour, I was back at home.

Word of my fortune preceded me. As the transport team escorted me to my house, inmates clapped and whooped and beat their tin coffee mugs with metal spoons. Inside we did not celebrate victories in football games or other sport. We cheered only when one of us survived.

They put me back in the cell on B-pod where I had lived before I got a date. Lilac was on the escort team with two new guys who had just moved over from population. Sargent was still living across the hall. He said, *Welcome back, Inocente. I told you your lawyer is the bomb.* My cell was empty. I asked Lilac when I would get my possessions. One of the new COs said, *You might be a little grateful you ain't dead yet, inmate, instead a makin' demands.* From inside his cell, Sargent laughed. After my door closed and Lilac took back her chains, a kite came skittering in. Sargent had folded four white pills tightly inside. He'd written, *I ain't never been so happy to lose so much dough.* He signed it with a smiley face.

It was midnight. I might have been dead for six hours. I hadn't slept in forty but I wasn't the least bit tired. I did yoga for an hour then whispered, *Thank you,* to Sargent.

He said, *It's the middle a the night, Inocente. Get some sleep.* Then he said, *And you're welcome.* I swallowed two of the pills, and when the breakfast tray arrived at a quarter to five, I didn't stir. The announcements for a count over the scratchy intercom were folded into a dream I had of flying with my papá back home. I didn't wake up until the transport team came for me at eight.

All three of them were there. Even Luther was smiling. I'd gone more than five years without touching anybody other than a corrections officer, but that was the first day it mattered. I wanted to hug them all. They told me the bandana had been sent off to a lab in Pennsylvania and that they would have results in less than two weeks. They stood up and touched their hands to the glass. I leaned forward and kissed it.

■ ■ ■

Day 2,019: For once my lawyers were wrong about the timing. Apparently, nobody's in any hurry to free guys from death row. It took the lab more than six months, but they had something to show for it. Technicians extracted well-preserved DNA from sweat that had dried on the cloth, and they constructed a complete genetic profile, like a fingerprint, but a billion times better. My lawyers ran it through a database of DNA from other convicted and accused wrongdoers. It matched a guy who had been found guilty of murdering a prostitute in a suburb north of Houston three months after Tieresse was killed. He had beaten her to death with a softball bat. He was serving a life sentence at a unit near Wichita Falls.

My legal team then requested additional DNA testing on the candlestick. A new prosecutor did not oppose it. In the years since Tieresse's murder, technology had gotten much better. New techniques allowed chemists to develop genetic profiles from a handful of skin cells. Analysts found four different profiles on the weapon. One belonged to Tieresse, one belonged to me, and one, not surprisingly, to the housekeeper. The fourth profile matched the DNA on the bandana.

Luther drove to Wichita Falls and interviewed the prisoner

on video. He was a middle-aged white guy named Lucas Gleason. He had sunken cheeks and sallow skin. He told Luther he had cirrhosis and expected to be dead in a month. He said he had killed Tieresse.

He'd been serving a ten-year sentence for robbery when he was paroled eight months before Tieresse died. He moved to Houston and paid sixty dollars a week for a single room in a boardinghouse in an industrial neighborhood on the east side of downtown. He washed dishes at a taqueria in the morning and in the afternoon parked cars at a fancy hotel. That's where he saw her. Tieresse routinely attended charity luncheons at that very hotel. Gleason told Luther he had noticed a ring Tieresse was wearing when she left her car at the valet stand. He wrote down the license plate number and used it to learn her address. When Luther told me all this later on I said, *The ring was a fake. I already told you all her rings and necklaces were costume.* Luther had replied, *I don't think Gleason had a jeweler's eye.* Luther asked him what had happened. Gleason said he had rung the bell and no one answered. He rung again. He did not think anybody was home. The front door was unlocked and he let himself in. He said he thought he might have the wrong house. Nothing looked fancy enough. But then he discovered a pile of what he thought were diamond necklaces in the closet. He had the right place after all. He stuffed the jewelry into his pockets and headed back out the front. Yet somehow, he took a wrong turn and ended up in an office.

I said, *He turned left instead of right.* Luther looked at me and continued.

Now in the parlor, Gleason paused to open the desk's deepest drawer. When he looked up, Tieresse was standing there, wearing a terry-cloth bathrobe, her hair wrapped in a towel. She had been in the shower. She must have heard him rummaging around. He jumped when she asked him who he was. He panicked and killed her. Luther asked him what time it was. He claimed he didn't remember. Luther pressed him. He said, *Listen, man, I ain't got nothin' to lose. If I knew, I'd tell you. All I know is it was just gettin' dark when I got there and had got pitch-black when I left. I remember that 'cause I could see inside with no lights on at first but I kinda stumbled around on my way out. I still can't believe I got 'way with it, well, at least up 'til now anyways.* Luther asked him how he had done it. Gleason said, *I reckon you already know I beat her to death.* Luther showed him five photographs: a wooden mallet, a fireplace iron, a crystal paperweight, a baseball bat, and the candlestick. He said, *Did you use any of these?* Gleason said, *Yeah,* and he put his finger on the murder weapon.

PART 3

...

On day 2,029 a transport team came for me at dawn. I'd spent one year, one month, and nineteen days in the county jail, and another five years, six months, and twenty-two days on death row. I was not yet convinced I wouldn't be back. I said, *What should I bring?* McKenzie said, *Are you kidding me, za-heater? Bring everything. It's moving day.* I put my diary and a clean white cotton jumpsuit in a box. I planned to hang it up wherever I decided to live, so I could see the letters *DR,* stenciled in black on the back, every day for the rest of my life. The hot plate and radio were for Mao. I asked Sargent what of my stuff he wanted. He said, *All I want, Inocente, is to watch your skinny ass walk out a here.* I could see he was smiling. I told him to please take the chess set because Águila had given it to me, and he said, *Will do, brother.* All my other possessions I left behind.

McKenzie said, *Hands.* In three hours I would be ordered released from custody, but they do have their procedures at the TDC. I squatted and offered my wrists. As soon as my door slid open, the row erupted. It was a sound of victory, and because

149

victories are so rare in our world, the sound was thunderous. Through the din I heard Sargent say, *Take care of yourself, Inocente*. His fist was pressed against the plastic slit in the door. If you read a newspaper story about him and what he did, you'll probably think he's just a cold-blooded monster. There's nothing like knowing a killer to create complexity. To me he was the best friend I'd ever known, not counting my parents and wife, and the only friend who had literally saved my life. I said, *I'll be back to visit. Count on it.*

And with two COs standing on either side of me and a third trailing behind with my things, I walked out the same door through which I had entered more than five years before. I turned around and looked at the squat concrete block, then across the field where the horses grazed and tracking dogs bayed from their kennels. McKenzie said, *Ready to go?,* and I said, *Yes, sir.*

The back door of the van opened. Three guards were sitting inside. As the transport team was guiding me to the rear bench, McKenzie said, *This ain't something that happens too often around here. Good luck to you, za-heater.* I said, *Seems like something that shouldn't ever happen at all.* The guard walking behind me said, *True that.* McKenzie shook his head.

He did not offer to shake my hand. The guard who had my things placed them on the floorboard and did. I looked at his nameplate as he pumped my arm up and down and said, *I appreciate that Officer Mullins.* He said, *Godspeed, sir.* In less than two hours, I arrived at the courthouse in Houston.

When prisoners like me talk about not being able to touch another human being, we are not talking just about sex, or even mainly about sex. We are talking about the things you don't notice: how the busboy uses his shoulder as he maneuvers past you to make sure you don't stumble into his path, or how the sous chef places her hand in the small of your back as she passes behind you with a sauté pan of brown butter to make sure you don't get scalded. We're talking about guiding a woman by the elbow through a crowd or having a buddy on the adjacent bar-stool drape his arm over your shoulder and pull you toward him so he can whisper a secret in your ear. We're talking about what's invisible until it's gone.

And so I felt my freedom begin when Olvido, Luther, and Laura, who were there to meet me at the courthouse's rear door, began hugging the breath out of me before both my feet had hit the ground. I tried to say *thank you* but I sobbed instead. Luther handed me a pair of jeans, a black T-shirt, running shoes, and socks. He said, *Might be a bit baggy.*

Thus it happened that, as the sun was rising over Buffalo Bayou, I stood on the concrete slab at the inmates' entrance to the Harris County courthouse, peeled off my prison garb, and changed into civilian clothes for the first time since the last day of my trial. Seven satellite trucks lined the street, reporting news of my exoneration as it occurred. All the major networks were there and even some from Europe. Olvido took in the scene for a moment, then held my face in her hands. She said, Rafael, I goddamn hate representing people who are innocent.

That morning I was inmate number 0002647, a resident of the Polunsky Unit of the TDC, otherwise known as Texas's death row. That afternoon, I was a free man.

■ ■ ■

Sitting at the head of a huge limestone table in a room packed with fifty reporters from across the country, one from Mexico, one from Canada, and five from Western Europe, I had my first press conference. Most of the questions were inane. *How does it feel to be out?* Great. *What are you looking forward to most?* Walking around without handcuffs. *What would you like to say to your lawyers?* Thank you. *How about to the people who are responsible for this tragedy?* I dodged that question by thanking the new district attorney, but the reporter, a thin man who spoke with a French accent, followed up and asked the smartest question I got that day, and the only one I could not answer. He said, *What do you think should happen to the officials who are at fault?* That turned out to be a question I could not get out of my mind.

Later I had my first celebratory beer. Olvido, Luther, Laura, and I sat outdoors at a bar on Main, and I savored a jalapeño cream ale from a brewery down the road. A black guy pushing a grocery cart and missing half his teeth stopped in front of us and pointed at me. He said, *I know you. You're President Bush's kin, ain't that right? Can you spare a penny or a dime?* I patted my hip, but I had no wallet and no cash just yet. Luther handed me a five. I asked, *Do you take paper money?* and his eyes sparkled. I said, *Good luck, chief.* He smiled and said, *Kin of the president. Right in front a my eyes. Check this out, people, kin a number forty-three.* And pushed his cart across the street to a new set of tables.

Olvido asked what I wanted for dinner.

I said, What I really want is to eat dinner after it's dark. You all decide where.

We took the train east to a cavernous restaurant with thirty-foot ceilings and a hundred kinds of tequila I was too scared to try, but the owner sent over a tray with a sample of five. Strangers who had seen the news made eye contact and nodded. Several came over to shake my hand. As we were finishing our coffee, the waiter told us someone had picked up the tab.

Luther handed me a duffel bag holding toiletries and clean clothes, and the four of us drove to a nearby apartment leased by a nonprofit organization devoted to helping former prisoners re-enter society. It was a one-room efficiency in a marginal part of town with a two-burner stove and a sofa that opened into a bed. It was mine for a month. The refrigerator and pantry were stocked, and there was an envelope on the table with five hundred dollars in cash.

Olvido had said, You do not have to stay here. I have an extra room. You are welcome to it for as long as you like.

But I was ready to be alone and unwatched, ready to use the toilet with the door open wide and nobody around, ready to watch TV in the middle of the night, ready to shower for however long I wanted at any time I chose. I was already planning to walk down the street to a convenience store at three A.M. and come home and make a bag of popcorn in the microwave. I said, *Thank you so much, Olvido, but this will do fine for now.* They hugged me and said they'd talk to me in the morning.

I set my duffel on the table and stood in the center of the room. I stretched my arms to either side because they wouldn't reach the walls. I opened the window despite the cold, again because I could. Horns blared and voices drifted up. Across the street a neon sign advertising beer with two missing letters flashed off and on. Three guys wearing micro shorts and leather jackets—I think they were guys—went roller-skating down the middle of the street and swerved around a bus parked at the curb. It was nearly midnight, and I wasn't the least bit tired.

The thin walls may as well have been screens. In the apartment next door, a young couple from Eastern Europe whispering in what I think was Polish tried without success to console their infant son. The woman sang, and I think the man played a mandolin. I grabbed two beers from the six-pack in the refrigerator, plopped down on the sofa, and turned on the cable news with the sound on mute while listening to the child cry all night. At four A.M. I walked over to the window and watched the stoplight change from yellow to red. A single car approached from my right. As it drew near I could see the driver was smoking. He was wearing a uniform, perhaps a security guard going home from work. He stopped at the light and turned his head up toward the window from where I watched. He noticed me there, nodded once, then idled on the empty street until the light turned green, white smoke curling up from his tailpipe. When the sky lightened at the false dawn and the traffic began to grow thick, I went to the bathroom and washed my face, then lay back down and fell deeply asleep.

A volunteer from the reentry group knocked on my door at ten holding two steaming cups of coffee and a paper city map. I thanked her for the apartment, the supplies, and the clothes, and reminded her I lived nearby not very long ago. She said, *Oh, I'm sorry, I didn't know.* She was embarrassed. I told her not to worry and to lighten the mood said, *Do people still use paper maps?* That might have made things worse. I said, *Okay, no more jokes from me,* and she smiled. She drove me to a government office where I got a new driver's license, then to a branch bank where I opened a savings account with a thousand-dollar money order donated by the volunteers. I didn't need the funds, of course, but I thought it might be bad manners to say so. So I said, *Thank you very much. I will pay you back as soon as I can.* She patted my forearm kindly. A month later I sent the charity an anonymous cashier's check for ten thousand dollars.

The night before, at dinner, Olvido had handed me an envelope. I opened it in the morning after the volunteer dropped me off. Inside were letters written by nine of the twelve people who had sentenced me to death. You might wonder what happened to the other three. I wonder that too. I brewed a cup of actual espresso and sat down to read. What would you say to someone whom you had grievously misjudged and caused to lose six years of his life? I admired these men and women for even trying to answer that impossible question. Tieresse used to tell me she judged people's sincerity by their effort, not their execution. The anguish and sorrow were evident in every letter I read. I knew these people had not acted in malice, and their antipathy toward the person they thought had murdered someone so good even struck me as a positive thing. Eventually I'd write back to every one of them with absolution. There were people I knew I would never forgive, but the twelve men and women who once believed I killed my wife were not among them.

I folded the letters and placed them back inside the envelope. I watched a small cockroach scurry across the kitchenette's linoleum floor. I clutched the envelope to my chest. The letters made me feel more alone, not less so.

A few years before I met Tieresse, I was watching the local news one night. Reporters were covering the story of a young man who had been convicted of rape and sentenced to prison for thirty years before new DNA testing established his innocence five years into his term. A crowd gathered outside the jail, awaiting his release. He emerged onto the street carrying all his possessions in a cardboard box. He was wearing a warm-up suit, horn-rimmed glasses, and an ear-to-ear smile. For a moment he took in the size of the crowd, then walked straight into the embrace of his mother, sister, and girlfriend, and disappeared. A reporter had interviewed the mom, who said she never had any doubt about her son's innocence. The only thing she didn't know was how long it would take her to prove it so he could come back home where he belongs. She placed her hands together and tilted back her head and said, *Glory be to God, all glory belongs to the Lord Jesus Christ,* and she was so certain and serene I smiled despite myself.

When I walked off of death row, the only people there to greet me were the guards, and when I emerged from the Houston courtroom a free man, there was nobody there at all. Reporters had to keep their cameras fixed on me. My parents and wife were dead. My friends were still in prison. Most of La Ventana's staff had testified for me at my trial, but they had been my friends, not my family, and unlike family, friends do move on. My restaurant and upstairs apartment were shuttered, and in another month I would sell them. I was glad to be out, but every remnant of my prior life was gone. What awaited me was emptiness.

I spent my first full day of freedom walking. Olvido had given me a cell phone, but except for a call from her to check up on me around noon, it didn't ring. I arranged with my offshore bank to have funds transferred to a new domestic account. I spent an hour reading the local paper in a hipster coffeehouse, surprised to see a quarter-page-size photo of myself taken outside the courthouse the day before. Six other patrons didn't seem to have any idea who I was, but the young man who brewed my drink bumped my fist when he came by my table to ask if I needed anything else. I left too large a tip and walked north toward Buffalo Bayou, pausing to buy a hamburger at a food truck along the way. By the time I got back to my apartment at close to five, my legs were so sore I struggled up the stairs. I drank a glass of wine while I drew a bath, and I fell asleep in the tub. There's a neighborhood pizza place that also delivers beer. I ordered a large pie with jalapeños and a six-pack of lager when I woke up at nine and watched basketball while I ate. Then my cell phone rang.

After the first DNA report came back, I received a letter from Reinhardt. It was the first time I had heard from him since arriving on death row. The letter held both a sincere apology and an unsparing flagellation of his decision to cut off contact with me. I read it out loud to Sargent. He said, *Damn, Inocente, some motherfucker beat my old lady to death I'd kill him too. Dude's stand-up, but he's got to chill.* I said, *Yeah, I know what you mean.* I wrote Reinhardt back saying I missed having him in my life.

I did not recognize the area code, but I answered anyway. Reinhardt said, *I hope it is not too late to call. I didn't know how to reach you. I finally got your number from your lawyer.* His voice was unsteady. I said, *I am glad you did.*

Reinhardt said, There are a lot of things I need to say to you, but the first task is to get you your money back so you can move on with your life.

He must not have known I already had more sitting in

Caribbean banks than I could possibly spend. I said, Actually, Reinhardt, that's very kind, but I do not need it, and I don't really want it.

He said, You can make that decision later, if you want to. Right now, I am arranging to transfer to you what my mother wanted you to have.

We spoke for nearly an hour, both of us crying at times, and made plans to see each other the following week. Before we hung up he said, *My mother was the happiest I ever saw her beginning the day she met you and lasting until the end of her life. It should have been obvious to me you could never have harmed her.* I recalled what Sargent had said. I said, *Reinhardt, if our two positions had been reversed, we'd be having the mirror image of this same conversation.*

The neighbors' baby was quiet that night, and I slept until the sun woke me the following day. I'd spent six years waiting for something good to happen, but believing I might jinx it if I made any plans. I no longer had an excuse. I took a cab to La Ventana to have one last look. Splotches of mold peeked out from cracks in the walls. The dial on the electric meter was still. The mirror that ran the length of the bar was tarnished and cracked, but the tables and chairs were mostly still in place, and I stared at the spot where I had first shaken Tieresse's hand. A homeless woman walked past and asked if I could spare some change.

I walked down the street to a boutique hotel and checked in for a week. I ordered a steak and a bottle of bourbon from room service and ate in bed while I watched a classic movie on a huge TV. That night, slightly drunk, I made a plan. I decided to say adios to Texas.

■ ■ ■

But it took a while before I could leave. Four TV networks wanted me on their morning shows. They flew me to New York in first class and put me up in a three-room suite overlooking Central Park. I sat down for interviews with NPR and the BBC, and my story was on the front page of *The New York Times*. Between shows I went to a matinee at a theater near Times Square. It was dark and loud, and I kept turning around to see what was happening behind me. I left before it ended. From a vendor on the street, I bought a candy bar and four newspapers and carried them uptown to the park. I sat on a bench across from a man who looked homeless and watched him throw crumbs to overweight birds. Although the temperature was in the sixties, he was wearing a threadbare overcoat, a polyester scarf, and an oven mitt on his left hand. I handed him my un-opened chocolate before I left. He looked at me, confused, glancing over my shoulder toward the pond. I think he said thank you in a language I didn't understand.

The day before I flew back to Texas, I had the beginning of an idea. At the time it was less an idea than an intuition, the way you can feel the extraction team coming around the corner before you see them. I was walking in Koreatown, looking for a place to eat lunch. At a bodega with wicker baskets holding carnations, roses, apples, and pears I bought a Nokia phone with one thousand minutes of talk time and two hundred texts. I paid for it with cash. I left it in its plastic wrapping and packed it in my suitcase for the flight back home.

Once I was back from New York, my newsworthiness faded to dusk. Other than talking to Reinhardt almost every day, my conversations were with waiters and cashiers. I had more space and more freedom, but no longer purpose or plan. I called Olvido, thanked her again, and told her not to worry if she couldn't find me for a while. She asked how long a while. I said, *I'll let you know*. I bought a small RV, food staples, clothes, and a bike. After an early cup of coffee the next morning, I checked out of the hotel, drove past La Ventana one last time, and headed east to Louisiana, the fastest way out of Texas. I crossed the Sabine, pulled into a rest stop, made a roast beef sandwich, and studied the map. I realized what I wanted to do first, what I needed to do first. I gripped the wheel, took a deep breath, and said out loud, *I'm coming, my love*. I drove north though Louisiana, into Arkansas and across Missouri, then I made a left turn and headed west.

It was after midnight when I crossed into Kansas. West of Kansas City, at a rest stop on Interstate 70, I pulled over for the night. I stretched my legs, had a sandwich, and drank a beer. Then I slept until nearly dawn.

The next morning, as the sky lightened behind me, I arrived at the property where we had planned to grow old. The pasture showed signs of six years of neglect, but the house itself was a pristine time capsule. When I had asked Reinhardt about it, he said he'd been too sentimental to list it for sale. I told him I was glad to hear that, it was where I felt I belonged. I lived in the RV for two days, working outside to clear brush and trails until the electricity, water, and gas were turned back on, then I parked the camper beside the hangar and moved back inside.

Reinhardt had had his mother cremated. I wish he hadn't. Maybe this sounds morbid, but I wanted to hold her bones, to go to sleep one last time with them lying next to me in bed. I have a different relationship to death than I once did. I'd spent seven years knowing the last woman I intimately touched was someone not my wife. I wish I could have changed that.

He sent me a box holding her ashes. I pushed my hand deep down into it. It was damp and cool, like rocky sand. I took a fistful of ashes and placed them in a clear crystal vase that still stood on the granite kitchen island beneath a patina of dust. I added a rose from a dozen Tieresse had dried and displayed. I put another handful in a small box from which I had emptied wooden matches. I took the remainder and scattered them where our garden had grown. I said, *Tomorrow, my love, I will plant,* and I wiped the ash from my hands.

I crossed the overgrown field to the forest and meandered down to the river. A love seat we had made from an old chairlift and a tractor-tire swing still hung from a massive oak. I took off my boots and socks and sat at the river's edge. The water was clear and cold. I saw a giant sturgeon and a school of rainbow trout. She never came to visit me in prison, not even once, but I felt her presence there. I smelled her too. I lay down and covered my eyes with my handkerchief. I pictured her the first time we had come here together, laughing, eating ribs with her hands, licking a dab of sauce from the corner of my lips. I heard her laugh again, and I smiled. I remembered our first night in Kansas, sitting outside, sharing a bottle of wine and staring up at the stars. I felt and I smelled and I tasted and I heard, and I smiled again, until I cried.

The next morning I cooked breakfast at dawn then walked to the hangar where we kept her plane. I drained and changed the oil and checked the fuel. I spent more than an hour inspecting the engine and frame. To start it up, I used an external power source because the battery needed a charge. The sky was cloudless, and visibility was unlimited. I checked the wind sock and took off to the west, and I flew for an hour.

To make my license current and knock off the rust, I enrolled in a three-day refresher course at a flying school in the southwest corner of the state, where nobody knew my name. I celebrated the three-week anniversary of my exoneration with a meat loaf sandwich and root beer float at a diner behind a gas station where they still filled your tank and checked your oil. The next morning, in the sky over Colby, heading east toward home, I discovered an important truth about myself. I've read interviews of exonerated men who spent years in prison before being released, and they always seem so serene and centered. They betray no hint of vengefulness or rage. They go on TV and say they harbor no malice toward anyone, and they mean it. They say, *Mistakes are made,* and they shrug. They say, *Shit happens.* They describe human tragedy with the passive voice. They say, *There's no point in being bitter,* and they aren't. They set up charitable foundations and go on the speaker circuit to urge reform of the criminal justice system. They write books and give the profits away. After years of being brutalized by a system that did not care about them at all, that denied their very dignity, they remain decent and good.

That day over Colby, this is what I realized: I am not one of them.

Years before, on that day early in our relationship when I first told Tieresse about my family and she told me about hers, I recounted the night my father caused the man who had leered at my mother in the marketplace to disappear. She seemed impressed by his primal act of retribution, not embarrassed on my behalf. I was surprised, and I told her so. Since reading Aeschylus in college I'd believed the urge to get even was a base impulse educated people could overcome. I said to Tieresse, *Not to be too cliché-ish, but don't you think there's some truth in the pacifist mantra that an eye for an eye leaves everybody blind?* Tieresse answered, *Yes, of course I do, Rafa, but not all acts of retribution trigger cycles of violence. Sometimes you can close the loop and get rid of the bad guy without injuring a good guy in the process. Maybe those instances are few and far between, but they do exist. I think your father found one of them.*

In three sentences, she undermined my entire understanding of why vengeance is bad. I didn't have to feel shame. It was okay for me to be proud of what Papá had done. Yet until that day flying home, the concept of just deserts remained mostly an abstraction. In prison I'd been too busy surviving to think about who was responsible for hurting me, or what punishment they deserved. Now, with nothing to do but fill the hours of my day, and the question the French reporter had asked lingering in my mind, the urge to get even took root, and it began in utter stealth. My subconscious was formulating details of the plan before my conscious mind realized a plan was there.

Powerful people had violated a moral code. They compounded my sorrow with pain. They deserved to pay. I believe Tieresse would have said that, too, was one of those times demanding retribution. I believe she would have approved.

So a few days later, I flew to Enid, Oklahoma, and drove a rental car to a convenience store at the edge of town. The intuition I had in New York had begun to take on a clearer shape. I bought a Motorola phone with five hundred minutes of talk and one hundred prepaid texts. I paid for it with cash. The same week, at a garage sale in Emporia, I found a brand-new

Dell laptop computer still in the box. At a big-box store in Topeka I paid cash for an Apple iPad mini. In the men's room of a truck stop on Highway 75 I bought a three-pack of tickler condoms for a dollar.

I put the phones in special foil packets the police use to prevent data from being remotely erased, and I placed the packets, along with the computer, the tablet, and a portable GPS, in a faux leather backpack. For the next seven months I stored the backpack in the luggage compartment of Tieresse's plane.

■ ■ ■

The first thing I needed to do was establish a routine. You could count on one hand, without a need for the thumb, the dividends from my time on death row. But there was undeniably one: Routine came easy to me.

The Main Street Diner, ten miles down the road, had been in business for seventy-five years, serving breakfast and lunch, from five in the morning until two thirty in the afternoon, every day of the year but Christmas, Easter, and New Year's Day. I started to go in three mornings a week, arriving between eight and nine. Unless it was raining the farmers were usually gone, but a few men in business suits would still be finishing up their eggs and bacon or asking for one more cup of coffee to go. It's a platitude, but it's true that news travels fast in a small town, and by my fourth visit, everyone I saw knew who I was. All three early shift waitresses, both busboys, and two of the cooks knew my name. I sat at the same counter stool every day and had coffee and cereal, and every now and again a homemade cinnamon roll or a cup of fruit.

I'd read the local paper someone had always left behind and use the free Wi-Fi to visit national news sites to learn what was happening in the rest of the world. A few former employees, including my sous and pastry chefs, had reached out to me, and I'd also connected with the families of some of the men I had met inside, so I would check my e-mail and social media too. After an hour or sometimes more, I would say thank you, leave money for the check and a tip at my place, and walk across the street to buy groceries and whatever else I needed for the day. Two or three times a month I would stop into the local hardware store. The owner and manager knew I almost always had a do-it-yourself home improvement project in progress. I was a fixture around town. People would have said I kept to myself, that I was friendly but quiet, that I seemed sad or diminished but not angry or bitter. The people who said those things would have been mostly right.

Thursday mornings I would leave. I would get in Tieresse's plane and fly somewhere for the weekend, always returning Sunday afternoon, unless the weather kept me away for a day or two longer. On Mondays the diner staff would ask me where I had gone, and if they didn't, I would tell them anyway. I showed them photos of small towns and national parks taken from five thousand feet. Sometimes I stayed in two-star motels in one-light towns and ate at local restaurants. Other times I flew to small cities and stayed and ate at chains. My favorite trips were to the wilderness, where I would camp and cook on an open flame. I was leaving a trail the weakest tracker alive could follow. I flew to places in Kansas, Nebraska, Oklahoma, Colorado, Utah, New Mexico, Arkansas, Missouri, Louisiana, and Texas—lots of places in Texas. Renata, a new waitress at the diner, once asked me what I was running from, and I told her that wasn't it at all. I was making up for lost time, seeing the whole country from the air and on the ground. She said, *Making up lost time for what?* and I saw Ramos, the busboy, whisper in her ear.

In the late afternoons, when the angle of the light made me melancholy, I would take a long walk around our property. In my jacket pocket I kept the box of Tieresse's ashes and a bag of unshelled pecans to feed to critters. In the early spring I scattered wildflower seeds in the grass. Most days I would linger in the tree swing by the creek and listen to the birds sing. At dusk I would have a drink or two on the porch and eat my dinner watching TV. I never invited anyone over, and in this town, no one ever stopped by unannounced. I would get in bed before eleven and read. I would rise with the sun, eager to start the long day ahead.

Years before, after Tieresse had seen this place for the first time, made a few phone calls, and bought the property with hardly a pause, the two of us returned to Houston. She came by La Ventana one night as we were closing, carrying blueprints and a 3-D model of the house. She said, *I just picked these up at the architect's office.* She unrolled the plans, spread them on a table, and said, *It's perfect, but are we sure the design will work on the land?* I had answered, *There's only one way to find out.* So the next morning, drawings in hand, we went back.

That was when we found it.

On the opposite side of the driveway from where we planned to put our house, hidden by a thicket of weeds, was a large manhole cover, nearly as large as a queen-size bed. It peeked out from the northern end of the mile-long concrete strip we planned to repurpose as a runway. After struggling without success to pry it open, I spied a small gearwheel covered by brush and brittle dandelions. Tieresse turned it, and the heavy steel door opened to the inside, revealing four hinges each a foot long. She said, What in the world is this?

We called the realtor, who had no idea what it was or even that it was there. I grabbed a flashlight from my flight bag and we lowered ourselves in. Tieresse had said, *I'll be darned. I bought a piece of history for a pittance.* We built the hangar for her plane right on top of her historical memento.

■ ■ ■

What we had found was a silo that formerly housed an Atlas F missile. Three decades earlier, a small structure on top had hidden the entrance, but the squat cinder-block building was long since gone. In the early 1960s, at the height of the Cold War, the US government had secretly built dozens of these silos, mostly in the Midwest. They held Atlas, Titan, and Minuteman missiles and were constructed to withstand a direct nuclear hit. Now that they were decommissioned and abandoned, the government declined to even acknowledge their existence. Ours did not appear on plans of the land, and nobody we asked could tell us when the weapon had been removed, but the silo's plumbing, electrical wiring, and ventilation remained in perfect repair.

The silo had eight levels, with a narrow tight spiral staircase descending the upper six, and steel-rung ladders welded to the walls providing access to the bottom two. The seventh and eighth levels held storage tanks, hot and cold connection systems, pressurization units, and overflow collection. The sixth level was the least crowded. It held a redundant heat exchange, a doubly redundant exhaust fan, and a diesel fume detector. All the equipment was against the northern and western walls. Tieresse had said, *If we didn't want to keep this place private, we could turn this silo into a bed-and-breakfast. It would be the hardest reservation to get in all the Midwest.* I had asked her whether she really wanted to do that. She smiled and kissed me and said, *Not in a million years. This spot of earth is yours and mine.*

Seven years and a few months later, it was exactly the same as we had left it. Wearing a headlamp, I walked up and down the eight stories, sketching each floor on a separate page of my drafting pad. My do-it-yourself home improvement project took shape. With sheet metal, cinder blocks, and stainless steel, I could turn the sixth level into exactly what I needed, something both secret and secure. It would become two adjacent cells. Together they'd be bounded by three solid concrete walls, with steel bars across the front. They would be divided into two separate spaces by a set of bars as well. They'd lack the built-ins I had on the row, and they wouldn't have a window, either. But I'd make them larger, because my prisoners would be there all the time. I couldn't risk taking them back and forth to a separate room for exercise or to bathe. I'd hang a shower curtain on each side of the interior wall so my prisoners could give each other privacy, or gain some for themselves, if they were so inclined.

Some of what I needed I bought from the hardware store in town. For the items that would have made the local owner wonder, I went to Kansas City or Overland Park. I bought the vertical bars from a company near Salina that sold fencing materials to construction crews. I bought sheet metal from a national chain in Topeka. I bought cinder blocks from a small home remodeling business in Tulsa. I paid for everything in cash. When a vendor acted suspicious of my stack of one-hundred-dollar bills, I told him I didn't like the idea of the federal government being able to keep track of me by getting records from the credit card companies. He shook my hand warmly and said that made perfect sense.

After six weeks, I had stockpiled my supplies, but I needed a disguise. I hired a company to put in a lap pool and hot tub. I can barely swim, but by heating the pool, or pretending to, I could explain heavy power consumption. Next, an outfit from Kansas City custom built for me a one-thousand-square-foot greenhouse where I planned to grow heirloom tomatoes, butter lettuce, and six kinds of chili peppers. Most important, though, it too would draw electricity and water.

With the subterfuges in place, it was time for me to build. Using a walk-behind, wet-cutting saw, I cut four three-inch-by-three-inch holes in the concrete floor of the sixth level down, beginning the construction of what would become the two impregnable cells. The holes would drain water and waste through pipes of PVC to the storage tanks two stories below. I ran a horizontal rod dropped eighteen inches below the ceiling across both cells. The inmates would be able to hang their portable shower bags from that rod. Set on top of two of the drain holes were camping toilets purchased in Oklahoma City that I had modified to fit the space.

In the ceiling I installed recessed LED lights. They were linked to a timer that turned them on at seven each morning and off at eleven each night, the same time the television would run. The electrical circuits were also relayed to my computer network through a router mounted on level 3. All the bulbs were outside the cells, so I could change them without having to go inside. I did not know how physically capable my adversaries might be, and I did not have any interest in finding out. Below the TV, bolted to the wall next to the door, was a digital clock that would count down the hours and minutes remaining until their release. Next to it was a battery-powered calendar showing the day, date, and time.

Vertical steel bars, spaced three inches apart, spanned the front. Each partitioned space had a gate with the highest-grade dead bolts money can buy. I bought them at a hardware store in Houston. The door built into their shared wall of bars had no lock at all. If they wanted to have conjugal visits, they wouldn't have to ask my permission. I bought cheap end tables for their cells at a flea market, and on top of each I placed a stack of books. In the drawers I left writing notebooks and a dozen pencils and pens. I bought two battery-powered camping lanterns, in case they wanted illumination after the lights shut off. Each cell had a straight-back chair, a rocker, and a stationary bike. One had a single cot, the other a sturdy bunk bed. The mattresses on both were warranted for twenty years.

A second row of bars, sixteen inches in front of the first, had a single door with two padlocks and a twelve-inch towing chain. It created a buffer zone between them and me and, more important, between them and freedom. I doubted they could escape from their cells, but there was something else important I learned on the row: the value of redundancy. The outer door leading to the staircase was from a bank vault. I rented a truck in Junction City to transport it to my property, and I paid three day laborers I hired in Kansas City to help me put it in place. When the work was done I bought them beer and tacos before driving them home, and I hoped they would not remember a single thing about me or what they had done that day. The vault door had a modified lock I could open myself by punching in an eight-digit code. Considering there are a hundred million combinations, I was fairly confident my code was secure. I used a drill with an industrial diamond bit to bore a peephole into the door so I could look in on my prisoners before entering their space.

One story up, on the fifth floor, I cut two four-inch-square holes through which food and water would be dropped into each of their cells once a day by an automated arm I scavenged from an electric dog food dispenser. The inmates would dispose of their waste and small bits of trash by dropping it through the drain holes in the floor of their living spaces, where it would fall into the storage vessel two stories below and be consumed by bacteria ordinarily found in backyard septic tanks. On the floors of levels 3 and 2 I laid a foot of sound insulation, and glued a foot more to the walls. Throughout the silo, I spread tiny remote-controlled cameras the size of a nickel attached to fiber-optic cable dropped down from level 1. The clock contained a camera I could remotely control to send me both video and sound. Smoke and fire alarms as well as carbon monoxide detectors were programmed to send me a text alert in case of danger. I was aiming to be a jail keeper, not a murderer.

Working four days a week, from late morning until early evening, construction took me nearly nine months. When my labor was done, I carried a radio down to level 6, tuned in the loudest music I could find, closed the vault, and climbed the levels until I was outside. I couldn't hear a thing. I pressed my ear against the manhole cover leading down and listened hard. I still heard nothing, except for a helicopter's rotors beating in the distance. I walked outside the hangar and looked up to see if I could spot it. I remotely activated the audio feed and heard the Rolling Stones singing "Satisfaction."

After coffee the next morning, I told the diner workers I

was excited about my next trip. I was going to head out to northern Arizona. The pictures I'd show them the following Monday I had actually taken a week before. So instead of flying west, I spent the next five days underground, three days in one cell, two in the other, testing everything out. The lights came on as programmed. My eye mask and earplugs shut out the light and sound of the TV. The food and water dropped on schedule. My shower bag filled every other day. The water and waste drained smoothly. The air was clean and fresh. I tried with both a baseball bat and a tire iron to hammer my way out, and I didn't make a dent. I couldn't imagine what kind of implement they would need to escape other than a key or a phone, and I didn't plan to let them get their hands on either one. The place was a fortress. I'd built a prison more secure than Alcatraz. If they could escape from this dungeon, they deserved to be free.

■ ■ ■

It was time to become familiar with the enemy. One I immediately had second thoughts about, but the other two I did not.

According to her official biography on the State of Texas Judiciary website, Sarah Moss had been on the Supreme Criminal Court for ten years. She attended St. Mary's School of Law, served as an assistant district attorney in San Antonio for six years, and ran for the position on the court after an unsuccessful bid to oust the Bexar County district attorney. She was a cheerleader at TCU, where she met her future husband, Harvey, who is the pastor of a megachurch in South Austin. The two have no children.

I did a web search to learn more. I did not find much news

of interest. The one exception was a story that broke when I was in my second year on death row. Moss's husband was sued by a former church employee who claimed she had carried on an affair with the pastor for six years and was fired when she decided to break it off. She accused him of fathering her six-month-old girl. The case was settled out of court for undisclosed terms. I tried to track down the mistress. As best I could determine, she and her daughter were living with her parents in Honduras.

According to his official biography, Leonard Stream graduated from Texas Lutheran with a degree in marketing. He played on the professional golf circuit for two years before starting a series of business ventures. He later attended law school at Baylor. Upon graduation, he went to work in the energy sector. A year before Moss was elected, the governor tapped Stream to fill a vacancy on the court when its senior member died.

My web search of Judge Stream was more fruitful. He started his business career operating fast-food franchises. A childhood friend of the governor, he bought, with the governor's financial backing, an established boot-manufacturing business, but the company declared bankruptcy after it was raided by immigration officials who determined that eighteen of the twenty-one employees were in the US illegally. Stream and his partner paid a fine for violating federal regulations but did not face criminal charges. Stream has an estranged son from his first marriage to a beauty contestant from Midland. Stream's second wife, a Dallas socialite, accused him of physical and psychological abuse in a high-profile divorce shortly after he was appointed to the court, but in the following election, Stream easily won reelection over a Green Party candidate. He

is now single, and rumors occasionally surface that he is secretly gay.

To all outward appearances, Stream and Moss were nothing
more than professional colleagues who voted the same way more
than ninety-nine percent of the time. Both were regularly en-
dorsed by police unions and prosecutors for their tough-on-crime
decisions. In nearly one hundred cases that had come before
them, including mine, neither Stream nor Moss had ever voted in
favor of a death row inmate. What Moss had written about me—
that I was a vile murderer who sacrificed one of God's most beautiful creatures to my selfish and rapacious desires—she had also
said, using the exact same language, of at least three black men
whose female victims had been white.

Her hostility to science might have even exceeded her indif-
ference to the Constitution. In one famous case that was broken
by the Brazos County newspaper crime reporter and subse-
quently picked up by the national media, newly tested DNA
evidence conclusively showed that a woman who had been
raped and murdered could not have been raped by the man
convicted of the crime. Moss voted against him anyway, specu-
lating the man convicted of the crime might have worn a
condom during the attack and laced the woman's vagina with
someone else's semen to throw investigators off track. Stream
joined her opinion, but a federal court intervened and granted
the inmate relief. Neither Stream nor Moss had drawn an opponent in either the primary or general election for the past
eight years.

But you can learn more on the ground than you can online.
So I told the staff at the diner I'd be gone for two weeks, visiting
national parks in Nevada and Utah. Instead, I checked the

contents of the backpack in Tieresse's plane, bought a car charger I could use for all the devices, and took off for the Texas Hill Country. I flew to a small airport south of San Antonio with no control tower, a potholed asphalt runway, and a rutty grass strip. Circling above the field at nine hundred feet to check out the wind sock, I thought the place looked deserted. According to an aviation website, the number of weekly arrivals and departures was zero, and there were no planes based at the field. I parked beside an empty hangar with a rusty padlock hanging from the open door. I planned to ride my bike to a used-car lot nearby and find something indistinguishable, but on the way there I spotted an old Ford pickup with a pop-up camper and a *For Sale* sign in the window parked on the side of a winding road. I pedaled up the unpaved driveway of a small ten-acre farm with two-foot-high alfalfa ready to be mowed. A potbellied man wearing denim overalls told me the truck had belonged to his elderly father who hadn't driven it for years. The truck was untitled, but the inspection sticker and license plates were current, and I bought it for fifteen hundred dollars in cash. The farmer threw in a case of oil. I tossed my bike into the bed and drove back to the field where I had landed and dialed a number off a sign I was pretty sure was not a working line. I was mistaken. My call was answered by the manager of a twenty-thousand-acre cattle ranch that dated back to the days when Texas was a republic. Until two years ago, the manager told me, the airport where I'd landed had been used by crop dusters, but it was abandoned when the ranch constructed a larger field capable of accommodating private jets ten miles to the north. I told the manager this one worked fine for me. He said, *You ain't gonna be runnin' no drugs or wetbacks outta the place, are ya?* I said, *No, sir, just looking for a bit of solitude to lick my wounds after a nasty divorce.* He gave me a grunt of sympathy and a PO box where I could send the rent. I leased a hangar for a year for the price of a fancy meal and paid for it in advance. Even with the plane, the truck, the camper, and a few pieces of old furniture inside, it had room to spare. I took a spiral notebook out of the backpack and wrote at the top of page one: *Things That Could Go Wrong.* On the first line I wrote, *Ranch manager?* The manager hadn't even asked my name, but it's the risks you don't notice that you most need to fear.

Keeping the speedometer needle five miles per hour below the limit, it took me less than an hour to drive to downtown Austin. I parked near the capitol and walked over to the courthouse. The entrance was set up like airport security. I took off my shoes and placed my phone in a tray. Nobody knew who I was. I sat down in the courtroom and watched the attorneys argue about whether the state's system for funding schools discriminated against the poor, and marveled yet again at how lawyers and judges can debate a question every reasonable person knows is undebatable. I left in the middle of the next argument, which had to do with whether a man who shot a woman in the leg could be charged with murder when the woman died three years later from an infection a doctor attributed to the wound. At dusk I walked to a fancy hotel and had a beer and a hamburger at a rooftop bar. Nobody recognized me there, either.

I slept that night at my hangar, inside a sleeping bag resting in the bed of the truck, and I returned to Austin the next day at dawn. Over time I would learn the judges were creatures of habit, and their daily routines barely varied from what I observed on that initial scouting trip. Both drove themselves to the

CONFESSIONS OF AN INNOCENT MAN

office. Stream alternated between a Porsche convertible and a Chevy SUV. Moss drove a BMW sedan. Their license plates identified them as judges. Most nights the local police left an empty cruiser parked at the curb outside each of their homes, and occasionally an officer would follow them to work in the morning.

Moss drove straight to the office and arrived at the court around nine thirty. Stream stopped every morning at a donut shop with a drive-through, but he always got out of his car and went inside. They left the courthouse for lunch around twelve thirty, but while Moss went to the same high-end restaurant every day and had a Caesar salad with grilled chicken and a single glass of wine, Stream usually picked up a meatball or salami sub and carried it back to his desk. They were never together, at least not that I saw, except in the world I was building. They left the office punctually at five. Stream would stop on his way home at a bar on Congress, stay for an hour or two, and pick up Chinese food, barbeque, or pizza on his way home. On Friday evenings, he often had guests. They always left before midnight. Twice a week he shopped for groceries. At the store, nobody seemed to know who he was. Once he made it home for dinner, he rarely left again before morning.

Moss's habits were a bit more varied. She and her husband went out every two or three nights, sometimes to an event or party, and other times to a quiet restaurant. Either he or someone else must have done the shopping, because I never saw Moss enter a grocery store. On weekends, she sometimes went to the mall and stayed all day. She did not go with her husband to church. Instead, on Sunday mornings, she went to a country club where she spent an hour on the driving range and then met three other women for a champagne brunch. The tuxedoed maître d' who guided them to their table always greeted her as *Judge*.

Although I had unhitched the camper from the truck and left it in the hangar, I still worried the old pickup might attract notice. So during my second week of reconnoitering, I bought a second vehicle, a low-mileage Lexus I found at an estate sale in Boerne. I paid for it with a cashier's check. The son of the previous owner signed over the title to me, and I put it in the glove box, where, as far as I know, it remains to this day. In my notebook of things that could go wrong, I wrote, *If I get pulled over, why am I here?*

When I got back to Kansas, I threw the notebook away. Trusting my imperfect memory seemed less risky than keeping a record of my concerns. At the diner I showed off my pictures of Arches and Zion National Parks and made a point of saying they were so vast and alluring, I intended to go back soon. Sitting at breakfast I made a mental list of items I kept in my cell while I was on death row and a separate list of items that were given to me each day. That afternoon I bought everything I needed at a local department store. In the razor aisle I paused. What if my prisoners despaired and tried to kill themselves, or worse, one tried to kill the other? During my time inside, one guy hanged himself and one overdosed on drugs, but no one succeeded in committing suicide with a disposable razor, so I bought a pack of twenty. I'd give them a new blade each week, after I made sure to recover the old one. If, despite my precautions, either nevertheless succeeded in killing him- or herself, I doubted I would lose much sleep, but the logistics of recovering and disposing of the body might be challenging. On Wednesday and Wednesday night I gave the prison another test run, making sure the amenities functioned and trying everything I could to break myself out. First thing Thursday morning I flew back to Texas.

Once I had landed and was inside the hangar, I removed the faux leather backpack from the luggage compartment of the plane and spread its contents on a plywood worktable the previous occupant had left behind. I created passwords to unlock the computer and the tablet: *IheartSarah* and *LeonardIheart,* respectively. They're maudlin, but they're easy to remember and, I hoped, easy for the authorities to hack. Just in case, though, I wrote the passwords on pieces of tape I stuck to the bottom of each machine. I used two different pens, two types of tape, and different handwriting for each reminder. I also created two e-mail accounts: one for JudgeMossTexas, and another for JudgeStreamTexas. The passwords for each were the same as for the computer and tablet. I made a note to get additional SIM cards for my own phone and dispose of the card I used on my trips to Austin once my mission was under way.

That evening, as Sixth Street in Austin was coming to life, I packed up all the electronic gear and drove the Lexus to the neighborhood in Round Rock where Judge Stream now lived. I parked three doors down from his town house and powered up the laptop computer. I was wearing a *Keep Austin Weird* sweatshirt and a baseball cap with a Texas flag. If anybody asked me what I was doing, I intended to say I was new in town and trying to find venue information about where I could hear a local band.

But nobody paid me any mind as I sat in my car and tapped the keys. Although I very much wanted to tell Reinhardt what I was planning and doing, for both our sakes, I didn't. I did, however, need his expertise. Earlier that year I spent half a day at his house in Princeton getting educated about cybersecurity.

Most of the questions I asked were innocuous, but one apparently struck him as more dangerous, and he wondered why I needed to know. I said, *It's better if I don't say.* He nodded, and he didn't ask again. He knew I was hiding something, but by then, he trusted me completely. As I was leaving, he said, *If you need anything else, let me know, okay? And be careful.*

Sitting in the Lexus near Stream's house, it took me five minutes to hack my way into his wireless router. Reinhardt would have been proud. I logged on to the e-mail account I had created for him and composed an e-mail: *Testing one two three. Please acknowledge.* I pushed send, closed my eyes for a moment, then headed to the high-end neighborhood Judge Moss lived in overlooking Lake Travis. It took me a bit longer to break into her network. Using the tablet, I logged on to her account. I wrote: *Message received loud and clear. I'm expecting a little more ardor next time, however <seductive grin>.*

I went back to Stream's block. I wrote a second e-mail: *Excellent! Can you get away this weekend? I know a charming B and B on the coast. (Does this meet her honor's expectations?)* I had one last e-mail to write, a reply from Judge Moss. She answered: *It does indeed, and that sounds perfect. Other than preaching to his flock, he will be playing golf all weekend and probably won't even realize I'm gone. Room service for lunch tomorrow at our usual spot?* I signed it with a winking smiley face emoji. I tried to think of what might go wrong, which notes seemed false, but nothing stuck out to me. I was good at this. Either I was a natural, or prison had affected me more than I realized. I shut everything down.

It was a cool, cloudless night. I got out of my car to put all the electronics in the trunk and to stretch my legs. Three bearded men were playing mariachi under a gazebo in a park across the street from the bus station, and I noticed my foot tapping out their rhythm. I bought shredded chicken tamales, frijoles, and two bottles of Carta Blanca at a taco stand on South Lamar and carried it back with me to the hangar as the aroma filled the car. I sat outside in a folding chair and studied the stars. My leg was shaking, and the eager anticipation I felt at that moment I had experienced only twice before: the night La Ventana opened its doors, and the day Tieresse and I became husband and wife. With half my second beer still left in the bottle, I fell into a deep and dreamless sleep. When I woke at sunrise, I was completely refreshed.

I drove the Lexus to a parking lot catty-corner from the courthouse and backed into a space so I was facing the street. I used Stream's Motorola to call Moss's Nokia and had a two-minute conversation with myself. Then I sent a text saying, *Nice to hear your voice, handsome. I'm running ten minutes late. Don't get started without me.* I signed it with the same winking emoji, then I texted back, *You're getting me so hot I'm not sure I can walk to the hotel. I might have to crawl <Smile>.* Two hours later, I sent another text from Stream to Moss: *That was an awesome opening attraction to our weekend.* She replied with a heart. I powered off the phones and placed them in their aluminum sleeves. I hoped that, in addition to preventing data from being remotely erased, the sleeves would also make tracking them impossible. I couldn't think of anyone who would want to track them, or of anyone who even knew they existed, but if there is a line between hypercautiousness and paranoia, I was willing to cross it to make sure I didn't get caught.

For the next eleven months, I flew south each Thursday

evening, drove from my hangar to Austin, and sent a text or two that day and an e-mail or two at night. I avoided toll roads and convenience stores with cameras. I wore a cowboy hat or a baseball cap with the brim pulled low. I'd leave Austin after midnight and go somewhere out of state, where I could charge a meal or a hotel room to my credit card, all part of my quest to explore the small towns of the Southwest—and leave a paper trail of my travels no place near the scene of the future crime. On my way back home to Kansas on Sunday, I'd make a quick detour to my hangar and drive again to Austin, where I would impersonate Moss and Stream one more time. Occasionally Moss would express concern her husband was growing suspicious and apologize for backing out of a scheduled weekend tryst. Stream always told her not to worry about it, that the most important thing was to be discreet. They were careful to describe their assignations in general terms—they'd talk about going to a hotel, or the beach, or the hill country—but never in a way that would allow their movements to be traced. Their caution ensured that investigators would not be able to interview any motel or restaurant employees about whether or when they had seen the amorous couple. Her e-mails and texts were flirtatious and coy, his were salacious and sometimes lewd. Scrolling through them, I felt like a sculptor who can see the shape hidden in the stone before he picks up his chisel.

Their Honors did not know it, of course, nobody did, but Judge Moss and Judge Stream were now having a digitally demonstrable torrid affair, and a pretty sordid one at that. I had created an excuse for them to be together and therefore a reason for them to disappear together. And I had a place to put them once they did. What I did not have, though, was any idea how I'd get them there.

■ ■ ■

And then I got lucky.

I had flown back to Texas so that the lovers could exchange a few e-mails and texts and reminisce about their weekend tryst at a West Texas B and B. It was Saturday morning. I was sitting in the Lexus outside his condo sipping coffee, writing something steamy and ridiculous about how great the sex in the back seat of his car had been as tractor-trailers rattled past them in a rest stop off I-10. I was trying to think of a better phrase than *take you,* when Stream got into his Porsche and left. On previous weekends I had tailed him while he ran errands in his SUV. I wasn't sure there was any more useful information for me to gather, and I was wary of taking unnecessary risks. But on the spur of the moment, I made the decision to follow him.

He put the cloth top down and headed east on Highway 71. In Bastrop he exited in front of a strip center with half a dozen fast-food places, but he did not stop to eat. Instead, he continued on, driving southeast on an empty two-lane road. I put half a mile of distance between us. Ten minutes later he turned. I kept on driving past him as he punched a code into an electronically controlled gate, and I parked on the shoulder two hundred yards down the road. It was a private field with a single runway that looked to be around three thousand feet long. Nobody else was there. Through a pair of binoculars I watched Stream spend ninety minutes doing touch-and-go landings in a high-performance single-engine plane.

Judge Stream was a pilot. The gods were winking at me, and my plan began to form.

For the entire two hours he was there, nobody else came or went. I wrote down the tail number of the plane and later learned Stream was its registered owner. Over the next few months I discovered he spent time in the air every other Saturday, weather permitting, so on a beautiful spring day, I flew to Bastrop to eavesdrop.

At airports without control towers, pilots communicate with one another on a common frequency, alerting aircraft in the area of their location and their plans. That way, two pilots will not try to land at the same time, and nobody will line up to take off as someone else is landing. I wanted to know how Stream phrased his calls. Ten miles north of the field, I flew in a tight circle at three thousand feet and listened to him on the radio, announcing his intentions to anyone who could hear. I made an audio recording of his calls on takeoff, approach, and landing. When he announced his final landing, I turned north and flew back home.

■ ■ ■

On my thirty-seventh birthday, Tieresse brought two glasses of fresh grapefruit juice into our bedroom while I was still asleep. She opened the shades and said, Rise and shine, birthday boy, I have a surprise.

We got in her car and she drove south toward the coast. I said, *Galveston?* But she said, *Shhh, no guessing,* and before we got to the causeway, Tieresse turned onto a pockmarked road and drove west. After a few minutes more we pulled into what I thought was a farm. Around back stood a prefabricated aluminum building, an unpaved runway, and a large twin-engine turboprop plane. Tieresse was taking me skydiving.

It was just the two of us. We sat in a space like a classroom with a dozen folding chairs and a whiteboard and played footsie as two jumpmasters lectured about safety precautions and things that could go wrong. After two hours they asked whether we wanted a bite to eat before going up and Tieresse said, I can assure you, young man, that would be a very bad decision. Now let's get in the air already.

Tieresse and I followed the two experts onto the plane. There were no seats, just two benches running parallel to the fuselage. The pilot was already on board, running through a checklist. Tieresse stared out the window as we climbed sharply and banked steeply to the left. She was giddy. I was not. At fifteen thousand feet, with my wife and myself attached to people I sure hoped were experts, we jumped. Within seconds we were falling at more than one hundred miles an hour. I saw Tieresse's mouth moving, she was saying something, but the roar of the wind in my ears drowned out her words. I tried to read her lips, but she just smiled. The young man I was attached to tapped an altimeter I was wearing on my wrist, reminding me to check the altitude so I would not forget to deploy the parachute at five thousand feet. I reached my right arm back, flailing for the rip cord. The jumpmaster took my hand and placed the cord inside. I yanked. The chute opened and we jerked to a slow descent, and soundlessness replaced the deafening noise of a moment before. I could hear Tieresse hyperventilating and my jumpmaster asking whether I was okay. To the north I could see Houston's downtown skyline, and then we pivoted 180 degrees and I stared out over the Gulf of Mexico to the south. We landed simultaneously in a field of cordgrass that sloped down to a brackish pond.

Tieresse ran over and hugged me while my arms were still shaking. She said, Happy birthday, my love.

I said, That was terrifying. Thank you, corazón.

She said, You're welcome. When you get your color back, let's do it again.

And so we did.

I remembered something else as well, a scene from my childhood. We were living in Chiapas. Mamá and I were standing at the edge of a field blooming with coca. The plantation was owned by the Mexican man my father worked for, but the field hands were mostly from Guatemala and spoke a dialect I couldn't understand. They laughed, and my mother eyed them warily. She held my tiny hand in one of hers, and with her other she shielded her eyes from the setting sun. She said, *Mira tu papá, él está muy bajo.* I turned to see my father flying parallel to the rows of green, not fifty feet above the ground. In an instant he rolled, and he was flying upside down. I believe I might have squealed with delight. The Guatemalans seemed to cower. As he shot by my mamá and me, he waved, and I could see his grin and the light in his eyes, and I jumped up and down and clapped my hands.

Out of those two memories came my plan. So early Monday morning I drove to the aviation academy near my home. I told the instructor I was not interested in becoming an elite expert in performing eight-point rolls or 180-degree inverted turns. I was merely interested in taking aerobatic lessons to be a better and safer pilot. I kept the real reason to myself. Aerobatics was my excuse to buy a parachute.

The following month I enrolled in a skydiving course. I paid cash in advance for a package that would have me certified after twenty-five solo jumps over two weeks. But once I was reasonably sure I could land more or less where I wanted to, assuming the wind was not terribly strong, I told the instructor I was having sinus problems and would have to take some time off. He said how sorry he was, but considering he had my money already, I held some doubt as to his sincerity. I told him I'd call him when I was healed, and I shook his hand. I planned to never see him again.

Days got shorter. Kansas got cold. Two feet of snow covered the ground. I spent another two nights in the silo to make sure it was warm. The timers worked, the temperature was comfortable, the water was clear. I did wake myself twice coughing, so I made a note to replace the air filters. If I hadn't had six years of practice (and, of course, the knowledge I could walk out whenever I wanted to), the claustrophobia of spending two nights belowground buried beneath the snow and ice would have made me suicidal. But the point is, I had.

I began spending more time at the diner, choosing a booth instead of a spot at the counter. I'd order a bowl of soup or a BLT, and I'd nurse my meal while I sat there and wrote. I told anyone who asked I was writing a book. It would be about my life with Tieresse and what happened to me when that life ended. Susanna refilled my coffee and asked if I had a publisher.

I said, Not yet, but I've got time.

In fact, three literary agents, two in New York and one in Hollywood, had gotten in touch with me and promised they could sell my story for a million dollars, which proved to me they didn't know my story, which is why I did not even bother to reply to their queries. A famous movie producer left a message on my phone. I called my lawyer and asked her to please not give out my number. She said, *I've never given out your number to anyone except Reinhardt and I don't intend to.*

I apologized and ended the call, and spent the rest of the week worried it was possible for strangers so easily to find me.

My book swelled to more than two hundred pages. The snow continued to fall. Farmers planted winter wheat.

Earlier that year I had started buying MREs from the army surplus store in Leavenworth, military meals, pretending these were what I ate when I traveled. I had accumulated enough food for two people to survive three years. The packages sat on industrial metal shelves on level 5 of my silo, next to the automatic dog food dispensers I had programmed to drop three meals a day. In another few weeks, I would have all the MREs I would need. According to the labels, they would expire in five years. But the ambient air temperature on level 5 was in the upper fifties, so I was thinking they might last a year or two longer. Either way, I wasn't concerned. If the meals expired, my prisoners could eat rancid food, just like I had.

On Christmas Day I flew to a town near Big Bend in West Texas, took a shuttle to the park, and spent ten nights in my tent. Before dawn broke I would look up at the stars that tiled the sky like a planetarium and talk to Tieresse. She told me not to do anything I might regret. I answered her by saying I had gotten to the place in life where regret has no meaning.

She said, There is no such place.

I said, I didn't used to think so either.

■ ■ ■

During my second year on the row, a few days after I'd paid McKenzie a hundred dollars for a six-pack of Valium, my house got tossed by a helmeted crew while he stood outside and watched. As they confiscated my stash and left, he said, Find a better hiding place, scumbag.

Sargent had been standing behind his door, watching. He'd been here longer than I had. He knew what I was thinking. He said, *Long as they be capable of pissin' you off, Inocente, they be winning, you feel me?* He sent me a kite with four small white pills and two Sufi meditative chants. The next week McKenzie sold me back the same pills I'd already paid for once. I hid them in the same place I'd kept them before.

For Christmas I bought everyone in the diner a gift. They were grateful and surprised. They knew my story, but not that I was rich.

During the first week of the New Year I was in Austin, sending forged e-mails and writing fake texts. Moss wrote she hoped next year they would be spending New Year's Eve together, *together and under the sheets,* she said, and she apologized again for not being with him two nights earlier. Stream texted back an emoji of a crying face and said, *I understand. But I'll see you for lunch tomorrow <grin>.* I took the truck and camper to a do-it-yourself wash, then, once back at the hangar, scrubbed every inch with bleach, inside and out. I would never drive or touch the truck again.

As I set up to land at my home back in Kansas, I put my right hand on the right seat and was surprised to feel Tieresse's thigh. She had visited several times since my release, and I talked to her often, but never before had I physically felt her presence. Again I wondered whether it was a sign of healing. She said, *In business, angry men make bad decisions.* I said, *I know, mi corazón. But I am not angry. I am indifferent, completely indifferent, and nothing could feel more liberating.* As I spoke those words to her, I felt her lips brush my cheek, and I knew for the first time beyond any doubt my plan would succeed.

It was now just a matter of time. Using different public computers around the state, I would periodically enter each of their names into a search engine. Most of what I learned was banal, like Stream being honored at the annual gala to raise money for the Fraternal Order of Police, or Moss giving the keynote address at the Constitution Day luncheon of the DAR. On Easter Sunday, though, I finally struck gold.

According to a newly issued press release, Judge Stream was scheduled to give a presentation on stand-your-ground laws at a program put on by the American Bar Association in Key West, Florida, the following May. I had just over a month to work out the details.

I flew to Padre Island and checked into a chain hotel. After breakfast the next morning, once my room had been cleaned, I hung the *Do Not Disturb* sign on the door and flew to the grass field where my car was parked. I drove to Austin, parked outside his house, and wrote her a text. It read, *Not sure if you saw I am giving a talk in Key West in May. One big boondoggle. How about coming with me?* I pushed send and drove across town. Parked on the block next to hers, I wrote, *I'd love to honeybuns. What are the dates so I can set up the story?* I headed back to his house. I wrote, *I love a meticulous woman. Let's work out the details Monday after our lunch.* He signed it with an emoji of a man winking and blowing a kiss. I flew back to Padre Island and got drunk enough that night to be noticed at an oyster bar on the beach. The next afternoon I flew back home.

I've never been a religious man. Even on my worst days on

the row I was never tempted to pray. But that night I did. I prayed for good weather for the third Thursday in May.

■ ■ ■

At the field where Stream kept his plane, I landed on Wednesday morning and parked across the strip from his hangar. Using a handheld radio to monitor the traffic, I trotted across the runway and checked the door. The main was locked but it didn't take me long to jimmy open the pedestrian door around back. From inside, the main hangar door opened with a doorbell button. I left it closed.

His plane was unlocked, and the key hung from the ignition. There were two headsets in the plane, top-of-the-line avionics, and paper sectional maps covering most of Texas, Louisiana, and Oklahoma in the back. Stream's flight bag holding his log book was in the luggage compartment. He'd made cross-country flights across Texas, and as far east as Alabama. The engine oil was clean, and both gas tanks were full. The pilot's operating handbook was in a pocket behind the right seat, and I opened it to the limitations section. Fully fueled and with five hundred pounds of passengers and baggage, the plane had a range of eleven hundred nautical miles. I quickly calculated how much fuel I would need to burn and hoped it would be enough.

My radio crackled. Someone was inbound from five miles north. I jogged back across the runway and waited by my plane. A taildragger came to a stop fifty yards away, and two slender middle-aged women emerged. I asked one if she knew whether there were hangars for rent here and whether there was fuel.

She gave me the name and number of the family who owned the field, and the cell number for a fuel truck that all the locals used. I said, *Thank you kindly, ma'am.* I tipped my hat and hoped neither was paying attention to my face or the tail number on my plane.

By the middle of the week, I had purchased paper sectional maps for East Texas, southern Florida, and all the area in between. A direct flight to Key West would be nine hundred nautical miles, but nearly all that distance would be across the open water. I wondered whether Stream was the kind of pilot who would fly directly across the ocean at night in a single-engine plane. I certainly wasn't, but he was going to prove a braver pilot than I.

I headed south. At a gun show in McAllen I bought a .45 automatic, a .38 revolver, and ammunition for each. I'd never shot a gun in my life. I'd have to watch a video to learn how to use them. From a different vendor I bought a knife with four-finger fist rings and a serrated six-inch tungsten blade. At a sporting goods store I bought a headlamp and, at a department store, a duffel bag, a small overnight suitcase, a casual dress, a navy sport coat, and underwear for a woman and a man. I divided the clothes into the two bags, along with toothbrushes, razors, and the three-pack of condoms I'd bought close to three years before, and I placed the bags in the back of Tieresse's plane.

Sargent had told me that several years before I arrived, back when death row inmates were still allowed out of their cells to work, five guys had tried to escape. They wrapped themselves in corrugated cardboard and duct tape and sprinted toward the fifteen-foot-tall razor-topped fence. Guards opened fire, shooting over their heads. Two of the escapees lay facedown and surrendered before ever reaching the fence. One dropped to the ground after climbing halfway up. The fourth dropped down on the other side but immediately raised his hands in surrender. The fifth kept running.

For a week and a half he was a legend. Texas troopers fanned out across the state searching. They formed a noose at the border crossing points to Mexico. They searched empty cabins and set up random checkpoints on the interstates and two-lane roads. Using tracking dogs and on horseback, prison officials scoured a perimeter that grew longer every day.

On the tenth day a fisherman found him floating in the Trinity River. His body was bloated with gas. The cardboard that kept the razor wire from disemboweling him as he flopped over the fence had grown waterlogged and heavy when he jumped into the river to hide his scent from the dogs. His mother later told investigators he couldn't swim. The lone escapee had probably drowned within an hour that very first day. Searchers had been chasing a corpse.

Sargent said, *Same shit that saves you can kill you if you ain't careful. Two faces a Janus.* I had said, *I only understand about half of what you tell me, Sargent.* He'd laughed and said, *That ought to be enough.*

I went over my plan again and again, certain I was missing something. What was the unknown that might kill me? It's not that I was afraid to die. I wasn't, and I had no fear. But I did still have my pride.

■ ■ ■

I'd been capturing his keystrokes with a program I had installed on his home computer when he clicked on a link in a phishing e-mail alerting him to suspicious activity on his credit card account. I wondered if I would have a chance to remove the program once he disappeared and, if I didn't, how big a risk it presented.

Judge Stream had bought a ticket to fly from Austin to Key West, with a stop in Miami, departing Thursday morning and returning Saturday afternoon. Because the real Judge Moss was not attending the conference, she had not bought any commercial tickets, but I had to do something about Stream, so I intended to cancel the reservation once I ensured he'd be unable to discover what I had done. And then I entered the danger zone.

On Wednesday morning I flew to the airport where Stream kept his plane for what I hoped was the third to last time. This was one part of my plan I couldn't entirely control. But I was lucky. Winds were calm and nobody was there. I taxied to Judge Stream's hangar. I entered through the back as I had done three times before and hurriedly raised the main door. There was just enough room for my plane, wing to wing next to his. I took the suitcase and duffel packed with clothes and loaded them into Stream's plane's baggage compartment. The day before, I had called the fuel truck, pretended to be Stream, and asked to have both tanks topped off for a long cross-country flight. Later I would spend a nervous two hours burning off that fuel, but first I needed to get my hands on the judge. I got on my bike and set off on the twenty-five-mile ride to his house. My backpack held the guns and the knife I had purchased in South Texas, a bottle of water, two pillowcases still in their packaging, three pairs of handcuffs I bought at a police surplus store outside Dallas, a wool blanket, and a roll of duct tape. If a DPS trooper decided to search me, I was probably going to jail.

Nobody was on the street. By remotely activating the camera on his computer I was reasonably sure he did not have an alarm or a dog. I rang the doorbell twice. The gate to the backyard was unlocked, as I knew it would be from watching the yardman open it every Friday morning. I hoped to get lucky and find an unlocked window or door, but I didn't. I looked around for a hidden key, also without success. I was prepared to do it the hard way, but until then, I was hoping I wouldn't have to.

At a few minutes after eight, as he had done every Wednesday since I'd been observing him, Stream arrived. I heard the Porsche's low rumble from two blocks away. I pressed against the garage's outside wall. I heard the electric door rattle up and the Porsche edge slowly in. A drop of sweat stung my eye. All at once, Stream killed the ignition and opened the door, and I was standing there before he could move, pointing the .45 at the middle of his chest. He said, *Take whatever you want,* and I said, *I plan to.* I told him to exit the car and turn around, and when he did, I cuffed his hands behind him. I pushed the button to close the garage door, and at last I relaxed. I said, *Shall we go inside?*

I was wearing blue jeans, a black T-shirt, and running shoes, and as we entered, I pulled on a pair of latex gloves. It was not yet completely dark outside, but I turned on a light in the kitchen anyway. I patted him down and took his phone. I said, *I'm surprised, I would have taken you for a concealed-weapon kind of guy.* He said, *I do not know if you know who I am, but you are making a big mistake.* I did not reply. He said, *I'm supposed to be meeting people for dinner.* I said, *Where are the keys to the SUV?*

I spun him around by his arm so he was facing me and

pressed the tip of the knife against his throat. I said, *Here's the thing: My first choice is not to kill you, but I can live with my second choice if I have to. Understand?* He nodded. I said, *Good. No talking and no noise.* I covered his mouth with duct tape and pulled a pillowcase over his head. I said, *Let's go,* and led him back to the garage. I put him and my bike in the back of the SUV and covered them with a blanket. I said, *If I hear any noise or I get pulled over, I'll shoot you in the head.* I opened the passenger door to the Porsche and retrieved a bag holding three cartons of hot Chinese.

As we drove back to the private field, keeping our speed a steady two miles below the limit, dusk turned to night. At the hangar, I put a second set of cuffs around his ankles and pushed him into the rear of my plane. I lifted off the pillowcase and peeled away the duct tape. I powered off his cell phone and put it back in his car. I said, *Prepare for takeoff, Your Honor.* He said, *So you do know who I am.* I said, *Same deal as before. You make a sound, I will kill you.*

Shortly before one A.M. we landed. I removed the leg cuffs and said *Watch your step,* and the two of us descended six stories underground, with me holding Stream's elbow in my left hand and a handgun in my right. I was wearing a headlamp. Except for the narrow beam it cast, the silo was dark as an underwater cave. I opened the padlocks and put Stream in his cell, and I locked the gate behind him.

I said, Hands, inmate.

He said, Huh?

I said, Turn around with your back against the bars.

After retrieving my handcuffs I said, *Step away from the bars now and face me.* I pointed my gun at his chest. I said,

Take off all your clothes except your underwear and drop them over here.

I handed him a thick cotton robe. I said, Lights and TV should come on at seven. There's a lamp on the table. See you tomorrow. Sweet dreams.

He said, What the hell is going on here?

I closed the bank vault door and climbed back upstairs. If he was making any noise, the silo's fiberglass insulation was absorbing every sound.

■ ■ ■

By the time Judge Moss's husband left their house for his church staff meeting Thursday morning at seven, I was parked across the street in Judge Stream's SUV. I used Stream's fake cell phone to send a text to Moss's fake cell phone, saying he'd pick her up in an hour. At eight, the garage door went up.

As soon as she closed the driver's side door, I turned into the driveway, parked behind her car, and got out with my gun. I said, *If you honk the horn or make a sound, I will kill you.* She said, *I do not have any money. You can have my ring.* I said, *Get out and turn around.* Once I had searched her, cuffed her wrists, and put duct tape over her mouth, I said, *I'm going to leave you this way for just a second.* I used the other set of handcuffs to attach her to the steering wheel of her car. I went back to the SUV and pulled it inside, parking next to her sedan. I said, *It's Leonard's. How do you like it?* Her eyes grew wide. I said, *No need to worry. He's perfectly safe.* I gave her the same speech I had given Stream. I dropped a pillowcase over her head, put her in the back of the SUV, and covered her with a blanket. I said, *I am going to tell you something. When I finish, I am going to ask you if you understand. If you do, lift your legs enough for me to see the blanket move.* I told her we would be in the car for around thirty minutes and that if I got pulled over, I would shoot her in the head. I told her when we arrived at our destination, she was to do what I told her to without making a sound. I said, *If you do exactly as I direct, I will not harm you. Do you understand everything I just said?* The blanket moved. I said, *All right then,* and I got behind the wheel.

Traffic was heavier than I expected. As we neared Austin's commercial airport, a highway trooper passed us going in the opposite direction. Involuntarily I glanced at the speedometer. I was well below the limit. I looked in the rearview mirror anyway. The trooper didn't turn around.

At Stream's airport, the electronic gate was already open when I arrived. My heart began to race. I rolled down the window and heard a buzz. Was another pilot doing pattern work? Would whoever was here wonder why I was pulling into Stream's hangar? I sat there at the keypad, cursing myself for not having a plan b. The buzzing noise grew louder. I slowly inched forward.

Across from Stream's hangar, a man wearing overalls and earbuds was on an air-conditioned tractor, mowing the grass. I raised my arm out the window and waved. I drove quickly into the hangar and lowered the door. I was shaking, trying to picture what the man on the tractor would have seen if he were looking.

I remembered the story Sargent had told me about the guys who tried to escape from the row, and how the one escapee had drowned. I'd said, *For all he accomplished, he might as well* have surrendered as soon as he cleared the fence. Sargent had said, *I s'pose if you're a utilitarian that might be so, but that ain't the way I see it, Inocente. If they plan on killing you no matter whether you're running toward 'em or away, I'd head away every time. Some victories cain't be measured in conventional terms.* I peeked outside, and the mower was still at work. I said to myself, *What he saw was Stream's SUV pull into Stream's hangar. Nothing out of the ordinary. I think I should be okay.*

I removed the pillowcase from Moss's head and held the knife to her throat while I asked her if she could send an e-mail from her phone. I said, *Nod once if you understand.* She did, and as I held the knife at my side, she wrote a note to her secretary saying she was going to a conference. At my instruction she wrote, *I apologize, it completely slipped my mind. I'll see you Monday.*

Outside, the noise from the tractor had stopped. I peered through the door, hoping he was not just taking a break. The mower was gone. I said, *It's like a hot streak at the blackjack table.* Moss said nothing. I said, *Okay, you're right. There's no such thing. It's all the law of averages. Come on, let's go. It's departure time.* I put her phone and her shoes into Stream's plane, where his phone already was, and said, *Up and at 'em.* Moss did not move. I pointed the revolver at her face and said, *That means I am ready for you to walk.* I guided her by the elbow and fastened her seat belt. Moments later, we were in the air.

Later that morning we landed at the silo. I said, *No talking until I say so.* I escorted Judge Moss down six flights and looked through the peephole. The lights and TV were on. Stream was sitting on the bottom bunk. But I was not going to take a chance.

I pulled the .45 from my waist. Moss gasped. I said, *Relax, Judge, I'm not quite ready to shoot anyone.* I opened the locks and swung open the door. Moss said, *Oh my God, Leonard, what is going on?* I said, *I don't recall giving you permission to speak, but I'll overlook it just this once.*

Stream looked like he had not slept at all. He was blinking repeatedly.

I said, Shit, do you wear contact lenses? I hadn't thought of that.

He said, No.

There were two unopened MREs on the floor in the cells.

I said, Looks like the timers are working.

Stream looked up to the ceiling but did not reply.

I said, I am going to ask you some questions I know the answers to. If you lie, I will shoot you in the knee, capiche?

He nodded.

I said, What day of the week do you practice touch-and-go landings?

He said, Saturday.

I said, Every week?

He said, No. Mostly every other week.

I said, When you fly cross-country do you file a flight plan?

He said, Not usually.

I said, Do you contact ATC for flight following?

He paused. He said, Sometimes.

I said, What about weather updates from flight services?

He said, Yeah, most of the time.

I said, You pass, Your Honor. Now turn around and give your colleague some privacy.

I put Moss in her cell and took her clothes. I gave her a

robe like Stream's. I said to them both, *I've got to run, so I'll give you the long explanation later. For now, I'll just cover the essentials.* I pointed at the shower curtains on either side of the set of bars separating their cells. I said, *Either of you can close the curtain for privacy. The toilets are the kind you find in an outhouse. They won't flush.* I pointed first at the ceiling then at the portable showers. I said, *Three meals will drop each day, along with a liter of water. When I'm around, I'll bring hot food every now and then. Those plastic bags hanging from the bars should fill with water one hour from now and every forty-eight hours after that. I have the nozzles set on medium. That will give you a six-minute stream. If you lower the pressure, you can make it last longer. You'll find soap, shampoo, toothpaste, and a toothbrush in those desk drawers. That's it for now. See you tomorrow.* I looked around to make sure I had locked their cells and not forgotten anything, and I started to leave.

Stream said, Do you plan to tell us what is going on here?

Moss said, My husband has probably already called the police.

I said, *I doubt that very much,* and I gently closed the door.

■ ■ ■

By the time I landed again at Stream's airport, it was getting dark. I used Moss's phone to send her husband a text. It read, *I cannot remember whether I told you I have to be at a conference today and tomorrow. I will be back Saturday.* I placed Stream's phone and wallet inside the flight bag, and Moss's purse next to her luggage. From the back of my plane I removed the parachute. I checked the fuel levels in Stream's plane one more time, then I said, *Here we go, Tieresse,* and I took off to the west.

I leveled off below three thousand feet and flew in a circle for three hours, burning fuel, then I climbed to forty-five hundred feet, flew west for ten miles, made a U-turn as I climbed to fifty-five hundred feet, and set the autopilot for a direct flight to Key West. I radioed flight service, identified myself with Stream's plane's N-number, and asked for a weather report over the western Gulf. It was clear below twelve thousand feet, with unlimited visibility and winds from the east. I thanked the controller and wished her a good night. I moved the baggage to the passenger seat and opened the suitcase and duffel. I put the clothes Stream and Moss had been wearing earlier that day on top. I double-checked my parachute, and when the GPS showed I was almost directly over Stream's airport, I opened the pilot's side door and jumped.

In seconds I was plummeting to earth. I was counting out loud but couldn't hear myself over the sound of the rushing wind, or possibly my pulse pounding in my ear. When I got to fifteen I pulled the cord, estimating my altitude at thirty-five hundred feet. I couldn't see anything on the ground except for highway traffic lights to the north. It was quiet and moonless. There was no breeze, and as I slowly drifted down, my fear of landing on the highway dissolved. In the distance I could see city lights in Austin and San Antonio, and I thought to myself, *This is beautiful.* Then I thought, *If I die, Stream and Moss are going to be in prison for the rest of their lives.*

I landed in a pasture, less than two miles from the field where I'd taken off. Cows were lowing but no people were around. I quickly refolded the parachute, loaded a map on my phone, and took less than half an hour to jog back to my plane. I touched down in Kansas as the sun was rising in an infinite and cloudless sky. No one was waiting for me. Everything looked exactly the same as it had two days ago. For the first time since the night before, I felt myself relax.

At almost the exact same time I was parking my plane in its hangar, Stream's was making its final descent into the ocean. According to a report by the Austin affiliate of NPR, a four-seat single-engine plane owned by Judge Leonard Stream, believed to be carrying him and one other passenger, crashed into the Gulf of Mexico three hundred miles from shore. Stream was thought to be en route from Texas to Florida, where he had a speaking engagement scheduled for the following day. The FAA reported there had been no distress signal or radio calls. According to an oceanographer at Texas A&M, the sea was deep in the area where the plane was believed to have gone down, but the water was warm, and if the passengers were alive on impact, they could survive for days. A coast guard official said a rescue mission was under way, and the NTSB announced it would begin an investigation once the wreckage was located. I clicked off the radio, took a long hot shower, and quickly shaved. Then I went to bed.

PART 4

...

Two brilliant yellow mourning warblers perched outside my window and woke me with their singing at eight. I brewed an Americano and carried it out onto the porch. Fifty meters away and six stories down, Stream and Moss were wondering where they were and why. It was time to tell them.

I left the trapdoor open and walked downstairs. Through the peephole I could see the lights and TV had come on. I opened the vault and said, Good morning, inmates.

Stream had dark circles beneath his eyes. Moss's eyes were red, and her cheeks were stained with tear lines from eyes to chin. I turned on the timer and flipped a switch, and its red digits began to count down to zero.

I said, We haven't met before, but I would like to introduce myself. You might recognize the name.

I told them who I was. Neither visibly reacted.

I said, A couple of years ago I came within minutes of being executed because you two jurists thought some arcane procedural rule mattered more than the fact that I did not kill my wife.

Still no reaction.

I said, Between the time I spent at county jail and the time I spent on death row, I was behind bars for more than six and a half years. To be precise, thanks to you, I was locked up for six years, eight months, and eleven days. That adds up to 2,444 days, you can check my math if you want, or 58,656 hours. That's how long you will be here.

I pointed to the digital clock.

I said, Oops, my mistake. I guess you'll be here a few hours longer, because I am just now starting the countdown. I hadn't thought about that. Sorry. I'll figure out later on how to make those few hours up to you. We have plenty of time.

Stream said, Yes. I do recognize your name. A jury convicted you based on the evidence before it, not Judge Moss and me.

I said, I'll let you explain the significance of that fact to me on some future occasion. Right now, I just want to introduce you to your accommodations before I head out for a while. Except for a few survivalists who fear Armageddon is at hand, I think you are the only two individuals in the entire US of A lucky enough to be living in a missile silo. I hope you appreciate the details. I did the work myself.

Moss said, Out for how long?

I told them I lived aboveground, just a few dozen yards away. I explained how the lights and the TV in their new home would operate. I used a remote control to demonstrate what I had briefly gone over last night: how MREs would drop down to them through a chute and how a reservoir in their cells would fill with water each day. I pointed to the tables where I had placed paper and pens and a stack of paperbacks. I gave them a short version of how the HVAC and waste systems worked and my own version of the warden's welcome. I said, If you behave yourselves, we'll get along just fine.

Both judges stared at me. Stream looked angry, Moss looked scared.

I said, Based on my observations, neither of you takes prescription medications, but if I am mistaken, let me know what you need and I will try to get it for you. Any questions?

Neither spoke. I asked them which news station they preferred, and when there was no answer, I put the TV on CNN.

I pointed at Stream and said, I'll call you John, and then turned to Moss and said, And you will be Jane. On the row the COs called us by our last names, or they tried, but I'll be honest: Your names stick in my throat. John and Jane feel better to me, and as you will learn, it is very much in your interest for me to feel my best.

Moss said, How do we get in touch with you if we need to reach you?

When I did not reply, Stream said, You will never get away with this.

I said, Actually, John, I think I might, but eventually you will get to know me well enough to realize I don't really care.

The door clicked shut behind me, and if they said anything else, I couldn't hear what it was.

Less than an hour later I was sitting at a booth in the diner, nibbling an apple fritter with my coffee and pretending to write to hide my excitement. I checked the Austin newspaper online and the local television news. There were no further updates. I went about my routine. I picked up a few items at the hardware store and bought my groceries for the day. I also purchased several books: the third in a historical trilogy of World War II, a volume of Neruda poems, and a novel nominated for the

Booker Prize. If I was acting abnormal, nobody in town appeared to notice. Back at home I listened carefully to see if I could hear any noise from my prisoners. All I heard were the birds.

For the next two days, I left them all alone.

■ ■ ■

On the third day of their sentence I went down to level 6. I peered through the peephole. Moss had wet hair and was sitting on her cot. Stream was doing push-ups. Both of them had eaten several MREs. I opened the vault door and walked inside. I unlocked the redundant gate and approached their cells. Through the bars I handed each of them two towels, three white cotton jumpsuits, five T-shirts, a hooded sweatshirt, a package of athletic socks, and a pair of flip-flops.

I said, I see you figured out the shower. I'll bring you clean clothes once a week and collect your dirty laundry. I am going to the department store later today, so if you tell me your size, I can get both of you underwear. I also have e-readers for you, but you will have to tell me what books and newspapers you want me to load onto them when I'm back aboveground. I'm sorry to say there is no public internet access down here.

Moss said, If this is about not getting the compensation owed to you, we can fix that.

I said, Jane, you can't fix anything. If you want to keep your house tidy, please put your garbage in here.

I held a trash bag up, and Moss reached through the bars and dropped her empty meal cartons inside. When I stood outside Stream's cell, he did not get up off the floor. I said, Suit yourself, John. But it's gonna smell awfully ripe in here over the next six years if you hoard your trash. I'm not sure your mistress there is going to be too happy about that.

Moss said, I am not Leonard's mistress.

I said, Actually, Jane, in a manner of speaking, you are. Don't worry, I'll eventually fill you in.

To Stream I said, *Last chance, John,* and I held out the garbage bag. He still didn't move. I shrugged and turned around. As I was closing the door I heard Stream. He was either whispering to Moss or hissing at me. The vault clicked shut before I knew which it was.

■ ■ ■

After lunch the next day I went downstairs carrying a duffel bag. I gave Moss two boxes of wine and a Swiss chocolate bar. I handed Stream a fifth of Scotch I'd poured into a metal flask and a can of nuts. I said, Sorry about the containers, but this is a glass-free zone.

Moss looked at the wine label with surprise. I said, You can learn a lot poking through someone's recycle bin. I do find it a bit ironic when people completely indifferent to legal rules and human suffering care enough about the planet to recycle, but whatever. Maybe there's hope for you. Either way, I had no way of knowing whether the wine is your choice or your husband's. If you prefer something else, let me know.

I looked at Stream and said, Same goes for you.

Moss said, *Thank you.* Stream only glared.

I gave each of them a copy of the papers my legal team had filed in their court, along with the opinions they had written denying me relief and the dissent of their colleague. I also handed them a copy of the order signed by the federal judge

halting my execution. I passed them the results of the laboratory's DNA testing, and a mug shot of the man who had murdered Tieresse.

I said, That picture is the thug who took my wife's life. He
doesn't much resemble me, does he?

I taped a third copy of the murderer's face to the wall next
to the TV. Both Stream and Moss stared at the photo.

I said, But if the two of you had had your way, we would
not know who bludgeoned my wife, and I would be dead.
I'll leave it here, so you don't have an excuse to forget. Any
questions?

Moss was breathing loudly through her nose. First her
neck and then her face turned pink on their way to red. Stream's
four-day beard was mostly gray.

He said, People will be looking for us, and the first thing
they will do is assume some disgruntled litigant is involved.

I said, I'm not disgruntled, and the people who are going to
be looking for you are not who you're hoping for.

I handed them each a page with an article I had printed
from that morning's Austin newspaper. It was a wire service
story, carrying a dateline from Houston. It read:

*Coast guard officials announced this morning they
have located the wreckage of the single-engine plane
that crashed into the Gulf of Mexico three hundred
miles east of Galveston nearly one week ago. The
plane is registered to Leonard Stream, a judge on
the Texas Supreme Criminal Court. According to the
Federal Aviation Administration, radar images in-
dicate the plane was en route from Bastrop, Texas, to*

Key West, Florida. Officials noted the pilot had not filed a flight plan, which is optional, but did ask for a weather report approximately two hours before the plane disappeared from radar. It is unknown how many others were aboard the four-seat aircraft, but Stream was believed to have been accompanied by Sarah Moss, also a judge on the same court. There is no sign yet of either one.

Officials said rescue boats will search for survivors during daylight hours while divers look below the surface for clues. They caution, however, that the depth of the ocean floor where the plane went down is more than 3,000 feet. An investigator from the NTSB, while declining to speculate on the cause of this accident, indicated that weather was clear below 10,000 feet, and that the agency would likely issue a report on its investigation within six months. Private planes like this one, according to the investigator, do not carry so-called black boxes, making the investigator's job more challenging. One source, who wished to remain anonymous, speculated the plane may have run out of fuel or the pilot may have been overcome by carbon monoxide poisoning. Stream had accumulated almost a thousand hours of airtime and had no reports of prior accidents.

Stream was first appointed to the court nine years ago and won reelection last November. He is divorced and has one grown son whose location is unknown. Moss, who also won reelection in November, is married to Harvey Salisbury, a self-taught pastor whose Sunday sermons are watched by an estimated 3 million people on cable TV. The couple has no children.

In a written statement, the Governor said his hopes and prayers are that Stream and Moss will be found alive and uninjured. He praised both judges as principled and conservative constitutionalists who place the law above their own personal feelings.

Moss gasped as she read it. A film of oily perspiration formed on Stream's upper lip.

I said, So, John, you can see why, given the circumstances, I doubt your first choice of an investigative theory will prevail. I'm waiting for my luck to turn bad, but three thousand feet of ocean is more than I could have hoped for, so it looks like the gods might be rooting for me.

Moss said, Why does anybody think I was in the plane? My husband will know this isn't true. He'll tell them I had no plans to be away. He knows I wasn't with Leonard.

I said, It's a constant source of amazement to me how spouses can lead double lives. I saw a story on a TV newsmagazine last week about a man who had a wife and two children in Dallas, and another wife and three children in Detroit. You have to admire his attention to detail, right? Anyway, Jane, you sent your husband a last-minute text reminding him you were going to a conference, and as you may recall, you told your secretary the same thing.

Moss lifted her hand to her mouth. Her eyes darted to the right, and then bored into mine. It took her only a moment to piece things together. In that moment, I saw her fear turn to anger.

I said, Eventually the authorities are going to realize you two were having an affair. They'll assume this trip was just another dalliance. If I am really lucky, they will also find your purse or wallet or cell phone somewhere near the crash site.

She said, Nobody will believe Leonard and I were having an affair.

I looked at Stream and asked, Do you feel insulted, John?

I said to Moss, I do feel bad about being cruel to your husband. He does not deserve that. I wish I could have thought of something better.

Stream said, Why are you bothering telling us all this? Do you want me to congratulate you on your cleverness?

I said, That's a fair question, John. But no, I am confident I can live without your congratulations. I'm telling you all this because I don't want you hoping someone is going to find you or is even looking. Hope is a balm, and you can't have any. Seven years ago I would have thought the worst thing about prison is being under someone else's control. But that's wrong. As I now know from experience, the worst part of being locked up is the complete hopelessness. I want you to have the entire experience. It's not the boredom that drives people mad; it's the certainty there's no escape, and the knowledge that the people who control your fate do not care about you or your ordeal. It is the daily reminder that, while you are here, they go home at night and drink a beer and watch TV. So no, I don't want you to congratulate me. I want you to realize you are going to be my prisoner until I decide to let you go.

I handed each of them a stack of pages on which I had printed all the e-mails and texts they had exchanged over the preceding fifteen months. Stream did not look down, but Moss did, and as she read, she began to shake.

I said, If the authorities search your homes and computers, they will find each of you had a secret e-mail account you used exclusively to communicate with one another, and a cell phone you used exclusively to talk and text to the other. The mystery will be solved: Two lovers die in a tragic accident while traveling to a secret rendezvous. Maybe instead of John and Jane, I should call you David and Bathsheba.

Stream said, Unbelievable.

Moss said, You are a cruel and evil man.

I said, No ma'am, I don't think so. I'm just indifferent. From your perspective there might not be any distinction, but from mine there definitely is.

I double-checked to make sure I had removed the paper clips from the pages I had given them, and I looked around to make sure I was not leaving anything behind.

I said, I'll be gone for a few days. When I get back, we can discuss those papers I gave you earlier. If either of you can persuade me there was a good reason to let an innocent man be executed, maybe I'll let you go. Otherwise, I'd advise you to get comfortable in your new home.

Stream said, Where are you going? If something happens to you we'll be trapped in here.

I paused in the doorway. I said, I guess you better pray I stay healthy.

■ ■ ■

Outside of Texas, after a brief story on the national news the day it happened, nobody was paying much attention to the crash of a small plane and the disappearance of two state court judges. Inside Texas, most papers were letting the Austin-based reporters do all the legwork. One wrote a story quoting a clerk from Judge Moss's office as saying Moss told her staff she would be at a conference. The same story confirmed Moss had sent a text to her husband with similar information. The press liaison for the Texas troopers confirmed Judge Stream had prepaid for a hotel suite in Key West for two nights, booking the room through the hotel's website and also that he had canceled a commercial air reservation. His SUV had been found parked at the field where he kept his plane. The story did not say whether police dusted for fingerprints, but I couldn't think of a reason they would, and besides, I had been wearing latex gloves so they wouldn't find mine. Investigators had not uncovered any evidence Moss was planning to attend the conference or made arrangements to be in Florida, but, they cautioned, the investigation was ongoing.

After leaving Moss and Stream, I flew to Texas to take care of a small piece of business. In the cab on the way to Olvido's office, I asked the driver to stop so I could buy a local paper. Inside on page three, a wire service story reported the most recent development: A shrimp boat captain based in Port Aransas, some two hundred miles south of Galveston, found debris eight days after Stream's plane crashed that included a piece of the plane's rudder and an expensive leather purse. The fisherman gave the purse to the local police, who in turn handed it over to investigators from the Texas Rangers. Inside the handbag officers found a wallet with thirteen dollars in soggy bills, two credit cards, a driver's license, Judge Moss's government ID, and two waterlogged cell phones. An anonymous source told reporters Moss's husband had been unaware his wife owned a second phone. I felt elation until I got to the part about the pastor, and then I felt a twinge of guilt.

But I remembered something Sargent had said one day when a feeble-minded effeminate inmate named Demerest who lived two doors down was being raped by a guard. Demerest said *no no no* and then started to whimper. Sargent read my mind. He said, *Listen to me, Inocente. Buddhists say the first noble truth is you cain't do everything to stop other people's suffering.* I said, *I know that, but get me close enough to that sadistic CO and I can at least stop Demerest's.* Sargent said, *True that, but it just be for now. Universe decides what's gonna happen once you gone.* I said, *Is there a lesson I'm supposed to take from that?* But he didn't answer. That night I heard Sargent whispering to the lieutenant. The next day, the guard who raped Demerest was fired. I heard he did time, but I don't know if it's true. I asked Sargent about it. He said, *I heard the same rumors as you.* I said, *Uh-huh.*

When I walked into their new office in Galveston, Olvido, Luther, and Laura were sitting in a conference room eating pizza. Laura saw me first and hugged me tight enough to pop my back. I said, *Nice digs. You guys take to representing the high rollers?* Luther smiled. Laura said, *I wish.* They asked what I had been up to, and I told them about the places I'd been to visit. Unless it's possible to lie by omission, everything I told them was true. We sat and visited for more than an hour.

Before I left I told Olvido I had a favor to request. I handed her an envelope containing several pages from a yellow legal pad. I had written the GPS coordinates for the entry to the silo and drawn a sketch of the building, with a thick arrow pointing to level 6. Below the arrow I wrote the numerical combination to the keypad lock on the door. I described exactly what I had done and how. At the bottom I wrote the day and date and a note saying no one other than me had been involved or had any knowledge of my plan. I printed and signed my name.

I said, I'd like you to put this in your safe and not open it unless a week goes by and you don't hear from me.

She said, Are you in some kind of trouble, Rafael?

I said, No, I'm just careful. Will you do it?

And she said, Of course I will.

I spent the night at a motel in Norman, Oklahoma, and watched the baseball team lose in extra innings to Texas Tech. I had a beer in a pub with free Wi-Fi and logged on to a Texas prosecutors' association discussion board. Reinhardt had taught me how to lurk on these boards anonymously, but I was extra careful and allowed myself to follow the gossip only from computers in public places.

There were more than one hundred messages dissecting the news about the discovery of Moss's possessions. Several posters said they were not surprised that Stream, a leading proponent of stand-your-ground laws, would be addressing the Florida conference, but nobody could make sense of why Moss, who was not on the program and who had no expertise in the area, would be going to a meeting pertaining to Florida law. Toward the bottom of the thread a prosecutor from the Rio Grande Valley wrote, *Maybe their relationship was, shall we say, not entirely professional <grin>*. The comment had an emoji of a smiley face with hands covering its eyes. Someone else responded, *Uh, I don't think so. Stream played on the other team.* Yet another prosecutor wrote, *Not that there's anything wrong with that.*

I closed the browser and erased the history. A day later, a reporter for a weekly independent had run with the story.

Courthouse observers said the rumors of an improper relationship between Moss and Stream were absurd. Moss's husband
said he and his wife were happily married. Office staff for both
judges said they never saw the two together.

Meanwhile, the coast guard formally announced that its
mission had been reclassified from rescue to recovery. If the
judges had survived the impact, they would have succumbed to
dehydration or exposure. Officials remained hopeful, however,
the bodies would be recovered, and they reported that a blue
leather jacket, believed to belong to Moss, had been found
floating twenty miles west of where the wreckage had been located. An official from the NTSB said the impact of the crash
had caused a wing to break off, making it impossible to determine if the plane had run out of fuel. Officials closed the investigation, describing the cause of the accident as *undetermined*.

For the next two weeks I went downstairs every morning
at eight, but I did not open the door to their cells. Through the
peephole I would watch Stream do push-ups and pedal the stationary bike. Moss sat in her chair with a plastic cup of powdered MRE coffee and read. Once, she pulled the curtain closed
between their cells and started to undress to shower. I pulled
my eye away from the door and walked back upstairs.

That moment, I think, was my first encounter with doubt.

■ ■ ■

One morning Stream said, I'll tell you the significance.

I said, What?

He said, The first day we were here, I said a jury found you
guilty. You asked me the significance of that fact. I'm ready to
tell you if you are prepared to listen.

I said, Knock yourself out, John.

He said, Your complaint is we should have gone along with the trial judge who ordered the DNA testing. But you had already been in prison for quite some time before that happened. I don't know how long, but I suspect you do. So even if you think Judge Moss and I should have ruled differently, we still had nothing to do with everything that came before.

I said, You're saying the punishment is excessive?

He said, Exactly.

I said, Like fining someone a million dollars for stealing a couple of thousand.

He said, Yes. It's disproportionate.

I sat down on the floor. It was the first time I had sat in their presence since capturing them. Moss was on her exercise bike, but not pedaling. Stream had his hands wrapped around the bars.

I said, I went to college and culinary school. I've never been to law school.

Moss said, I don't think what Leonard is saying requires a law degree to understand. It's simple morality.

I said, The guys my father worked for were probably psychopaths. They figured out a truck driver who had access to their warehouses was a spy, planted by the federal police. They killed him, of course, but that's not what I remember. I was only nine years old. They cut off his head and left it outside the local substation. Just a head, sitting on the ground, with a sideways baseball cap on top.

Moss covered her mouth with her hand. Stream was clenching his teeth. I could see his jaw muscles flexing. I knew he knew what I was about to say.

I said, I think in law school, they refer to that as deterrence.

■ ■ ■

The next evening I brought homemade lasagna, garlic bread, and a bottle of Chianti down to level 6. I was feeling magnanimous. I intended to ask them how much time they thought I should shave off their sentence. But I never got the chance. As soon as I opened the door, Stream said, Am I supposed to be getting a roommate?

My original plan had been to imprison three of them: Stream, Moss, and the district attorney who had opposed testing the DNA. That's why Stream's cell had bunk beds. But in the course of my research, I read the obituary of the DA's wife. She had died from a burst aneurysm at the age of forty-two, leaving her widower as the single father to three young kids.

I said to Stream, The DA has twin boys and a daughter in middle school. So you get to keep your single.

Moss said, Your combination of compassion and callousness is incongruous to me.

I felt the pressure in the room suddenly drop. When Moss said *callous*, I flashed back to the night I was with Britanny. That had never happened to me before. The two of us were in bed. The TV was on, showing a movie in black-and-white. I looked over Britanny's shoulder at the screen. Lucas Gleason was picking up the candlestick, examining it, turning it over in his hands. Suddenly Tieresse was in the frame. The towel fell from her head. Gleason was beating her. The TV volume was turned all the way down, but I could tell what my wife was saying. She was screaming, *Help me.*

It was as if Stream had read my mind. He said, If the man who butchered your wife had been sentenced to death, how sympathetic would you have been to his last-minute appeals?

I did not know what to make of the fact that every possible answer to that question seemed wrong.

■ ■ ■

Just as I reached the top of the stairs, I threw up. My neck was damp and I couldn't catch my breath. I believed I knew why. The stress of being a jailer was taking a surreptitious toll. It was the only thing I hadn't prepared for. How could I? I remembered what Sargent told me about Gandhi and hunger strikes. I needed to find a way to either cope with the pressure or let them go, and I knew exactly whom to ask.

There had been one guard on death row who was different from the others. Her name was Irene Johnson. I mentioned her earlier—she was the guard who practiced correctly saying my name—but I didn't tell you why she was special. On days when my lawyers would visit, I would sometimes see Ms. Johnson hugging family members of other inmates. I never heard anyone mouth off to her. Inmates fantasized about injuring practically every other CO except for her. She and Sargent were especially close. When no other guards were around she would call him by his first name. I once said to him, *Looks like you have a bit of a school crush on CO Johnson,* and he said, *Don't even be joking around me with that shit, Inocente. Miz Johnson be like Joan of Arc. You know who that is? You can admire the sister, but you cain't mess with her, you feel me?* I knew exactly what he meant, and he had nailed it. She exuded compassion. I had no idea how someone like her ended up working here. I had said, *You bet I do.* Irene Johnson was saintly. If anybody could help me out, she would be the one.

Like most people who use social media, Johnson was easy to find. She lived in a nondescript apartment building across the street from a row of inexpensive chain restaurants. One stayed open twenty-four hours a day, and I quickly learned Johnson had two cups of coffee and a piece of pie every afternoon at three thirty. She must have been working the early shift. I got there at three and took a seat with a view of the door. I ordered a BLT from a waitress who said, *What'll it be, handsome?* Ms. Johnson did not appear to notice me when she walked in, but when I picked up my check and walked to the cash register to pay, I pretended to accidentally drop my keys as I passed her booth. She looked up, and her eyes fastened on mine. She said, *My Lord Jesus, if it ain't Mr. Zhettah.* I stopped as if shocked to see her. She invited me to sit down.

My cover story was I was writing a book about my time spent in prison, and I was in town to do some research. I told her about how I had been spending my time and how I was hoping to talk to some of the guards. She said, *I wouldn't go gettin' my hopes too high if I was you, Mr. Zhettah. Most a the COs ain't too big on visitin' with former inmates, even the ones that ain't done nothin' wrong.* I told her all I really wanted to ask is how they deal with the responsibility and pressure of having someone's life in their hands.

I said, Do guards ever think about things like that?

She said, Child, they ain't bad people. It's just a job so's they can put food on the table. There ain't too many other opportunities out here.

I said, Pardon me if I am stepping over a line, Ms. Johnson, but it seemed like more than that to you.

She smiled. She said, My papa was a preacher. I s'pose that's why I know those men can be saved. All it takes is someone to try.

I don't know what I had expected to learn, but it definitely was not that. Saving Moss and Stream was not on my agenda. I told her it had been nice to run into her. I paid my check and I surreptitiously paid hers, and then I flew back home. That evening I made two turkey and Swiss sandwiches and carried them down to level 6. I looked through the peephole and was surprised to see my prisoners staring at the TV.

CNN was reporting investigators had recovered sexually explicit text messages from the phone found in the handbag believed to have been owned by Judge Moss. They had determined the phone was used to make calls and send texts to a single number. An anonymous source inside the Austin Police Department said the working theory was that the number belonged to Judge Stream, but investigators were not yet certain. Another source at the state police said investigators had questions because the phone had been sold at a bodega in New York and they had not yet been able to place Moss in that city at any time in the preceding year. Moss's husband, appearing exhausted, insisted to a scrum of reporters congregating in his driveway that he and his wife were completely faithful to each other.

I hadn't thought they would care enough to trace the phone back to its point of sale. I didn't even know that was possible. I felt my neck grow damp and my heart start to race. It must have showed. Stream said, You fucked up, as all fuckups do.

Moss said, Harvey looks exhausted.

I said, People buy all kinds of things online. There are a

million ways she could have gotten it and not a single one has anything to do with me. I'm liking my odds here.

That's what I said, but it wasn't at all how I felt. Every tiny mistake was an earworm of a bad country song. I could not foresee what would happen if investigators tugged on that thread. Probably it would lead nowhere. Yet I worried it might. I could hear my pulse beating in my ears.

But the last thing I was going to do was let my prisoners see my fear. That would be throwing them a life raft. It would give them hope. It wasn't going to happen. I forced myself to remember the day I flushed my disposable razor down the commode.

I said, I brought y'all sandwiches. I roasted the turkey and baked the bread myself. The tomatoes and the basil in the pesto are from the greenhouse. Hope you enjoy. When I check in on you tomorrow let me know if there is anything you want from town.

Back in my kitchen I heated water for coffee and turned on the news. CNN had moved on. They were covering a story about political upheaval in Venezuela. The other stations were all carrying local news. There was nothing online besides what CNN had reported. There were more than four million people in Manhattan the day I was there buying the phone. Millions of secondhand phones are sold online. I took a deep breath. For ten minutes I focused on my breathing, convincing myself there was nothing to implicate me. Then the phone rang.

Sargent and I were once fantasizing about escape. He said I'd have a harder time readjusting to the free world than he would because in my former life I made plans. I said, *Everybody makes plans.* He said, *Uh-uh, Inocente, not the way you think.*

Middle-class white dudes make plans to go to college, get married, have kids, all that Ozzie and Harriet shit. I said, *I'm not white.* He said, *Ain't the point. You akse a corner kid where he wants to be in a year you know what he says? He says he wants to be right where he's at. Here, everybody says that. 'Fore you got here, you thought about the future, ain't that right? Now what? You just thinkin' 'bout that shower tomorrow. Tell me I'm wrong.*

But Sargent wasn't wrong. I'd firmly entered the prisoner's universe. The crazy guys kept making plans. That's one way you knew they were crazy. But like most people who have no hope, my concept of the future didn't extend beyond tomorrow.

Sargent had been right about another thing as well. When I finally did get out, I had to relearn the concept of the future, and how to plan for it. Some of it was easy. In the restaurant business, you order from a supplier the food you need for a week. You just sit down with a paper and pencil and plan the menus and do the math. The other kind of planning is hard. What do you do when a diner doesn't tell you she is allergic to the hazelnuts you've finely ground atop an amuse-bouche of asparagus bisque? Call for a doctor, dial 911, or scream for epinephrine? You have to react right away and triage. If you haven't thought in advance about how you will deal with an emergency like this one, the patron will die while you ponder options. That was my mistake. I hadn't seen the tiny hole in my fabric of a plan, and now it was growing, and there was no way for me to stop it.

I answered after the second ring, and the instant I heard his voice, I relaxed. Reinhardt said, I am giving a talk next week at KU on security issues with open networks. Want to come and then have dinner after?

I said, I wouldn't miss it.

■ ■ ■

In a large conference room in the computer science department, packed, to my surprise, with more women than men, I sat and listened as Reinhardt discussed new measures designed to defeat MAC spoofing. MAC is an acronym for media access control, and every computer on a given network has a distinct MAC address. As best as I could tell, Reinhardt was talking about how hackers fake a MAC address to gain access to a network, and then, once inside, can do all kinds of mischief. After about two minutes, I could barely comprehend what he was saying, but I enjoyed listening to him all the same, like being at an opera where the arias are in a language I don't understand. The professors and postdocs in attendance seemed in awe.

On the drive back to my house I said, Your mom told me you were like a rock star. I chalked it up to maternal pride. I wish she'd seen that.

Reinhardt said, Me too.

We had a late dinner of barbequed brisket and beef ribs we picked up on the way home. I told Reinhardt about the first time Tieresse and I had flown to Kansas and gotten food from the very same place.

He said, I know. I talked to her the next night. She told me about the property she bought and the rings she braided. I had never heard her sound so happy.

I said, You have no idea how much I miss her.

He said, I think I do.

We sat outside in Adirondack chairs on the front porch and drank ice-cold beer. Fifty meters away, seventy feet underground, my prisoners were in the dark.

I said, Reinhardt, I've given my lawyer a letter with instructions to open it only upon my death. I do not think she will forget, but please remind her if I die.

He said, Are you sick?

I said, Not that I know about.

He said, Then why are we talking about this?

I said, I used to think nothing could surprise me.

He said, I get that.

We talked about the Kansas City Royals and the Atlanta Braves. Reinhardt's second love was computer science. His first was baseball. He had signed a contract with the Royals to create some kind of database they were using to decide which players to pursue and how much to pay them. He described it to me in what he considered a layperson's terms. For the second time that day I realized how the things that interested him most were utterly incomprehensible to me. I felt Tieresse sitting right there beside me, saying, *See what I mean?*

He thought I was laughing at him. He said, What's funny?

I said, Sometimes I feel the presence of your mother.

He said, Yes, sometimes so do I.

I said, I mean physically, like she is actually pressing against me. Is that normal?

I placed my hand on top of his arm, and we sat that way for some time. Finally he grew tired and got up to go off to bed. As he was walking to the guest cottage I said to him, Thank you for forgiving me, and for being my friend.

He turned toward me, placed his hands together as if in

prayer, and stood perfectly straight. He said, Rafael, you have no idea. The pleasure is mine. And you have the direction of the forgiveness exactly backwards.

The next morning, after coffee, I offered to fly him home. I watched him as we pulled the plane out of the hangar, looking to see if he would notice the flap I had cut in the large rubber mat designed to keep oil and gas from dripping onto the concrete floor. But he did not, and there were no sounds from below. I pictured the woman in the Hitchcock TV episode who kills her husband with a frozen leg of lamb then roasts it and feeds it to the police. I was fighting a powerful urge to tell Reinhardt what I had done.

He said, Is something bothering you?

I put my arm around his shoulders and said, Not a single thing. Let's get out of here.

By evening I was back at home. There was no more news on CNN. There was nothing online. The prosecutors on their discussion board were talking about other issues. At last I felt myself again relax.

■ ■ ■

Hopelessness is not caused by a single thing. The opposite is true. It is caused when there is not a single reason to go on. The day after Demerest was raped in his cell by a malignant guard, the state court turned down my appeal. Sargent told me about something called the Stanford experiment. He said, *You think it's a coincidence that just about every CO in this joint gets a hard-on when they get to suit up?* I said, *It's not a coincidence. You have to be a certain kind of person to want to do this work.* Sargent said, *Uh-uh, Inocente. You got the causation backwards. Doing this work makes you into that certain kind of person.* He described how researchers at Stanford University, using twenty-four volunteers, assigned twelve undergraduates to play the part of prison guards and another twelve to be the inmates. It was role-playing. Nobody had broken any laws. People were assigned to one group or the other arbitrarily. Yet within a matter of days, the prisoners began to exhibit signs of madness, and the guards became sadistic and cruel. The behaviors were so dramatic, the experiment had to be canceled. I said, *What's your point? That I should have more sympathy for the guards?* He said, *Nope. That ain't what I'm sayin' at all.*

That afternoon, a trustee came by my house with a stack of pamphlets. I told him I hadn't ordered anything from the library. Sargent said, *It's on me, Inocente. I thought you could use some illumination.* I sat down with the material. Sargent had sent me a collection of death penalty decisions involving Judges Moss and Stream.

I read a case. I said, *Shit.* Sargent said, *Keep reading.* So I did. I read about a case involving an inmate whose lawyer kept falling asleep during his trial. Several jurors, the court reporter, and a bailiff all signed affidavits confirming they had witnessed the lawyer with his head on the table during testimony snoring quietly, saliva dripping from his open mouth. Judge Moss said it was impossible to tell whether the lawyer had missed anything important, so where was the harm? Two years later, a different judge determined the inmate was innocent.

Another case involved an inmate whose lawyer arrived at court in the morning already drunk. Stream wrote the opinion ruling against the inmate. He said, *Requiring trial judges to monitor the sobriety of every lawyer who appears before them is insulting. We see no reason to add tedious burdens to their already heavy workload. Our state's judges can be trusted to run their domains efficiently and fairly.* Moss added a warning. She said, *In recent years, lawyers representing inmates on death row have adopted terrorist tactics of spamming the courts with numerous and frivolous appeals. This abuse creates unjustified stress for the courts and judicial personnel, and for the family members of the victims of these heinous murderers. I take this opportunity to admonish defense counsel they may be found in contempt of court if these behaviors continue.*

The next case involved a trial lawyer who had been sleeping with the wife of his client. The two had sex for the first time in the lawyer's office a week after the defendant was arrested. The conflict of interest was as obvious as they come: If his client wound up on death row, the married lawyer could keep his mistress. Judges Stream and Moss didn't see it that way. They agreed the lawyer's conduct was questionable, but, they continued, it was not nearly as reprehensible as what his client had done.

The last opinion in the stack dealt with a guy I knew, a guy so mentally impaired he routinely forgot to get undressed before showering. Every guard on the row knew he was feeble. Judge Moss denied the appeal. She said if the criminal had been smart enough to commit murder, he was smart enough to get executed. And then she ruled the inmate's lawyer was in contempt of court and fined him five thousand dollars.

I said, I don't think most of the lawyers who work on these cases even have five grand.

Sargent laughed. I said, What's funny?

He said, As usual, Inocente, you're missing the point.

I said, Which is what?

He said, Ain't no environment shaping those two. It's cool

to hate. You just got to make sure you be hating the right moth-erfuckers.

I had not kept copies of their opinions, but at the public library in Kansas City, I printed two sets of several highlights. The morning after Reinhardt's visit I went downstairs and gave each of my prisoners a copy.

I said, I've got a deal for you. If either of you can persuade me that even a single one of these ridiculous opinions you wrote makes sense, I'll shave a year off your sentence.

Stream said, We don't owe you any explanations for anything.

I said, John, were you listening to what I said?

He said, You're nothing more than an arrogant punk.

Moss was looking at me like she wanted to say something.

I said, Are you familiar with the Stanford experiment?

Moss said, I am.

Stream sat in his chair and pretended to read.

I said, Congratulations, John. You have single-handedly given me empathy for the COs who used to toss my cell and steal my things and gas me for grins. I'll see you around.

Moss said, Can you please wait for just a moment, please?

I said, Sorry, Jane. I'm afraid not.

■ ■ ■

Days passed, and then weeks. I didn't want to hear their voices. I didn't want to see their faces. I went downstairs only to collect the trash and bring them clean clothes.

In theory there's a difference between an argument crafted by a lawyer and a judicial opinion. One is supposed to seek a certain outcome, the other is not. Lawyers are not expected to be neutral. Judges, on the other hand, claim to be principled and driven entirely by the rule of law, not by a desire to see a particular party prevail. The collected works of Stream and Moss obliterated the distinction. I continued to give them copies of their handiwork, but I resisted the urge to engage. Some narratives are already too far along to be rewritten by the time you arrive on the scene. Take a guy like Taylor, my Nazi neighbor from the row. A black CO might literally save his life, but Taylor still wouldn't ever break bread with a shooter from the Crips. Same with Moss and Stream. If they couldn't see for themselves how they'd eviscerate as many legal principles as they needed to in order to keep prisoners locked up, I didn't see how a former prisoner like me could possibly give them any pause.

After a month, though, my resolve weakened yet again. When I brought them fresh clothes Stream said, I realize you believe I have to justify myself to you, but I am wondering whether you can first explain to me how your intentional misdeeds are justified as a response to our unknowing mistake.

I said, Don't you think it's a little mild to characterize allowing an innocent man to be executed as an *unknowing mistake*?

He said, Fair enough. Is that your answer?

I should have said *Yes* and left the room. Instead I said, No. My answer is that I am not trying to restore balance or order to the moral universe. This is all about teaching you a lesson, in case you are ever again in a position where it matters.

Stream said, That's bullshit. If your holier-than-thou rationalization were true, I wouldn't be stuck here, staring at a digital countdown.

I said, Teaching you a valuable lesson and scratching a vengeful itch are not mutually exclusive.

He said, Exactly.

I rehearsed pithy answers in my head. I wanted to say, *Winning the debate and being right are not one and the same,* but it was too late. He had done it again. Did the bodega have security cameras? Was there video of me sitting across from the courthouse or stalking the judges around town? Would Stream's plane's wreckage still contain my DNA? Maybe the paper trail I had left across the western US was so obvious any investigator would know it was a decoy. Only by staying preoccupied could I keep doubt at bay. I looked into opening a food truck. I thought about going to law school. I considered whether I had any skills Tieresse's foundation could use.

In the end I did none of those things. Part of me thinks some other part of me knew I wouldn't have time. Or maybe, like the Stanford students, I had simply grown to enjoy being the jailer.

■ ■ ■

Six months after the crash, the coast guard announced it was calling off the search and would resume only if new evidence or debris surfaced. A month after that, the NTSB issued its final report, declaring that while the reason for the crash remained undetermined, neither pilot error nor carbon monoxide poisoning could be ruled out. Private pilot discussion boards were more inclined to find Stream at fault. One pilot's theory was that he had run out of fuel due to stronger than expected headwinds. This explanation was plausible, but as another pilot pointed out, it did not explain why Stream had not issued a distress call. Someone else speculated that the best cause of the radio silence was that he had turned on the cabin heat to combat the external air temperature, which was in the upper thirties, and a heater malfunction filled the cabin with carbon monoxide, rendering both Stream and Moss unconscious as the plane lost power and fell into the Gulf.

The story was on page one of the state news section of the Austin paper and was carried on the local TV stations, but no major national outlets picked it up. I felt safe once again. I went downstairs and read it to my prisoners.

I said, Here we've been together half a year, and I think I can finally stop looking over my shoulder. What do y'all think?

Moss said, Gloating is an ugly thing.

I said, You're right, Jane, it is. But it's like I've committed a crime and can't be prosecuted because the statute of limitations has expired. Do you realize how exhilarating that is?

Stream had said, There are ways around those statutes.

I said, That attitude, John, is precisely why you're here.

I resumed my routine. I flew to Cortez, Colorado, and spent a week in the wilderness of the San Juans. I rented a bike in Moab, Utah, and stayed in a one-room cabin heated by a wood stove. I went to New York and saw three Broadway shows in two days. Once a week, on Wednesday afternoons, I checked in with Olvido to say hello.

Around the same time our romance turned serious, Tieresse began selling the numerous pieces of her sprawling business. I asked her whether she was worried about being bored. She said, *I have a weakness many driven people have. I cannot cut back. If I have a company to run, all I will do is run it. But I want to read more books and see more films and go to more museums. Unless I sell all of it, I won't do any of those things.* I said, *I am worried you will resent me.* She kissed me and said, *Don't flatter yourself, amor. It's a priceless luxury not to have to worry about all the little things. The only way I can afford it is to go cold turkey.*

With nobody looking for Stream and Moss, I felt free to stop worrying about the little things. I decided to go back to Austin. I rented a room in a four-star downtown hotel and leased a car. Stream's house appeared to be vacant. The lawn was manicured and mowed but the windows were dark. At Moss's house, on the other hand, every light seemed lit. I drove by again in the morning and saw her husband get in his car. He had grown gray around the temples. I thought about leaving him a note.

There's a scene in *Raging Bull* where Jake LaMotta is trying to adjust the television antenna while eating a sandwich. He's won the middleweight championship and lost it again. LaMotta's potbelly spills over the top of his shorts, and his brother mocks him. You can't be tightly disciplined forever. But if you cross the line between venting the pressure and growing complacent, you'll wake up in a cell. On Saturday afternoon, driving back into the city on US 183 after a barbeque lunch in Lockhart, I was pulled over by a Texas state trooper.

He removed his aviators and asked for my license and proof of insurance. His eyes were cobalt. His cheeks were shaved so close they shone. He took my documents, told me to remain where I was, and walked back to his car. His boots clicked on the asphalt. In the rearview mirror I could see him talking on the radio and tapping on a computer keyboard. If I fled, they would catch me. If they arrested me, would they let me go in exchange for information? I rehearsed how I would offer to make a deal. I'd say, *You know those judges whose plane crashed? Yeah, well, they're alive, and I know where they are.* I watched as he strode back to my car. He said, *I remember you,*

Mr. Zhettah. You're famous around here. I'm going to let you off with a warning this time. Speed limit's sixty-five, though. Okay? Have a good day, sir. I looked at the stripes on his sleeve. I said, *Thank you, Sergeant.*

That night I drank all the whiskey in the hotel room's minibar and ordered room service. In my isolation, I'd begun talking to Tieresse more and more. I said, *Well, my love, I got lucky and learned my lesson without having to pay a price. I won't take the risk again. There will be no more complacency for me. From now on, I never stop sweating the little things.* She said, *Weren't you paying attention, amor? It's the little things that will steal your joy.* I said, *I believe I already consumed my earthly allotment of joy.* She said, *I do not want to hear that from you, Rafael,* and I felt her lips brush mine. Before the sun came up the following day I was on my way home.

■ ■ ■

At the grocery store I bought a dozen fresh eggs and an unsliced loaf of country bread. I cooked a frittata with sundried tomatoes, garlic, red chiles, and feta cheese and carried it down to level 6 with a spatula and three plates and forks. I said, *I'm a little late, but I've been busy. Belated happy New Year. I fixed breakfast,* and I handed each of my prisoners a plate. Moss said, *Thank you.* Stream said, *We had eight thousand cases filed in our court last year.* I stopped chewing. He said, *Five thousand of those were petitions for a writ of habeas corpus.*

I said, Okay, I'll play. I used to serve a thousand meals a week.

He said, Do you believe human activity is contributing to global warming?

I told him of course I did. So he asked whether I think vaccines cause autism, whether the earth is flat, and whether I accept the theory of evolution. I told him no, no, and yes. Then he asked me whether I am a scientist.

I said, That's an interesting question, John. Most great bakers are chemists at heart, and I've met two or three chefs who are pretty scientific. If you ask me, they are soulless. But I guess I'm old-fashioned. Is there a point here?

He said, Yeah there is. You rely on experts just like we do.

I looked over at Moss. She had eaten her eggs and half a piece of toast and placed her fork in the middle of the plate. Stream appeared to be waiting for me to say something. I had a bite of frittata.

He said, We rely on lower court judges to do their work, and we rely on our staff attorneys. We don't have the time to review every appeal ourselves. Everybody alive depends on experts, including you. You pretend to be a self-righteous avenger. I think you're just a cheap hypocrite.

His outburst surprised me, and for a moment, I admired his fervor, but it did not take long for admiration to morph into disgust.

I said, Here's the problem with your argument, John. The trial court judge to whose expertise you supposedly defer ruled in my favor. She wanted to test the DNA. You and Jane here reversed her.

Stream said, Because she was wrong.

I said, One of your colleagues didn't think so. The way I see it, two of the state of Texas's finest judges wanted to make sure they got it right, and two others didn't.

Stream said, And your fellow citizens elected Judge Moss and me to be two of the three ultimate decision makers. I'm not seeing much of a line between your moral outrage and an embrace of authoritarianism.

Before I knew very much about my lawyer, Sargent filled me in on her background. She had been mentored by an Ivy League–educated Texan who had been a captain in the marine corps infantry before attending law school. He kept a tall brass spittoon on the floor in his office, and it was not for decoration. He had been the subject of an award-winning documentary, and Sargent had a copy of the biography on which the film was based. One evening a guy we called Javier was set for execution. Javier had confessed to shooting a cabdriver somewhere in West Texas, but for the past few years had been insisting he had not really done it. The day before the execution, the investigator from the case called Javier's lawyer and admitted he had tortured Javier to extract the confession. The cop was apparently on his deathbed and anxious to clear the deck. The lawyer filed a last-minute appeal. The case went all the way up to the Supreme Court, and they did not reach a decision until after ten o'clock. They ruled against Javier, by a vote of five to four. Javier was pronounced dead around eleven. When word got back to the row, there was no raucous protest. There was just stunned silence. Sargent said, *Yo, Inocente, listen to this.* He read a passage from the biography quoting Olvido's mentor. *You tell the jury your client was not even at the scene, but if he was, he was not the one who pulled the trigger, and even if he did, he had a good reason. You give them A and B and C. The courtroom is not a laboratory where one answer is true and the others are false. It's a baseball game where you don't care whether you get a hit, take a walk, or get hit by a pitch, just so long as you wind up on first base.* I was depressed about Javier. I said, *As usual, compadre, your point is eluding me.* He said, *It ain't only the cops and DAs who think this is a game. It's our side too. Reason Javier ain't back here is on account of this shit is just a sport to the dudes who know for sure they ain't never settin' foot in the place. You know who the Sophists were?*

I did, of course. They were philosophers. According to Plato, the Sophists cared more about crafting a winning argument than about identifying the truth.

I said to Stream, Maybe the difference is not obvious to you, but it sure is to me. You know what Churchill said? The best argument against democracy is a five-minute conversation with the average voter. He might have added with an average judge, because what neither you nor the people who voted for you can even begin to comprehend is the real-world impact of your sophistry.

Stream said. Churchill never said that.

I said, Maybe you're right, John. Maybe it's apocryphal. But who said it isn't the point. The point is, it's true.

As I was gathering my things to leave Moss joined the fray. She said, I assume you are aware your lawyer has a bit of a reputation. She has gotten too close to the line too many times. Most judges are not inclined to be generous to someone who takes advantage of the system.

I said, Jane, you fined a lawyer five thousand dollars for pointing out his client was mentally retarded. I knew the guy. I've never seen a person so impaired in my life.

Moss said, Your lawyer is not the only one who throws Molotov cocktails.

I said, Let me make sure I understand: You resent

aggressive lawyers, so you hold their fervor against their clients, but you will pay close attention to crappy lawyers, even though they don't have anything to say. Do I have that right?

Stream said, Guys like you think a lawyer is crappy if he doesn't raise a hundred issues. The reality is that most lawyers do not raise many issues because most issues are frivolous, and they recognize raising a weak claim is at least as harmful as raising no claim at all.

My parents were not devout, but they both believed in good and evil. Maybe that's why I felt so at home in college in Utah. The Mormons who surrounded me had a very clear vision of right and wrong. I didn't share their religious beliefs, but I could easily relate to their morality. It took being convicted of murder to realize how mistaken I had been.

I asked Stream, How many guys are on death row?

Stream said, I'm not sure.

I looked at Moss. She shrugged.

I said, Three hundred and forty-five. If I were to shoot you two right now, three hundred and forty of them wouldn't even bother looking up from their checkers games. They'd be certain I had done the right thing. You know what that tells you about moral absolutes?

Stream said, A prison full of murderers are who you look to for moral authority?

I said, Actually, lots of guys on death row believe in the death penalty just as much as you do. But not a single one of them thinks it's too much to ask that you be absolutely, positively sure before giving the state the green light to execute somebody.

Stream said, I'm not ever absolutely, positively sure of anything.

I said, Well I am. I'm absolutely, positively sure I did not kill my wife.

I paused. I turned and pointed at the picture of the killer I had hung on the wall beside the TV. I looked at Stream and said, And I am absolutely, positively sure of something else too. If you and Jane here had had your way, I'd be dead, and neither you nor anyone else would know I'm innocent.

Moss said, That's true, Mr. Zhettah. I see your point, I really do, but we have a system where a jury makes decisions based on the evidence before it.

I said, It must be easy to trust twelve strangers as long as it's not you they're misjudging. Maybe that makes me an authoritarian in your moral universe, but I'd rather be a dictator trying to do the right thing than someone who follows a mob to the pyre.

I dropped my plate into the plastic garbage bag. I said, I'll see y'all later.

Stream said, Thanks for the eggs.

I left quickly so they wouldn't see me seethe.

■ ■ ■

In my own mind, I had won the debate, but I wondered whether the reason was because they hadn't asked me the hard questions: If this is about teaching us something, exactly what lesson is it you're expecting us to learn? And if it's not about learning, then why are we here? I was worrying I was the Sophist.

During my years on death row, I talked about my family to Olvido only twice: the day we met, and the day she came to tell me we had lost our state appeal. She said, *And here's the bad news*. It wasn't that we had lost. It was that state court had been our best hope. I said, *I heard federal judges are more fair.* She said, *It has nothing to do with fairness.* In Olvido's opinion, our best shot had been state court, because in federal court, the judges do not care whether you're innocent. I said, *What?*

She told me how, in the 1990s, the Supreme Court ruled the US Constitution does not prohibit a state from putting an innocent person to death, so long as the trial resulting in the conviction and sentence was fair. I said, *If an innocent person is sent to death row, isn't that inherently unfair?* She said, *You would think.*

I told her about the last time I saw my father. I'd gone home for Christmas vacation during my freshman year. I spent a lot of time studying because our exams were in January. One morning my nose was buried in the complete Socratic dialogues when my father, who did not even know what philosophy was, asked what I was reading. I told him there were all these really smart people who spent their time thinking about what it means for the government to treat people fairly. My mamá walked into the room and he was beaming. He said, *Quizás mi hijo va a ser un profesor.* My grades were not nearly good enough for me to have been a professor even if I had wanted to, but I was not going to say anything to dampen his pride. My mamá, though, was the more practical of the two and had no such qualms. She said, *Qué loco. You think he can earn a living discussing whether the glass is half-empty or half-full?* Papá laughed and kissed her head. He put my neck in the crook of his arm and tugged me close to him. He smelled like motor oil and leather and freshly mowed grass. He said, *En mi vida, el vaso siempre está medio lleno.* And it was true. For him, the glass always was half-full.

He did not know it at the time, but the federal police and

the army were on their way. Thirty-six hours later, he lay dead, but he lay there smiling. I said to Olvido, *You know why?* She nodded. She knew. He had served his purpose. He had loved and provided for his wife. He had sent his son to America. I said to Olvido, *He wouldn't have believed me if I'd told him in America it doesn't make any difference whether you're innocent or guilty. When I asked you and the others not to go to Mexico and try to find my relatives, I was worried they would be ashamed. Now I realize I would have been.* Then she told me something surprising. I asked her why state court was any better. And she said, *Because, believe it or not, Texas has its own rule that says you can't execute someone who's innocent.*

I called her the afternoon of my heated exchange with Stream and Moss and said, I have a quick question. Does Texas still have the rule you can't execute someone innocent?

She said, Same rule. Why are you thinking about this now?

I said, I don't know. I haven't been able to sleep. Maybe I have PTSD. I'm trying to figure out why I'm alive.

She said, You're alive because you got lucky we found a federal judge with balls.

I said, And because I had a pretty awesome legal team.

I pictured her smiling. She said, Well, that too.

Our conversation put an end to my self-doubt, at least for the moment. I made a pitcher of fresh lemonade, poured a tall glass with crushed ice and muddled mint, and carried it down to the creek. A cloud of dragonflies hovered over the surface, and I watched a bass arc through the air and gobble down three. I knew I was right. Maybe that was enough.

I wondered whether I should let them go.

If the point of my scheme had really been deterrence, as I'd said to Stream, hadn't I already met that goal? And if I hadn't, would I ever? But if I did let them go, what would that mean for me?

Stream had been right when he called me a fuckup. I had fucked up. But not in the way he thought. I plotted the opening and the middle, and, if I say so myself, I did that pretty well. But I neglected to fully imagine the end. Their crime didn't warrant death, but I had no intention of going back to jail. My mistake had been to not recognize that those were the only two endgames, and neither endgame worked for me. Sure, if I did go back to prison for kidnapping state officials, I'd be a celebrity with the other inmates, but I didn't foresee the corrections staff making my life easy. I remembered their gratuitous cruelty and the pleasure they took the first time I was gassed. I recalled the taste of chemicals, the jagged edge of a broken tooth, tear-filled and sulfurous burning eyes. Moss and Stream had it easy by comparison. They drank Scotch and wine and from time to time enjoyed a home-cooked meal. They had books and TV. And most important of all, I had allowed them to keep their dignity. But when I envisioned my trial, I knew none of my kindnesses would matter.

I finished my lemonade and decided. If I had to choose between being either a hypocrite or a prisoner, I'd take the former every time.

The next morning I went down to check on the MRE supply and take out the garbage bag. Moss said, Today is my twenty-fifth wedding anniversary.

I held the garbage bag open so she could deposit her trash. I said, I was married only fourteen months.

She said, What would you have thought if she had just disappeared? What would she have thought if you had?

I said, Are you and John going to play good cop, bad cop with me from now on?

She glanced at him, then said, I'm wondering why you seem indifferent to how cruel you are being to my husband, who never did anything to harm you.

I said, I'm not indifferent, but I can't think of any way to punish you appropriately that won't also injure him, can you?

She said, Perhaps not, but I did not injure you intentionally.

I said, When you ruled against me, my lawyer said our best chance for victory was behind us, because unlike the federal courts, Texas has a rule saying you can't execute someone who's innocent.

She said, Mr. Zhettah, I am sorry for what happened to you. I wish I could take it back.

I said, People like you say everyone finds Jesus on death row. I noticed you haven't answered my question.

I held up the garbage bag outside Stream's cage and said, *Trash?* Without getting out of his chair he said, *You didn't ask a question.*

Hadn't I? I was trying to act nonchalant, except something Moss said had started the humming back up, but I wasn't sure what it was, or why.

We'd been seeing each other about three months when Tieresse said, *Why haven't you ever asked me about my marriage? Aren't you curious?* I said, *You've never asked me about girlfriends.* She said, *One day soon I might just do that, but it's a silly comparison. I'm assuming you did not take a vow to be together with one of your girlfriends 'til death do you part.* She smirked when she said the last part. I said, *Okay, then. Tell me about it.* She said, *If you insist, amor.* And she smirked again.

She'd been in Germany negotiating a deal to import frames and trusses manufactured from softwood lumber, like pine. He was a C+ student who would have been destined for middle management except his father left him a lumber company. He was recently divorced. He delegated just about all his duties to others so he could be out the door every day by five and on his barstool hitting on women by five fifteen. Tieresse said, *He was charming in a roguish kind of way, and I was vulnerable as a child. I'd had sex with three people in my entire life, two of whom were women.* She saw him when she traveled overseas, every three or four weeks, and when he traveled to the US or Canada, just as often. The second time they slept together, she got pregnant. She said, *I thought about getting an abortion and never even telling him. I don't know why I didn't.* When she broke the news, he opened a bottle of champagne and said he'd been intending to propose marriage anyway. She demurred, concerned about the logistics, and unsure about his motives. He said he would do whatever she required. She said to me, *His charm was blinding.*

Two months into their marriage, he hit her. She said, *I suppose if he had immediately fallen to his knees and wept, I would have accepted his apology. But he demanded I apologize to him.* I asked her for what. Tieresse said, *He told me my commitment to business over his welfare was insulting.* I reminded her about the man who had disappeared the day after he leered at my mother in the market. Tieresse said, *I remember that story well. I sometimes feel my own desire for vengeance is primitive. I admire your father. I detected the same loyalty in you the day we met.* I said, *I'm not as strong as he was.* Tieresse said, *You might surprise yourself, just as I did.* She left him two months before Reinhardt was born. She said, *Any questions?* I said, *Yes.*

Did your father know? She said, *Some marriages are loveless. The people who have them, people like my father, think nothing of it that others have them as well.*

That was my mistake. I'd just assumed Moss had been in a marriage of convenience, that she needed it for her career, and that her preacher husband needed it for his, and to tamp down the rumors he was a serial philanderer. When I saw them walk together into a restaurant, they never held hands or even touched. I never saw them do anything remotely romantic, and so I assumed, because I did not see it, it must not ever have happened. I made assumptions about her capacity for love based on her insensitive rulings. I made assumptions about his based on my stereotype of a megachurch preacher. Now I was wondering whether I had been wrong, and not just by a little bit. I'd assumed she would not worry that the story of her disappearance might wound him. Maybe she was playing me. Perhaps I'd been right all along and now she was just pretending. But what if she wasn't? She seemed genuinely in agony, and I felt a need to fix it.

I said to Moss, I really do feel bad about your husband. But some problems can't be mended. I'm sorry about that.

■ ■ ■

At a bar called the Cask in Lincoln, Nebraska, a young woman sat down next to me and asked whether I intended to buy her a drink. I'd noticed her earlier, sitting at a round table with six or seven other girls. I nodded toward the table and said, *You made a bet with your friends?* She said, *Nope. We're calling it an evening, even though it's early.* I said, *Tell you what, I'm flattered by the attention, and I will buy you a drink, but then I'm going to have to say good night, because I teach at St. Gregory,*

*and they'll kick me out if I buy you more than one, as much as
I'd like to.* She said, *No shit? You're really at St. Gregory.* I said,
Looks can be deceiving. She ordered a vodka collins and told
me she was finishing her master's degree in social work, special-
izing in helping victims of child trafficking. It reassured me to
know there were people like her in the world. I listened intently
and told her so. Then I paid the tab, kissed her on the cheek,
and said good night.

Not counting waitstaff, she was the first person who had
spoken to me at a restaurant or bar outside the diner since I
settled in Kansas. I wondered whether she was an investigator or
was recording our conversation. But that would have been impossible. Even I didn't know I'd be drinking there until I walked
in the door. I couldn't remember if I'd ever seen her before. Once
you begin to see the hand of God, you see it everywhere. It's also
known as paranoia.

When I got back to Kansas the next day, I took a legal pad
downstairs and handed it to Moss. I said, *I'm going to read
what you write, but if you would like to say something to your
husband to make him feel better, I will deliver it for you. I'll be
back for it in a few days.* When I closed the door, Moss sat
down in her chair, with the pad on her lap and pen in her hand.
She said something to Stream I couldn't hear. I also couldn't
make out his reply, but I could see he was agitated. He punched
holes in the air with his index finger and leaned forward from
the waist. I peered through the peephole for a few minutes more
until their conversation appeared to come to an end, then I
headed upstairs. Two floors up my left knee locked and I had a
coughing attack. I had to stop to catch my breath. That night my
throat felt raw and sore. Before I went to sleep, I put a lozenge

under my tongue and ordered a rowing machine online. A month later, I still hadn't taken it out of the box.

When I came for Moss's letter, Stream asked whether I could also deliver a message to his son. I told him I was already taking a big enough risk with Jane's husband.

He said, Every night for the past ten years I've dreamt of our reconciliation.

He told me his son blamed him for the bitter divorce that left his former wife working two jobs to pay the rent. They hadn't spoken since the day he moved out. The son was now a large-animal veterinarian in Kentucky, catering to wealthy horse owners who traveled around the country competing in dressage.

I said, I read somewhere about a Catholic who committed suicide. The priest assured the man's family he would still go to heaven because the victim might have changed his mind and prayed for absolution between the time he pulled the trigger and the moment the bullet entered his brain.

Stream said, I'm not following.

I said, The human capacity for self-delusion has no bounds. You've had a decade to fix things with your son.

Stream looked down at his bare feet and said, You're right about that.

I said, Write the letter. I'll see what I can do.

■ ■ ■

Mamá started reading me the classics before I could walk. The local one-room library did not have Dr. Seuss, but it had Hemingway, Yeats, and Jane Austen. She read me *Pride and*

Prejudice when I was four and *For Whom the Bell Tolls* when I was six. She read me the poem by Donne the year after that and *The Second Coming* every night before bed. Whenever I picture her, she is at the table reading, drugstore glasses perched on her nose, but the only book I ever saw her read cover to cover more than once was a slim volume of Talmudic sayings she said had been a gift from her grandfather and was inscribed by a famous man whose signature I could not comprehend. I found it in the kitchen when I returned to Kansas after prison. I could not remember how it got there.

I put the book and the letters from Stream and Moss into my flight bag and took off to the south. The tiny unattended airport in Livingston is directly across the road from death row. I crossed the two-lane highway and walked toward the prison's front door. I felt guards in the watchtower staring down at me over their rifle sights, but when I looked up, nobody was there.

Inside, I walked through a metal detector and took off my shoes. The guards who searched me and looked at the bottoms of my feet had no idea who I was. A female CO took my driver's license and gave me a plastic ID, which I hung around my neck. It said, *Visitor.* I walked through an electronic door, another door, a locking gate, two more electronic doors, and I was there, standing on what inmates call the free world side of the glass.

I was back at death row, visiting for the very first time.

On the other side, you hear guards chattering and the clinking of irons. Most days, you hear noise from the pods. It smells of urine and bleach. The phones are sticky and have flecks of mold on the mouthpieces. On this side, it's like a hospital waiting room: cold, sterile, and whisper-filled. Ms. Johnson was not on duty. The guard watching the visitors was new.

Sargent and I had been corresponding since my release. A few weeks earlier I told him I was finally ready to visit. He wrote back a letter with three words. *About damn time.* He signed it with a smiley face.

I heard him laughing when he was still a good distance away. When he squatted so the guards could remove his cuffs, I could read his lips. He was saying, *Goddamn, Inocente, you look great.* I did not recognize two of the guards on the transport team, but Lilac was there too. Her face lit up when she saw me, and she discreetly waved. Sargent stood and rubbed his wrists, then he leaned forward and kissed the glass.

He said, This might be the first time in my life I don't know what to say. You look great.

I said, You do too.

He said, Tell me something I don't already know, Inocente.

We caught up, like the old friends we were. He told me about how the guys I knew were doing. I asked him what he was reading. He told me he still had not heard back from his daughter Charice. He asked about Reinhardt and where I was living. I told him about my trips—about all of them except for the ones to Austin. At last I held up the book of rabbinic stories.

I said, Being that you read more than any guy I've ever known, I brought this for you. I already got permission to leave it.

I told Sargent the book was called *Pirkei Avot.* He said, *You gonna translate?* I told him it was a collection of ethical vignettes from the Talmud called *Ethics of the Fathers.* He said, *Shit, Inocente. I thought you was a, what's the word, a wayward Hebrew.* I said, *This was the only book I ever saw my mamá read more than once. I found it in my kitchen. I didn't know I still had it. It turns out there are little nuggets of wisdom lying around everywhere.* Sargent grinned. He recognized the bastardization. Years earlier, what he had actually said to me was *There be some smart motherfuckers in every church, you feel me? You just got to ignore the supernatural hocus-pocus and focus on the wise shit they say. Tell you the truth, 'cept for God and them miracles, ain't really nothin' wrong with religion.* Now, sitting across from him, I said, *A smart dude I know taught me that, once upon a time.* He said, *I don't think that's precisely how the smart dude phrased it.* He wiped his hand across his mouth and added, *I'm touched, Inocente. I mean it.*

I told him how Mamá used to read the epigrams out loud to Papá and me at dinner, translating to Spanish on the fly. My papá's favorite was where a rabbi named ben Zoma says a rich person is someone who is satisfied with what he has.

I said, He liked that because it explained how he could have nothing and also be so happy.

Sargent said, Only reason you can say something so dumb, Inocente, is on account a you ain't got no kids yourself.

I said, Could be. I'm leaving it here because you measure up better than me.

Before I got to the row, there were two guys named Lucas and Antonio who got exonerated within a few days of each other. I'd seen them on the news. I told Sargent about a chapter where the rabbis say a strong man is one who masters his emotions, and I asked him whether he knew either of the guys.

I said, You got any insight into how they kept from being angry?

He said, How you know they weren't? It ain't like you can see what's happening inside a brother's soul based on whether he's smiling at you. Just 'cause some shit the rabbis say is smart don't mean everything they say is. You akse me, anger is severely underrated. Be a better world if more people was to get pissed off now and then, give the masters some serious shit to worry about.

There'd also been two other guys I knew who got released. Both died in separate car crashes months after winning their freedom. I said to Sargent, What about Toney and Guerra? You think the way they went is a coincidence?

He said, Yeah. Matter a fact I do. Anybody who says anything different is a mail-order shrink. Brothers didn't crack up or kill their selves on account a they forgot how to boil rice. 'Til they got here, all their luck was bad. Why'd you expect that to change just 'cause they walked out instead a being carried?

I said, You're the one who told me some people plan for the future and others don't. Maybe those guys died because they suddenly had tasks they weren't capable of performing and there was nobody around to show them how. That's how I feel, anyway. My papá was always happy despite having nothing. I have more than I can possibly spend but can't get past the feeling something's missing.

He said, Yeah, motherfucker. Your old lady.

I said, That's not what it is. I spent weeks mourning her. Nothing's changed.

He said, Inocente, you was inside here longer than you been out. You got brothers who spend like one year in Eyewrack and they be fucked-up rest a their lives, you feel me? Talk to me in six months. I tole you it'd be hard for someone like you. I didn't say impossible.

We sat in silence for several minutes, until I said, *Okay, six months,* and then we were quiet a moment more. Finally I said, You remember the guy who picked up the SPU case?

Sargent said, Course I do. Brother named Nelson. What's he got to do with it?

I said, I'm writing a book about my time here, and I wanted to tell that story, except I couldn't remember the details.

I felt bad about lying, but I couldn't very well say, *Hey, you know those two judges who disappeared in a plane crash? Well, I'm holding them hostage.* Sargent reminded me about Nelson. He'd been on the row four years and had lost his appeal. His lawyers were just going through the motions, and Nelson was desperate, so he wrote directly to all three judges on the Supreme Criminal Court, insisting he was innocent. He said if they let him die they'd be murderers and have to answer to God. Moss felt threatened and contacted the Special Prosecution Unit, the office that investigates crimes committed by people behind bars.

I said, How is writing a letter a crime?

Sargent said, It ain't. What happened was they come by his cell to akse him a few questions, and they find he's got the judges' home addresses and the names a their kids, and it goes from there. Thing is, Nelson didn't have nothin' to do with it. Some Latvian chick, I think, was writin' him practically every day and sendin' porno pictures of herself with her own goddamn daughter, if you can believe that shit, least that's what McKenzie said. Way I hear it, she printed out a bunch a pages 'bout his case off a the internet, and that's where the information 'bout the judges come from. Brother Nelson couldn't barely even read. Wadn't how SPU saw things, though. They moved him to level, threatened his wife and kids, tole him they'd have his nuts in a vise he didn't say who was helpin' him.

I said, And?

He said, And nothin'. Brother got executed two months later.

I said, A guy I knew in county paid a CO to mail letters to people he wasn't allowed to contact.

Sargent said, Okay.

He didn't want to ask, I could see that, but he knew from the non sequiturs I was hiding something.

I said, It's nothing, man. Like I said, I'm just thinking about writing a book.

I got up to use the bathroom and wash my face. I hoped the recorders were on. I needed them for insurance. I wrote a note on a paper towel using a pencil I had hidden in my sock. When I got back to the visiting booth, I checked to see whether the guard was watching, then held it up to the glass. On it I had written, *Please do me a favor and read the next three sentences out loud.* The next three sentences said, *If it's cool with you, can you write my two pen pals in France and let them know what's going on with my case? I tried to write 'em myself but I think the mail room here is messing with me. If you don't want to do it, I understand.* Sargent did as I asked.

I said, Of course I'll do it.

He tilted his head and said, For real, Inocente, you cool?

I said, As ice, my friend.

We'd been talking for two hours. The guard in the visiting area caught my eye and tapped her watch. I stood up and touched my hand to the glass. I said, I swear, I'm good. I'll be back soon to tell you why, okay? Meantime, stay off of level.

He said, I cain't make no promises, and you better.

On the way out, I bought a bottle of water from a machine and flushed the towel down the commode. In the hallway, a trustee stepped to the side and stared at his shoes until I passed.

I retraced my steps to the entry. When I traded my visitor badge for my driver's license, there was a new guard in the booth. She recognized me and said, *Mercy me. Praise Jesus.* I said, *Actually, her name is Olvido.* I didn't wait for the CO to respond. I walked outside and crossed the highway, but instead of getting into the plane, I stood on the shoulder of Farm Road 350 and held out my thumb. A passing pickup with four Mexicans wearing overalls and smelling of hay stopped for me and gave me a ride to a cluster of fast-food restaurants down the street from city hall. I bought them a bag of burgers and fries, said *gracias,* and crossed the street. On a yellow pad, holding a felt-tipped pen with my left hand, I wrote, *Preacher, Whatever you might hear about your wife having an affair is not true. She has always been faithful to you.* I signed it, *Somebody who knows.* I folded the sheet in thirds and put it in the envelope Moss had addressed. In the other I placed a sheet on which I wrote, *Dear Lucian, Your father has always wanted to get straight with you. He loves and admires you, no matter what you might think.* I signed it as I had the first. I bought a book of stamps from a vending machine and added more postage than the letters required. I wet my finger with water to seal them and used a tissue to wipe away any fingerprints and, I hoped, to eliminate skin cells that might contain DNA. Using another tissue, I lifted each envelope by the corner and dropped them into a blue mailbox in the parking lot of the US Postal Service.

That evening, back at home, I lit a fire in the grill and tossed the letters Stream and Moss had written into the flames. Once the coals were gray, I cooked a half a chicken and a pot of beans and washed it all down with two bottles of Mexican beer. If you had asked me right then and there, I would have said I was a wealthy man in more ways than one. Later I would wonder why I was not at least a little bit angry.

■ ■ ■

There's a town I've forgotten the name of near Tulsa where Tieresse and I once spent a week in a lake house owned by a college roommate of hers who made a fortune in the oil business and died when the driver of a tractor-trailer fell asleep at ten A.M. and struck her SUV head-on speeding around the curve of a two-lane road. Tieresse's stated goal was to teach me to water-ski, but she gave up after half a day and said, *There's also a sailboat. Let's try to master that.* I planned to fly down and see if I could find the house, but I woke to a burning sensation below my belly button and a headache so bad my vision was blurred. So I swallowed four aspirin and fell back asleep. When I awoke again that afternoon I decided I'd just stay around the house. I gathered ripe tomatoes from the hothouse and several heads of lettuce and took a care package into town. I also bought ingredients for a cake.

As I was paying for the groceries, Margaret at the cash register asked me if I felt okay. I said I just had a bit of a fever. But the room was spinning and I had to bend over from the waist and put my hands on the conveyer belt carrying my purchases to the sacker to keep from falling down. At home, I got back in bed without bothering to put the things away.

By evening, though, I felt better, and after an early dinner, I baked. The next day I carried the cake downstairs.

I watched the digital clock as it counted down. When it hit 49896:00:00, I said, One year down, five and a half, more or less, to go. Look, I brought cake.

I said, I mailed y'all's letters.

I expected at least a touch of gratitude, but neither even looked at me. I said, *Happy anniversary, Jane,* but Moss said nothing back. I said, *You too, John,* and Stream said nothing back as well.

I cut the cake in thirds and put their two pieces on two paper plates. I stuck a plastic fork in each slice, like a birthday candle. I said, *Y'all enjoy, now,* and I slid each plate into their cells. I said, *The Bible says to feed your animals before you feed yourself.* I took a bite of cake.

I said, The cream cheese frosting doesn't have very much sugar; I don't like it too sweet. The black flecks are Madagascar vanilla, no expense spared.

Still neither spoke. I said, Some recipes call for nutmeg, but I leave it out. I'm not a fan.

I said, I'm thinking we'll have angel food next year, red velvet the year after that, followed by apple, then coconut for our fifth anniversary, and German chocolate, that's my favorite, for our sixth. But I'm open to suggestions.

More silence. I said, And we can have devil's food a few months later to commemorate your liberation. Funny, huh, devil's food?

Not even a smile. They were both in a bad mood.

I tasted the cake. They each put a piece on their forks at the same time. Moss said, *Thank you.* Stream said nothing. Even though it's been a year, I still can't figure out whether Stream's frequent hostility is calculated or sincere. He might be manic. His swings remind me of Taylor. I also can't figure out whether Moss has a twinge of genuine regret, or whether that's calculated too. Honestly, though, I couldn't care less. I've surprised myself, but it's true. I really could not care less.

Finally Moss said, Thank you for mailing our letters.

Stream nodded and took a bite.

I said, You're welcome.

On the flat-screen TV molly-bolted to the steel-fronted cinder-block wall, CNN was previewing its upcoming coverage of the tenth anniversary of Hurricane Katrina. I was still locked up when New Orleans got flooded, so I stood and watched video of a scene I'd never seen before. There were people on boats floating in the French Quarter, still photos of an abandoned amusement park, and what looked like a refugee camp inside the Superdome.

I said, Unbelievable.

The advertisement ended. I said, See you around, Your Honors.

Neither one of them laughed, but I did, just a little hint of a chuckle. *Your Honors.* I do still amuse myself.

By the time I got back upstairs, a thin sheen of sweat covered my forehead. I was breathing hard, and I was dizzy again. I hadn't seen a doctor in ten years. It was probably about time.

■ ■ ■

In college my freshman roommate was a black army brat born in Mississippi who went to high school in Connecticut. He told me in the South you know who the racists are. They're obvious. In the North, you have to learn to read the subtleties. I never had, or at least not very well, but still, something about Moss's manner made me suspicious. She went from glum to grateful way too fast, as if she was saying thank you to elicit a reply. But about what? Whether I had really mailed the letters? Might I have perhaps inadvertently transmitted a secret code? Had they tricked me into doing something I'd regret? I was conscious I had crossed the line into full-blown paranoia. But I also remembered Heller's line from *Catch-22*. Someone might really be out to get me.

I sat at my desk and did a search to learn whether the cable and satellite companies keep track of the shows we watch. I could not get a clear answer, so I worried what I was about to do might be incriminating, but Moss had gotten under my skin again, and I could not resist the temptation.

I cued up the three most recent Sunday-morning sermons Moss's husband had preached to his flock and watched them back-to-back. He was very handsome. He could have been a model. He began with a funny, self-deprecating story, then opened his bling-adorned King James and strutted around the stage. His conversational style was easy to listen to. In the first service, he told his congregants not to let labels imposed by others limit their ambition. *Define yourselves,* he said, *instead of letting others define you. God gave every one of you the power to do anything, so long as you put your trust and faith in Him.* In another, he prodded his flock to break out of their comfort zone. He said, *We are not serving God if we are always comfortable. Noah took a risk, built a boat, and did not even know how to swim. Abraham took a risk, leaving his father and comfortable life behind. Joseph lived in the house of Pharaoh. That's what Jesus asks of you. Do not be satisfied merely by dropping a dollar into a mendicant's cup. Engage. Engage with the homeless mother and the wandering veteran. Engage with the stranger. God told the Israelites they too were strangers in a foreign land. You might think you have nothing to say to the down on their luck, nothing in common with the hungry or the poor. But you do. Say what it is,* and the congregation thundered, *We are all God's children.* In the last sermon I watched he told the story about Moses rescuing the lamb, and how we are the lamb and Israel is Moses. All in all his preaching owed far more to Norman Vincent Peale than it did to Jesus or the Old Testament, but I was not interested in what he was saying. I was interested in how he was saying it. And if this was a guy hiding pain or grief, he was the Laurence Olivier of the church.

I said to Moss, I watched your husband preach.

She said, What on earth for?

I said, You don't sound very proud of him.

She said, I fell in love with him watching him preach.

Stream said, What Sarah means is you do not act like a Christian.

I ignored him and said to Moss, I saw his most recent sermons. He doesn't seem especially sad or distraught.

She said, And you, Mr. Zhettah, do not seem especially innocent.

■ ■ ■

A few months into our romance, I was fretting over a mediocre review La Ventana received from a national magazine. Tieresse sat next to me and said, *What is there in the article you can learn from?* I'd said, *Nothing.* She said, *Really? Nothing?* I said, *That's why it's so infuriating. The guy doesn't like the paint shade or the flatware or the fact I'm not selling French wine. His only complaints about the food were he wished the garlic on the potatoes had been sliced instead of crushed and the roasted lemon had been removed from the fish before service.*

And for that he takes away a star? Tieresse took the magazine from me and said, *I'm going to throw this away. You get to decide who lives inside your head, amor. Don't cede the valuable real estate to anyone who does not have something useful to offer.* I said, *So this strategy explains why you are always happy.* She said, *It just seems that way to you. See if you can figure out why.*

I needed to evict Moss from my brain, and I knew the perfect place to do it. The Blue Spring Trail in the Mark Twain National Forest was one of Tieresse's and my favorite hikes. It was lush and quiet, and it paralleled a perennial creek. I put my tent and camping gear in the truck and headed off for south-central Missouri. On the way there, I made a fateful choice.

Every two years, to keep my pilot's license legal, I was required to have my health checked by a certified aviation medical examiner. These physical exams are not what you would get from your family physician. They are perfunctory checkups taking less than fifteen minutes. They check your eyesight and your weight and listen to your heart. There happened to be an AME on the way to Missouri, and I decided to stop. An elderly doctor examined my eyes and took my blood pressure. He wrote down my height and calculated my BMI and asked me questions about what medicines I take. He asked how much alcohol and caffeine I drink and how many hours I sleep. He sat at a computer and entered the information on the FAA website. Then he put the stethoscope in his ears and listened to my heart and lungs. He said, *When was the last time you had a complete physical?* I told him I didn't remember. He said, *I think you need to get one.* I asked him what was the problem. He said, *Probably nothing, but I am hearing some wheezes. You might have some fluid buildup. Have you been coughing lately or had difficulty breathing?*

The truthful answer was yes, but I might have been in a bit of denial. When Reinhardt had come to visit, he asked about my cough. I shrugged it off. I was getting more easily winded, but I was no longer a young man. If I had known this doctor better, I might have recognized the alarm in his voice, but his question gave me hope. If I had pneumonia or an infection of some sort, bed rest and medicine would restore me in no time.

I said, *Why can't you just order the tests here?* He said, *Son, I'm mostly retired. I just keep my license as an AME to keep guys like you in the air. You need to see a certified internist. It's very important.* So I did. I spent three days in the woods, feeling mostly pretty good, and on the way back home, I stopped at a public health clinic in Wolf River. I explained I had been coughing and was short of breath. A nurse took a complete medical history, but given that I had not had a checkup in more than a decade, there was not a baseline of comparison. He took my blood pressure and gave me an EKG. The results were normal. When the doctor came in, I told her I sleep well, I've never smoked, I drink in moderation, I avoid fast food, and I still wore the same size jeans and T-shirts I had since college. She asked about exercise. I told her I used to take long walks but lately they'd grown shorter.

I did not tell her that climbing the stairs after visiting my prisoners left me breathing hard. I knew the explanation for my shortness of breath, and the explanation wasn't medical in nature. The stress of being a jailer was something I hadn't anticipated, and my quick visit with Irene Johnson had not revealed any useful coping mechanisms. I remembered how, on the first day I locked up Judge Moss, I told her I was indifferent. Looking back, I might not have known myself quite so well as I thought I did.

I stripped down to my boxer shorts and the doctor examined me. She checked my patellar reflexes and the bottoms of my feet. She had me bend over and touch my toes. She peered in my ears and nose and throat. She was making small talk, asking me about my life, and I told her I was retired. Then I discovered she wasn't a poker player, or a good one anyway. When she asked me to take deep breaths with the stethoscope pressed against the back of my rib cage, I felt the fingers on her free hand stiffen.

She said it might be an infection. I could have pneumonia or bronchitis, or perhaps a small obstruction. There were many possibilities, so the first thing I needed was blood work and a chest X-ray. She gave me the name of a doctor at the university clinic in Kansas City.

She said, If I were in your position, I wouldn't wait.

After the X-ray, they sent me for a CT scan and had me spit into a cup when I hacked up phlegm. Two days later they gave me a short-acting anesthesia and performed a bronchoscopy: The doctor slid a lighted tube down my throat and into my lungs. While I was still under, she used the images from the CT scan to guide her as she pushed a needle through my chest wall and gathered cells from my lungs. Three days later I sat in an overstuffed leather chair in her office while she told me I had stage IV non–small cell lung cancer.

I said, I've never smoked a day in my life.

She said, I know. I'm sorry.

She told me they could drain the fluid around my lungs and that would improve my breathing a bit. Chemotherapy might extend my life, but there was no known cure.

I said again, But I am not a smoker.

She said, We've discovered that around twenty percent of lung cancer patients never smoked.

I asked questions. I asked how often I would need chemo and about side effects and how much longer it would give me. She said they'd use a two-drug cocktail, and I might lose my hair and notice food tastes different. In the short term, I might be even more tired than normal. I'd receive four sessions of treatment that would last two days each, with a week of recovery in between. I noticed she did not say anything about whether it would help.

I said, And if I go that route, what are the odds?

She said, The five-year survival rate for people with your kind of cancer is less than one percent. But everybody is unique. Many people live far more than five years.

When I said, *I don't guess I need a doctorate in math to understand what you're telling me,* she looked down at her hands folded in her lap and whispered, *No, I don't suppose you do.*

I stood up and shook her hand. She asked whether I had someone who could take me home.

I thought to myself, Unlike most cancer patients, this is not the worst thing that has happened to me.

I said to the doctor, Thank you for your kindness, but I can drive myself home. I will let you know what I decide.

■ ■ ■

The piece of pop psychology about how most criminals have a secret desire to get caught is a bunch of crap. Criminals get caught because they make stupid mistakes. I got away with my first, but I wasn't so sure I'd be as lucky the second time around.

The letters had been a huge blunder born of hubris and unde-served compassion—or maybe unconscious guilt. Either way, if they caught me after all this time, I would have only myself to blame.

Shortly after I was exonerated, Olvido called and told me Detective Pisarro wanted to apologize. She asked whether I was willing to talk to him. I said, *Go ahead and give me his number,* and I called him that night. He said he knew it probably wouldn't matter, but he still wanted me to know how sorry he was. I said, *Actually, it does matter. In my experience, most people in your profession seem to think if they do not admit the existence of a mistake, the mistake will not exist, law enforcement's answer to Heisenberg.* There was an uncomfortable silence for a moment, then he said, *I'm not sure I know what you mean, but I'm not going to make any excuses for my own failure. I should have figured this out. I didn't know what Cole was doing, but in hindsight, I blame myself for missing the clues.* I said, *I appre-ciate your willingness to reach out to me, Detective. I do not blame you at all.* He said, *I'm grateful, sir.* I expected I'd never talk to him again.

But ten days after I mailed letters to Moss's husband and Stream's son, local and national news outlets reported the as-tonishing development. I carried a cup of coffee downstairs one morning when the news was on CNN. Moss said, *I don't un-derstand. They're saying the letter my husband received was anonymous.* I said, *Are you still surprised the media gets prac-tically everything wrong?* I felt a stab of guilt for misleading her. Stream didn't believe me. He said, *Every judge learns after a week on the bench a universal truth. I told you before, fuckups fuck up. It's only a matter of time.* I said, *How long do you guess you'd live if I turned off the food and water supply?*

He said, If some lowlife murdered my loved one the way your wife was killed, I'd peel off the guy's skin a layer at a time. You seem more interested in skipping over the puddles.

Give the guy credit. He did know how to push my buttons. I left without answering and headed to Mesa Verde National Park in southwest Colorado. I spent two days exploring cliff dwellings, sleeping under the stars, and wondering whether I was mad at the wrong people. I wondered what Sargent would say. I worried I was betraying Tieresse yet again.

Late the following Sunday afternoon, as I was lining up to land back at home, I saw a black sedan parked next to my house and a man wearing a sport coat sitting on the porch. Who was there? In this part of the country, people don't just drop by. I came in too fast and too high and had to abort the landing. Circling around for my second attempt, I thought I saw backup units on the way. Backup units for what? My brain was playing tricks on me. I told myself to stay calm. I read the items on the checklist out loud. I kept my eyes glued to the runway and my instruments, and by the time I touched down, I had assured myself nobody else was there.

But in fact there was. Detective Pisarro met me at the hangar and asked if I could use a hand. He had aged, but I recognized him instantly. He made a note on a pad, the plane's N-number I think, then slipped it into his breast pocket. Without my asking, he helped push the plane inside. He didn't pay any notice to the rubber pad covering the sealed passageway leading below. He said, They told me in town you usually come home Sunday afternoons. Your face is red. Do you feel okay?

I said, I'm surprised to see you, Detective.

He said, Two years ago I retired from HPD and took a job as an investigator with the SPU. Lots of travel, more than I care for, but pay is good, and I've got two kids in college. Can you believe that?

I was making notes in the plane's logbook and shutting everything down while he was talking. I said, This is all very interesting, Detective, but you are telling me this why?

He said, You know what the SPU is?

I said, Of course I do. I was an inmate, as you may recall.

He said, Right. Well, I guess you heard the news about the letters sent to the husband and son of the missing judges.

Pisarro was waiting for a response. I was not going to help him. I didn't fill the silence.

He said, My captain got the idea a guard at Polunsky mailed the letters. The reason is that both letters had a Livingston postage stamp from the same day.

I hung my headset over the yoke and closed the plane's door. I pointed at the hangar door and said, You want to help me with this?

We walked back toward the house. I said, I have to go into town for some supplies, but can I offer you something to drink before I head out?

He came inside. We sat at the kitchen table with two bottles of beer. He said, Did you know they have video cameras at that post office?

I thought he might have been bluffing, but I quickly reconsidered. He was here after all. If he was here, he had to have a reason. My going to see Sargent couldn't have been enough. He must have been telling the truth.

I said, No I didn't. Is there a reason I should care?

He said, A few days ago, I was looking to see if I could find video of a CO mailing a letter from downtown, and imagine how surprised I was when I saw you.

I said, I went to visit a friend of mine. I'm guessing you know that already. He asked me to send a couple of letters to his pen pals in Europe. Is that against the law?

He said, Were you worried they might have germs?

I didn't answer.

He said, You probably know the prison records conversations death row inmates have with their visitors.

I thought to myself, *Thank God*. And I said to Pisarro, The whole time I was there, the only visitors I had were my lawyers. You're telling me the prison is listening in to those meetings?

He said, No, not legal visits. You mind if I have a look around?

I said, I don't mind at all. Help yourself.

He said, Anybody staying in the guesthouse?

I said, Not right now. But the door should be unlocked. If it's not, the key is in the planter.

He said, Interesting that you're a pilot. Been flying long?

I said, Since childhood. Want to go up sometime?

He said, Seems like you've been traveling a fair amount.

I said, I'm trying. It's a big country. Lots to see.

He put down his beer on the counter. I sat at the kitchen table and pretended to read through my e-mail. I watched Pisarro go into the guesthouse, the greenhouse, and the hangar. He walked around back, and I lost sight of where he was going. Fifteen minutes later, he came back inside. He said, Mr. Zhettah, do you know anything about the disappearance of Judge Stream and Judge Moss?

I said, Detective, I don't expect you to understand, but I could not possibly be less interested in the goings-on of the Texas criminal justice system.

He said, I understand. I'm sorry to bother you, sir. Maybe I'll see you again. You have yourself a good day.

I stood to walk him to the door. He placed his card on the table and shook my hand. He said, My cell number is on the back in case you want to reach me.

I said, Good luck at the new job.

He got in his car and drove away. I heard gravel crunch beneath the tires. I was breathing slowly through my nose. My heart rate was sixty-two. I poured a glass of ice water, sat down at the table, and drained it in a swallow. I replayed our conversation in my mind half a dozen times. I had answers for everything. It did not matter what he suspected or knew. He couldn't prove a thing. I felt bulletproof.

I made a list and drove into town. At the grocery store I bought a grass-fed rib eye I intended to stuff with blue cheese and grill over oak, a russet potato to roast, and spinach I'd braise in butter and cream. The day I learned of my cancer was the day I quit worrying about my diet. While the fire burned down I mixed a pitcher of martinis and had my first sitting on the deck. I wondered what Stream and Moss had been doing while Pisarro and I were standing on top of them talking. In the morning, I intended to ask.

■ ■ ■

People take risks because they do not see them as risks. Consider my father, for instance. He put his life in danger by speaking frankly to homicidal drug dealers who had as much regard for other human beings as they did for roaches or ants. He confronted armed men twice his size if they insulted or disrespected someone he loved. He flew in canyons where the distance between sheer shale walls and the tips of his wings could be measured in inches. Some people won't even wade into the ocean if they don't know how to swim. Others will strap on a life vest and get on a raft in class VI whitewater. It's not that people we call risk takers weigh the danger-reward balance differently from people we think of as prudent; it's that they are oblivious to the danger. When I woke up the morning after Detective Pisarro had stopped by to visit, I finally knew how they felt. I heard my father whisper, *Cuidado, hijo,* and I said out loud, *It's okay, Papá. They cannot hurt me.*

Moss said nothing when I told my prisoners about Pisarro's visit, but Stream did. He said, If you made the mistake of getting yourself caught on video, you made others. One thing I've learned over the years is that bad guys don't make just one mistake. That means the detective will be back. The walls are closing in on you, Zhettah.

I said, I bet you were one of those Little League baseball coaches who told your players they still had a chance when they were behind by fifteen runs with two outs in the bottom of the ninth inning and two strikes on the hitter.

He said, You bet I was. Ain't over 'til it's over.

I said, It's a paradox, John, but sometimes it is.

Moss said, Can you explain to me about the letter?

I said, I don't know. Maybe the police were putting out bad information so someone with knowledge would come forward and correct them. Unfortunately, I might call too much attention to myself if I tried to learn the answer, so I am afraid we are going to have to live with the uncertainty. I learned a bit about Buddhism during my years of incarceration, thanks to a polymath who lived across the way.

Stream said, A polymath on death row, huh?

I said, One night Tieresse and I were watching a documentary about the Boston Strangler. She could not get enough of those true-crime shows, but they tended to make me morose. I said to her, *Don't these programs make you think our species is irredeemable?* You know what she said? She said, *Amor, the price we pay for Bach and Shakespeare is Manson and Dahmer.*

Stream said, I'd happily trade Bach to get rid of Dahmer.

I said, That is a terribly bad trade, John, but you're missing the point. Picasso was a misogynist, Eliot and Wagner were anti-Semites. Genius and evil can coexist. That's the point. People are not either good or bad. They contain both good and bad. So, to answer your question, yes, a polymath on death row, a man who is superior to you in every possible way.

He said, Do you even know the details of what your friend did? I bet you don't, because then you would have to justify calling him a friend. Say what you want about me, but I did not commit murder.

I said, You did come close, though.

Stream's ears grew red. He said, It took me a while, but I finally understand why the jury convicted you. They looked at your face expecting fury. Instead they saw a flat line. Maybe you can explain why you hate Judge Moss and me more than the man who murdered your wife.

I said, I don't hate either one of you, John.

Stream said, As usual, your narcissism blinds you to the central point.

I said, Which is what, exactly?

He said, People who do not hate the murderers who slaughter their loved ones are not advanced or superior; they're enablers of evil.

Moss was silently biting her lip. Stream was staring at me,

waiting for my response, looking almost feral. If the night I heard cries coming from Demerest's cell as he was being raped was the first time I felt capable of murder, standing four feet from Stream right then was the second.

I left without saying a word.

That evening, swinging in the chair by the creek, I wondered whether the only way to evict them from my brain was to stop going downstairs.

■ ■ ■

Three months passed. If Pisarro was still investigating me, it was without my knowledge. The reporters appeared to have moved on. Moss was devouring three or four novels a week. Stream had been requesting biographies of Civil War generals and a multivolume history of the First World War. I still went to town most days but hadn't taken a trip away since Colorado. Some days I spent fourteen hours in bed.

My cough grew worse. I hacked up blood-laced mucus and occasionally teaspoons of frothy blood. Pain spread from my chest to my shoulders, and then to my back, and to ease the pressure, I took to sleeping in a chair. I had pain in my throat and upper chest when I swallowed, and pain in my belly after I ate. I met with the doctor to tell her I had decided to do nothing further.

She did some tests and told me the cancer had spread to my esophagus. I did not yet have symptoms it had invaded my brain, but she said that could happen, and I could have seizures or lose my sight. She gave me the number of a hospice center and a prescription for a painkiller. I said, *Don't I need to be careful with this stuff? I've heard it's highly addictive.* When she stared back at me, I said, *I'm kidding, Doctor. I appreciate everything you have done for me.*

I called Olvido and asked her to get the others and put me on speaker, and I told them the news. Laura gasped, Luther was silent, and Olvido asked what they could do. I told her beginning tomorrow, I would check in every day by phone, e-mail, or text, and if I missed a day, they should read the letter I left with her. She said they would. I said, *Y'all saved my life. Thank you.* When I hung up, it sounded like all three of them were crying.

I wrote Sargent a letter. It read, *I'm not going to lie. I did it for myself. But not just for myself. Please tell the guys I did it for them too. You're about as good of a friend as a man can have. Thank you for being mine. More than anything, I hope you and your daughter connect. I suppose the name you and Molina called me is no longer deserved, but still . . .* I signed it, *Your friend forever, Inocente.*

I called Reinhardt and filled him in. He said he was going to fly out right away. I said, *That's silly,* but the following evening, I was sitting in the glider on my deck, drowsy from two shots of whiskey and two of the pills, and his rental car came gliding up the driveway. I stood to greet him, but my head spun, and right away I sat back down. He'd brought a pizza and a six-pack of beer. After a single bite I told him the rest was his, and he looked at me with alarm. I tried to look nonchalant. I drank a swallow of beer and I said, *I have to tell you something, Reinhardt. I've done something that is going to be discovered soon, and you are going to think less of me when you learn what it is. I want to apologize if it causes you embarrassment.* He said, *Rafa, what are you talking about?* I said, *It's better if I don't say.* He said, *There is no way I will think less of you, and it might be better if you do.* I sipped the beer and leaned back in my chair. I said, *I loved looking at the stars with your mother.* He looked up at the sky. I said, *You know the story of those judges who disappeared in a plane crash?* His eyes grew very wide. He said, *You killed them?* My laugh turned into a cough, and when it stopped I said, *No, I did not kill them. They're alive.* He looked up again. He said, *If it was me, I might have killed them.* I said, *That might have been smarter. I'm like one of those mothers who's promised she'll finally have closure when they execute the murderer of her son. Then the execution happens, and she wakes up the next day, as diminished as she was the day before.* He said, *Remember when I told you about the support group I went to after Mother died? The one word we were never allowed to use was* closure. I laughed again. I said, *I sure wish you'd have told me that sooner.*

He asked, *Where are they?* I said, *I'm not going to tell you that. But they are safe, and it won't be long until they're found.* I told him all the details, except where I was holding them. He said, *I had a feeling something was up when you were so curious about LAN hacking.* I said, *I could tell you were suspicious and just being too polite to prod.* He said, *It's pretty damn impressive, Rafa. I remember when Mother told me about the time she took you parachuting. It's as if she had a finger in this.* I said, *I hadn't thought of that.* He said, *You're promising me they're okay.* I said, *Safe and sound. I promise.* He said, *I'm not going to worry about it, then. Let's play.* He removed a portable chess set from his backpack. I remember opening with e4 and he answered with the Sicilian Defense. I played knight to e3, and he said, *I've heard of that but never seen it played.* I don't remember anything else. I woke in the morning in my bed to the smell of coffee. Reinhardt came in and said, *I love you, Rafa,* and I said, *I love you too.* The following afternoon, he flew back home.

Stream was reading the third volume in the World War I trilogy I had bought him. Moss was reading the previous year's winner of the Booker Prize. I said, *I have good news and bad news. Which do you want first?* Neither answered. I said, *On second thought, it might all be bad news. Or actually, it might all be good. Shit, I might have a brain tumor, but it really is very confusing.* They were still not saying anything. I said, *Well?*

I said, Fuck it. I have cancer. I doubt I have very long.

Moss said, Oh my God.

Stream said, What kind of cancer?

I said, I have a confession. I did not deliver the letters you wrote to your son and husband.

Stream said, I didn't think so.

I said, But I did write your son and told him you love and respect him.

Stream looked at the floor. He appeared almost ashamed.

I said to Moss, And I wrote your husband and assured him you were not having an affair.

She said, Thank you for that.

A spasm of coughs shook me, and I sat down heavily.

Stream said, How long do we have until our food supply runs out?

I said, Half the guys who got executed when I was on the row had appeals pending the day of their executions. They got moved over to the holding cell, a few feet from the execution chamber, and paced back and forth for five or six hours, wondering. Almost all of them prayed. A couple like me got lucky.

Most got a phone call from the lawyer saying they lost. A few had a lawyer who didn't even bother calling, so they found out when the transport team came to take them to the gurney.

Stream said, If you've expected me to gain some sympathy for your murderer friends during my time here, you've miscalculated.

I said, Have you had enough time down here yet to come up with an explanation for why less than one percent of the people who commit murder in Texas even face the death penalty?

Moss said, There isn't a good explanation for that.

Stream turned and looked at her. She did not meet his gaze.

I said, Or why we kill poor guys who never had a chance but give the rich or the privileged slaps on the wrist?

This time Moss said nothing. She stared at the ground.

I said, If Detective Cole had died one month later than he did, I would have been executed and the three of us would have never met. Einstein might have been right that God doesn't play dice with the universe, but he sure likes to shoot craps with individual human lives.

Stream turned back to me and said, Are you going to answer my question about meals?

I said, I did answer it.

■ ■ ■

That evening I made roast beef sandwiches and a fresh tomato salad and carried the food downstairs. I said, I'm trying to get rid of my perishables.

Stream said, The least you can do is tell us whether we should conserve our food. Even in prison you know you are not going to starve.

I said, The second guy I knew who got executed was a black guy named Michaels.

I took several deep breaths. Moss said, Mr. Zhettah?

I said, You ever go fly fishing where it's catch and release? You might catch the same trout five times. How dumb is a fish that keeps getting caught?

Stream said, I think you should call a doctor.

I said, The day they took Michaels to the Walls, he stopped by my cell. Know what he said? He said, *See you tomorrow.* I thought he was being spiritual, so I said, Yes, friend, I will see you down the road. He said, *Naw, man, I mean back here. I'll see you tonight back here on the row. I got something planned for these guys. Supernatural intervention. Be sure to listen to the news, you dig?*

Stream said, Half the guys about to get the juice act like they're too crazy to be executed. You notice that?

I got to my feet and vomited into the plastic garbage container. My stomach was empty. I threw up gastric acid and blood.

I said to Stream, The problem with you is not your ignorance. It's that an ignorant person can become a judge and hold another man's life in his hands. That's one fucked-up system.

I closed the vault door while he was still answering. It took me fifteen minutes to climb the six flights of stairs. When I got to the house, I lay down for a quick nap and fell asleep until the following day.

■ ■ ■

I spent virtually all of the next two weeks either in bed, in the glider on the porch, or on the tree swing by the creek. I ate very little. I had pain pills, but the pain was tolerable, and I rarely used them. I checked in with Olvido every day and talked to Reinhardt every night. I stopped checking my e-mail or listening to the news. I felt like I might be a dog, looking for the right place to die.

At the diner the people who knew me looked alarmed. I told them I was ill but managing. Lorena, who brought me coffee most days, said she and the others could do my shopping and bring things to the house until I recovered. I worried that anyone who came to see me would be a suspect once I died. I said, I appreciate that, but I have what I need.

According to the experts, the Stockholm syndrome develops gradually. Over time, a victim of domestic violence, or a prisoner of war, or a common hostage, develops a bond with the captor. Psychologists do not fully understand the phenomenon, only that it happens. In my years in prison, I had not experienced it, but I now wondered whether it could come about quite suddenly and in reverse.

I hadn't been able to get Stream's anxiety about starvation out of my mind.

At the grocery store I bought a roasted chicken and prepared vegetables and potatoes. The smell of garlic and rosemary filled the truck on my drive home, and twice I pulled over because I thought I might retch, but I carried it downstairs without incident. I placed it on the floor beside their cell.

I asked Stream and Moss to tell me about what they were reading. Stream spoke first. He said, Why are you all of a sudden interested?

I said, I've been interested from day one. All that's new is I'm asking, probably because we do not have much more time.

I thought I detected a flash of sympathy. He said, *Okay,*

and he told me a story about an Australian general named John Monash who was involved at Gallipoli and was later an architect of the Battle of Amiens, which led to the end of the war. When he finished I said I'd like to know more about the guy, and he slid the book he was reading under the bars. I said, *Thanks,* and I looked at Moss.

She said, In my case, it's a funny thing. I have always loved reading fiction, but I never wanted to be a novelist. I wanted to be a critic. In college I wrote a monthly book review for the paper. If I'd been good enough at criticism, I don't believe we would know one another today, Mr. Zhettah.

I said, In that case, I wish you had been more talented.

I meant for it to sound lighthearted, but it might have come out mean. So I said, *That was a joke,* and I told them a story about Tieresse. She had built several subdivisions in Davenport, Iowa, and was worried the middle-class homes were going to squeeze out the homeless and the poor. So she had this idea of also building affordable housing, with small single-family homes surrounding a common quadrangle with a playground and a community garden. Working mothers could help one another co-parent. She bought twenty acres north of the university, and in addition to the small houses, she also built a food cooperative and a job-training center on the same piece of land. The project succeeded beyond her wildest dreams. The mothers got jobs, if they did not already have them, and one hundred percent of the kids who grew up there went to college. St. Ambrose University contacted her because they wanted to bestow an honorary degree. The only reason I knew about any of this was I read the letter from the provost Tieresse left lying on the kitchen counter. When I congratulated her, she said, *I declined.* I asked her why.

Tieresse had said, *It is really quite ironic. I think the university is truly committed to liberalism and does valuable work in the community, but I just can't get over the namesake. Ambrose was a raging anti-Semite. A mob near the town where he lived destroyed a Jewish synagogue, and the emperor Theodosius was going to punish the criminals and compensate the victims, but Ambrose talked him out of it. He basically said the Jews rejected Jesus, so they deserved whatever happened to them.* I asked her how she knew all this. She said, *I studied early Christianity in college. That's why I'm an atheist. Anyway, maybe it's silly. I just don't want my name on a diploma next to his.*

Moss said, She was quite a person.

I said, That she was.

Stream said, Ambrose ranks with Augustine as one of the greatest theologians of his era. You think it's fair to measure people from the fourth century using modern moral standards?

I said, At long last, John, we've discovered something we have in common. We're both moral relativists.

I said, Thanks again for the book. I'll let you all divide that food.

I went upstairs to take a nap.

Maybe telling the story about the honorary degree is the reason she finally came to visit in my dream. We were at the one and only political fund-raising event she had taken me to. Young women and men wearing white gloves circulated through the crowd with trays of caviar and bottles of champagne. By the standards of the superrich, it was not especially ostentatious, but I think Tieresse saw me doing the math in my head. She said to me, *Half the people who grow up with great privilege come to embrace many values of socialism. The other half become monarchists.* I asked her what explains who chooses what. She said, *Some people fear the other, some don't. It all depends on how they're raised.* I said, *Your upbringing doesn't seem responsible for how you turned out.* She said, *Thank you for noticing, amor. But parents are only one variable in the equation.* A few moments later, we left. She never told me what the other variables are.

The next morning, when I went downstairs, I realized I had left the vault door open. I said, I didn't hear either of you shouting for help.

Moss said, What would have been the point?

I shrugged and said to Stream, What did your father do for a living?

Stream said, He taught high school history. Why?

I said, I had a dream last night about my wife. Anyway, I have to make a quick trip away. I should see you back here in a couple of days.

Moss said, Are you supposed to be traveling?

I said, Probably not.

■ ■ ■

As weak as I was, it was a foolish and dangerous thing to do, but despite having learned that closure is a malignant illusion, the drive to pursue it is nevertheless a blinding and powerful force. I filled a thermos with soup and another with coffee and put them in my flight bag, and I flew to Houston for what I was sure would be the final time.

A hedge fund manager with a gorgeous wife and fraternal twins was living in our old house. I knocked on the door. A housekeeper wearing a gray uniform swung it open and said,

How may I help you? I apologized for stopping by unannounced, but explained I had no way to call. I told her who I was, that I lived here before, and asked if I might have a look around. She asked me to wait a moment and disappeared upstairs. On the wall in the entryway hung an enormous Matisse. Tieresse would have loved it. A moment later, a woman wearing a tennis dress came down, trailed by a boy trying without success to carry his sister on his back. She saw me examining the painting and said, *My husband thinks all great art should be hung in public museums so everyone can see it, but I love that piece so much he made an exception.* I said, *My wife would have agreed with both of you.* The woman introduced herself and greeted me warmly. She asked if I cared for anything to drink, and when I said no thank you, she took me on a tour.

The parlor where Tieresse had her desk, where she had been killed, held six theater-style seats, a large TV, and a turntable. I said, *You listen to vinyl?* Four electric guitars and one acoustic stood along the wall. She said, *My husband is a frustrated rock musician. He swears it sounds better. To me, it just sounds louder.* I said, *You know who I am, right?* She said, *I do.* She guided me by my elbow into the bedroom, which was unchanged from how we had arranged it, then downstairs, through the kitchen, and into the backyard. She said, *The twins would swim all day every day, if we let them.* They had hung at least half a dozen bird feeders from thick branches of live oaks that had grown enormous in the years since I had seen them. I said, *Whatever you are feeding the trees agrees with them.* She said, *The kids have that one singled out for a tree house,* and she pointed at a gnarly trunk where two squirrels were chasing each other in a widening spiral. I said, *Thank you*

*for your kindness, ma'am. I would have called first if I had
known how to reach you.* She said, *The pleasure is mine. I wish
my husband were home. We both adore your former house.
Please stop by anytime you like.*

From there I went to La Ventana. It was now a renowned
sushi restaurant with every table reserved three months in advance. When I stepped inside, the hostess told me all the seats
at the bar were taken at the moment, but if I'd care to wait one
patron had asked for his check. Before I could answer, the chef
recognized me and came over to say hello. He invited me to sit
and I felt guilty telling him I was afraid I did not have time, but
would definitely be back soon. He bowed, and when he stood,
I offered him my hand.

Back at the airport I visually checked the fuel tanks and
was suddenly too tired to fly back home. I lay down in the
lounge for a short nap. When I woke it was past midnight,
and there was no one there but a security guard who looked
to be at least seventy-five. I thanked him for letting me sleep,
then checked the weather and took off into a cloudless, moonless
night.

■ ■ ■

Tieresse and I didn't have a honeymoon. We intended to. We
were going to go to North Dakota. It was the only state in the
country she'd never visited. She said, *I feel like we should go
somewhere together where neither of us has ever been.* Any-
place would have been fine with me. But she tore her ACL
playing tennis the day before we were supposed to leave, and
we had to postpone. Our backup plan was to go on our first
anniversary, but the date came and she was overseas, closing

her German subsidiaries. When she finally got back from Europe she said, *Amor, I don't care if the entire planet is on fire next year, we are going to Dakota for our second anniversary.* That was the first anniversary we never had.

I looked through the peephole. Moss and Stream were sitting in their cells, talking. I opened the door and said, I'm not sure how much longer I have. I gave my lawyer a letter confessing to kidnapping you, and detailing how I did it and where you are. If she doesn't hear from me for more than twenty-four hours, she will remove the letter from her safe and read it.

Stream said, You're sure about that?

I looked at my phone. I said, I'll be right back.

I climbed the stairs, pausing on every floor to see if I had a signal. Not until I got completely aboveground was there service. I sent a text to Detective Pisarro. It read, *On one out of two occasions, Detective, you showed impressive instincts,* and it included GPS coordinates for the silo's trapdoor. I left the phone on the ground and went back down.

Moss said, Is everything all right?

I said, Redundancy.

I closed my eyes, I am not sure for how long, and when I opened them I said, You ever have an Etch A Sketch? One of those kids' games where you use two knobs to draw a picture and then shake the machine to erase it and start over again?

Moss said, I loved my Etch A Sketch.

I said, From the time I was a little kid, I could press my eyes closed really hard, and it was like erasing whatever bad thing was happening. I'd open them, and everything would be better. I'd forgotten all about it until the day Tieresse proposed marriage.

I asked Moss where she and her husband had gone on their

honeymoon. She said, I like spas. Harvey likes crowds. So we went to Vegas.

I said to Stream, You?

He said, Neither of my marriages is anything I want to revisit.

I told them about North Dakota.

Stream said, There's a Minuteman missile launch site in Cooperstown. Seems ironic given our predicament.

I hadn't known that. It felt like it meant something. I turned and looked at the digital clock, counting down the seconds.

I said, I was really looking forward to sharing more cakes with you. Did you know I already picked the flavors?

Moss said, Yes, you told us.

My breathing was very shallow but didn't feel labored. I might have even felt a bit better. Tieresse told me with her melanoma she felt her very worst right before she entered re-mission.

I said to Stream and Moss, Maybe I'll be the one person who beats the odds. Somebody has to. But in case I'm not the guy, it's time for plan b. I've reached the point I either need to kill you or let you go.

They looked at me with alarm. I said, *Relax. I had to watch a video to learn how to load a gun. I still don't know how to shoot it.* I placed the keys to the padlocks on the floor beside me.

I said, I'm not exactly sure what I was hoping to accomplish. Maybe I achieved it.

I looked at Stream. I said, Although in your case, probably not.

I muted the TV. Stream cracked his knuckles. Moss stood from her chair, which continued to rock without her. I said, When I gave this place a trial run, and the TV and lights went off, it was like being buried alive. No light, no sound. I found it peaceful. I feel that way now.

Moss said, Mr. Zhettah?

My eyes burned and felt heavy. I looked at Stream. I said, *My best friend wants nothing before he dies except to reconcile with his daughter. I hope things work out with your son.* I said to Moss, *Please tell your husband I apologize to him and wish I had been smart enough to think of another way,* and she said, *I will do that.*

My eyelids fell shut, then flickered open, and through the matted lashes I saw the two of them, standing there, pressed against the bars. Stream was still scared, but Moss was not. I slid the keys into their cells.

I said, When I am gone, you can use those to let yourself out. My lawyer might have already opened her safe. Detective Pisarro is probably on his way. And I'm going to leave the vault door open when I head back up.

They were watching me carefully, but neither was fearful any longer. I took another breath and closed my eyes for a moment. When I opened them I said, *Goodbye, Your Honors. Hah. Your Honors. Even now I amuse myself.* My laugh turned into a spasm. I felt a cauldron tip in my gut.

Clutching the railing, I slowly climbed the stairs. I heard no sound or activity from below. I considered calling down to reassure them it was not a trick, but there wasn't any hurry. They'd come up when they were ready. I went inside the house and grabbed the box of Tieresse's ashes from the counter. I walked into every room and opened every closet door. I put one of Tieresse's dried roses in my pocket. Then I turned on all the lights and walked outside. I smelled verbena and cudweed and maple blowing in on the western wind.

She was already there, sitting in the plane. She was wearing the same yellow sundress she'd had on the day I met her. I wanted to say, *I remember that dress.* I climbed in next to her and handed her the flower. I felt her mouth brush my ear and she whispered, *Where to, amor?* A tiny fleck of salt glistened on her lower lip. A thick purple scar ran down her left cheek. I said, *I think we've waited long enough,* and I set a direct flight plan to Cooperstown, North Dakota, five hundred nautical miles away. She smiled, and I gasped as the scar on her face disappeared. She said, *I want you to do something for me, amor, something you did for me once before very near to this place. Will you do it?* I wanted to say, *Of course, my love, I'll do anything,* but I was tired, so very tired, so I simply nodded my head.

And before she could ask I closed my eyes.

ACKNOWLEDGMENTS

When I was in graduate school, I studied with the great historian Edmund S. Morgan. Professor Morgan used to warn his students about gonna-historians. A gonna-historian is a historian who is gonna write this book and gonna write that book, but who never actually writes any book. I was heading firmly in the direction of becoming a gonna-novelist until my course was altered by my wise, smart, and supportive agent, Simon Lipskar. He believed in this book when it was still only an idea, and his steady encouragement is a major reason it exists.

Simon arranged for me to talk to John Parsley. After a few minutes of our first conversation, I knew I wanted to work with John and his team at Dutton. I've been fortunate in my life as a writer to have had several truly wonderful editors. None is better than John. To him, Cassidy Sachs, the copy editors, the fact-checkers, the artists, and the rest of the Dutton team: Thank you.

I'm lucky to be able to park myself among two very different yet equally supportive sets of colleagues: the faculty and staff in the history department at Rice and at the University of Houston Law Center. I am especially grateful to Dean Leonard Baynes and

Associate Dean Greg Vetter at UH, and to Carl Caldwell, Alida Metcalf, and Lora Wildenthal at Rice, for their steady support of my work. I also have the benefit and honor of working with a superb team of lawyers at both the Texas Innocence Network and the Juvenile and Capital Advocacy Project, including Christina Beeler, Katya Dow, Cassandra Jeu, Jeff Newberry, and Ingrid Norbergs. Charlette Jefferson and Lillian White provide unsurpassed administrative help.

I realize that the scene in *Amadeus* where Salieri discovers that Mozart's manuscripts have no erasures is made up, but I still think of it every time I begin to count the number of people who made this book better. My wonderful and wonderfully loyal friends who freely shared advice, encouragement, insights, and occasional browbeating, include: Seth Chandler, my brothers Mark Dow and Stuart Dow, Abby Schusterman Dow, Jon Liebman, Deborah Musher, Sandy Guerra Thompson, and Ron Turner. I relied most of all on the keen eye and keener sensibility of Katya Dow, whom I'm also lucky to be able to call my wife. Our son, Lincoln, was more helpful than any high school kid should be when talking with me about the ethics of Inocente's conduct and the mechanics by which he carried out his plan. Inocente's familiarity with *Pirkei Avot* is a result of numerous energetic conversations around the Shabbat dinner table of my youth, presided over by my mom and dad, who knows pretty much the entire text, as well as the commentary, by heart.

I'm not going to express an opinion about whether Twain was right to urge authors to write what you know, or whether Twain even actually said it. What I will say is that while I do know a fair amount about capital punishment, this book is a novel, and so far as I am aware, Inocente, Sargent, Moss, Stream, and all the rest exist only in its pages.

ABOUT THE AUTHOR

David R. Dow is the Cullen Professor at the University of Houston Law Center and the Rorschach Visiting Professor of History at Rice University. As the founder of the Texas Innocence Network and the Juvenile and Capital Advocacy Project, Dow and his team of lawyers, students, and interns have represented more than one hundred death row inmates in their state and federal appeals. Recognized internationally as an authority on capital punishment, Dow's TED talk on the death penalty has been viewed more than three million times. Dow has addressed aspects of his work in two previous memoirs, including *The Autobiography of an Execution* and *Things I've Learned from Dying*. He lives with his wife, their son, and their two dogs in Houston, Texas, and Park City, Utah. *Confessions of an Innocent Man* is his first novel.